A Treasure to Die For

The Third Something To Die For Mystery

D0026929

Radine Trees Nehring

St Kitts Press   Wichita, Kansas

PUBLISHED BY ST KITTS PRESS
A division of S-K Publications
PO Box 8173   Wichita, KS 67208
316-685-3201   FAX 316-685-6650
stkitts@skpub.com   www.StKittsPress.com

The name St Kitts and its logo are registered trademarks.

This novel is a work of fiction. Any references to real people and places are used only to give a sense of reality. All of the characters are the product of the author's imagination, as are their thoughts, actions, motivations, or dialog. Any resemblance to real people and events is purely coincidental.

Edited by Elizabeth Whiteker
Cover design by Diana Tillison
Cover art by Cat Rahmeier

First Edition 2005

Library of Congress Cataloging-in-Publication Data
Nehring, Radine Trees, [DATE]
    A treasure to die for / Radine Trees Nehring.-- 1st ed.
       p. cm. -- (The third Something to die for mystery)
    ISBN 1-931206-00-7 (pbk. : alk. paper)
    1. McCrite, Carrie (Fictitious character)--Fiction. 2. Ozark Mountains--Fiction. 3. Elderhostels--Fiction. 4. Older women--Fiction. 5. Arkansas--Fiction. 6. Widows--Fiction. I. Title. II. Series: Nehring, Radine Trees, [DATE]   Something to die for mystery ; v 3rd.
    PS3614.E44T74 2005

                        2004015316

ADVANCE PRAISE

Nehring's delightful novel, the third in her Something to Die For series, features history and romance with murder thrown in. Who would have imagined an Elderhostel could be so dangerous? A winning combination and fun read.

—PATRICIA SPRINKLE, President of Sisters in Crime, bestselling author of the Thoroughly Southern Mystery series

The treasure here is Radine Trees Nehring and her plucky crime solver, Carrie Culpeper McCrite. Carrie and her partner in detection, Henry King, are attending an Elderhostel in Hot Springs, Arkansas. Someone is after an ill-gotten treasure, and they're willing to kill for it. If Carrie and Henry survive long enough to discover who's behind the mayhem, maybe they'll solve the mystery of what kind of partnership they've gotten *themselves* into.

—J.M. HAYES, author of *Plains Crazy, Prairie Gothic*, and *Mad Dog & Englishman*

This carefully crafted, intriguing tale links what could have happened during the colorful days of open gambling in Hot Springs to what would have happened during a modern Elderhostel there (except for the scary events that reach back to the past and make the week terrifying for the characters...and the reader). Just as compelling are the subtle shades of meaning in friendships, romantic adult relationships, and the heroine's struggle between independence and belonging. The characters are as alive as present-day Hot Springs. I couldn't put it down.

—DR. DOJELO C. RUSSELL, Program Coordinator, Univ. of Ark. Elderhostel programs in Hot Springs, Ark.

ACKNOWLEDGMENTS

Writing about the adventures of imaginary people I enjoy spending time with is just part of the fun in my life as a writer.

Another enjoyable part is spending time with real people who help me build story locations and tell you, the reader, about what happened there. My stories may grow from imagination, but the settings are as accurate as I can make them within the confines of the story being unfolded. It takes real people to help me depict those settings. In *A Treasure to Die For*, that means, first of all, the dedicated staff and volunteers at Hot Springs National Park, Arkansas.

First, thanks go to Curator Sharon Shugart, who quickly caught the story dream along with me and guided me into private and public places in the Fordyce Bathhouse. The Fordyce closed as a bathhouse in 1962 and re-opened as the Hot Springs National Park Visitor Center and Museum in 1989.

Sharon was amazingly patient as I walked and crawled into every corner of the Fordyce, and she helped me picture what could happen in those places, extending from the rooftop to the back-of-dark beyond in the mechanical area of the basement. With Sharon's help I have been everywhere Carrie and Henry go inside the Fordyce. Sharon's own book, *The Hot Springs of Arkansas Through the Years* (Department of the Interior/National Park Service, Hot Springs National Park, 2000) was a tremendous help. You'll meet Sharon as Park Curator/Historian Shirley Sandemann in this book.

My thanks go also to Interpretive Ranger Jeff Heitzman, who becomes Charles Hawkins, "Ranger Hawk," in these pages. Jeff is the one who initially tickled my imagination when he told our Elderhostel group the ancient-to-modern story of Hot Springs. He also helped me "see" the inside of the Quapaw by showing me floor plans of this beautiful bathhouse—closed to the public since 1984.

There are many others who were patient and kind with an author who could, most certainly, ask a lot of questions. Ranger Mark W. Blaeuer and Interpretive Secretary Gail Sears are two friends I met this way. Law enforcement Ranger Joseph Kanopsic was especially helpful as he explained various jurisdictions, responsibilities, and legal procedures in the event (so unlikely!) that any crimes like the ones I imagined herein had actually occurred within park boundaries.

Other law enforcement information was provided by members of the Hot Springs Police Department, primarily Corporal Mike Buck and Sergeant Michael Bingham.

Federal Bureau of Investigation Special Agent Charles S. Falls outlined the probable FBI role in this story, though I admit my own imagination built on the background knowledge he shared. Any departures from real probabilities rest on my shoulders, not those of Agent Falls, and he was not the model for either Agent Colin Bell or Agent Willard Brooks.

This book would not have been possible without the understanding support of Dojelo Russell, long-time coordinator for the many Elderhostels held in Hot Springs each year. "Doj" has been a part of this story from the beginning. When my husband John and I arrived at our first Hot Springs Elderhostel I told her that the event and our fellow Elderhostelers were probably providing research material for a novel just then in its planning stages. Throughout the three years since our first contact, Dojelo, an author herself, has been a supportive friend, though until recently she hadn't a clue to what kind of book might result from our work together. (In no way is Carrie and Henry's own Elderhostel Coordinator, Greta Hunt, modeled after Dojelo Russell, though Greta's concern for her Elderhostelers is characteristic of those in her position, most especially of Doj.)

I also want to thank the many staff members at the Garland County Historical Society who provided information and guided me on a tour of their building. Finally, thanks to Jan Hendrix at Oak Lawn Park who gave me a brief peek into horse racing in Hot Springs.

Back home in Gravette, Arkansas, several willing experts provided help. My special thanks go to Dr. Jeff Honderich and Lou Honderich. Thanks also to pharmacist Ron Teasley, Gravette Police Chief Trent Morrison, attorney Dan Yates, Arvest Bank Branch Manager Susan McPherson, and Gravette resident Estelle Marney. Estelle lived in Hot Springs for many years.

To each of you, old friends and new, named and unnamed, I say thank you for your time and expert help. The need to adapt to plot considerations may have altered what you told me, and I hereby acknowledge that any mistakes resulting from this are mine alone.

A final word...but then, words can never sufficiently thank my St Kitts editors, Laurel B. Schunk and Diana Tillison; my cover artist, Cat Rahmeier; or, most especially, my husband, John, who is always there to support me. So, without words to say more thanks, I guess that's all for now!

As for money being hidden in the Fordyce basement... see what you think. Here's the story.

DEDICATION

To family members who have supported and encouraged me along the way, especially:

My Aunt Myra, who praises just enough to make me feel good but not so much that she sounds insincere. She gives copies of my books to everyone she knows and to more than a few she doesn't know.

My sister-in-law, Cat, who thinks of all the right words to say just when I need them, besides being the world's best cover artist.

My cousin, June, another book sharer and encourager. She's a brilliant and talented lady; I still can't figure out why she seems awed by the fact her cousin writes books.

Always to my husband, John, and here, words fail me, because he does so much—though just the fact he's here would be enough.

And finally to my mom. She didn't live to see any of her daughter's books but began the process all those years ago when she told me stories.

PROLOGUE

He stood in his pool of blackness and watched the flashing lights on Central, heard the shouts, the sound of glass breaking, metal being smashed.

Blood-sucking maggots! They were taking away the very life of good working men and their families. For more years than he'd been here, the established way of life in Hot Springs had boomed along. They were trying to kill that.

Oh, yes, there'd been showcase raids, but everyone knew how to get past those. Close some houses, kick a few people out of town, keep going to church, smile at the ladies. Hug your children in front of all the church ladies.

But now? Who'd have thought this smash-up would come when the country was so caught up in the mess of Vietnam? They should pay attention to fixing that, not be bothering about the way of life here in Hot Springs. Folks wanted diversion, didn't they, especially in bad times like these?

Lights flashed closer along the row, but he knew they

weren't looking for him. Yet. No one except Mark, Will, and Hank knew what he was about. Even they didn't know where he was, what place he'd chosen, and the cop who'd warned him thought he only needed enough time to get out of town.

So now he watched the lights, feeling safe in his pool of blackness. He'd like a cigarette, but didn't dare risk it. Little things, like a small glow or drifting smoke, could foul a man up, big time. He knew what was what. That's why they'd chosen him as guardian over...he looked down at the pillow cases by his feet. How much was in them? He had no way of knowing. They hadn't taken time to count, just shoved money in the cases, grabbing stacks of hundreds and fifties while a hidden door held off the chaos outside.

Like the big guys said, paying a cop pays off. And he'd been ready, saving empty baking powder and cocoa tins for more than a year, just in case.

He'd count the money before he hid it all away. Almost all. He needed traveling funds, something for his family to live on until he could find a new stake.

Now *that* part might be hard. He'd grown up in the houses, learning the trade from the best, including his dad. All he knew was bookmaking.

He laughed but was careful to make no sound doing it. Hey, he could be a bookkeeper! He knew how to keep track of money. And Hot Springs would open up again. It always had.

Meanwhile, get out of town. He'd been very good at his job and he'd be on the list, noticeable to the state police, the governor, and all those maggots bent on looking virtuous. They'd have their pictures in the paper, the sucking maggots. He just didn't want his picture to show up there.

Time to be busy. He went to the window he knew would

open and shoved his money bags through, letting each one drop on the floor of the silent, empty building. He slid in behind them, holding the pillow case full of cans carefully, then moved away from the windows. Couldn't let light or rattling cans betray him.

He'd already hidden the sack of concrete and jugs of water in the basement. He knew what was what. Oh, was this a plan! No one would be inside this place for months, if then, and all four of them had agreed to be patient.

He heard a siren. Probably the governor, come to have his picture taken among the virtuous.

He struck a match, touched it to the lantern wick. Time to start making holes. He needed to get out of town before daylight.

CHAPTER I

HENRY

"Meatloaf?"

"That's what I said. How does meatloaf figure into Jason's sudden enthusiasm for this Hot Springs trip of yours and Eleanor's? He told me..."

"In a minute, Henry." Paper rattled.

He squeezed his lips together to stop himself from either laughing or saying something he'd have to talk his way out of later. Instead, he concentrated on watching the winding asphalt highway disappear under the car as his fingers beat a syncopated tap, tappity-tap on the steering wheel.

Sometimes the woman sitting beside him could make simple things into stuff that would befuddle a sage. Why didn't she just say right out, "Eleanor convinced Jason to go along with this vacation idea when she...when she..."

Whatever. Maybe it was too silly to repeat. Probably was.

Tap, tappity-tap tap. Tap, tappity-tap. They were driving through a forested area now, and touches of early September color hinted at fall glory yet to come.

More rattling paper signaled that Carrie's immediate concern was map reading. Finally she said, "About four more miles. Turn east on U.S. Highway 270."

Paper sounds, then a quick puff of exasperation from her side of the car. "Oh, for good garden seed, I've always wondered what idiot figured out the way maps are designed to fold."

"It's a logical system," he said, "very simple. A back and forth pleat. That way you can re-fold the map to any section you want to read."

He glanced over at her, hoping his words hadn't sounded too patronizing, but now Carrie was concentrating on making pleats. His eyes returned to the highway, and he said no more until she had the map conquered and the paper sounds stopped. Then he asked again, "Tell me about meatloaf. Jason said meatloaf was what convinced him to go along with the Hot Springs Elderhostel idea, and that sure sounds peculiar to me. How did meatloaf break down our neighbor's resistance to attending a school for elders?"

"Henry King, it is *not* a..."

"Okay, okay, you know what I mean. Now what did Jason mean?"

After a pause, she said, "Eleanor makes very good meatloaf."

He said nothing but "Hmmm?" hoping she'd feel compelled to fill any awkward silence with explanations, as humans so often do. The silent method had worked well for him with suspects throughout his many years in police work, and he still found it useful at times.

Tap, tappity-tap.

But not useful with Carrie. "Henry, is that Morse code, or should I put in a music tape so you can play along?"

No, silence wasn't going to work. For one thing, he'd done too good a job teaching her his police methods. He'd told her about the silence thing and how it got people to talk.

"Come on, Carrie, what is it with the meatloaf? Surely it's not a secret. It just sounds silly. After all, Jason is no gullible fool."

"So ask Jason. He was the one who brought it up."

He laughed at that. "I'll bet you know. In fact..."

She went on as if he weren't speaking. "I can make good meatloaf. You liked my Magic Two Meatloaf. You certainly ate enough when I served it."

He stopped as a memory flashed into his head.

"Carrie Culpeper McCrite! You made that the same night you asked me to come to this Elderhostel with you."

"Did I? All I remember is, *whenever* it was, I wanted you to try it with me so you could help me decide if I should write down the recipe. We both thought the idea was worth keeping. And I asked you to this Elderhostel—whenever I asked you—because I thought we'd have fun. I was in the mood to celebrate. You can't have forgotten that your daughter had just called to tell me her office finally figured out all the angles of that stock theft mess, and she'd traced most of the investments Evan stole from me. So, during one phone conversation, I went from worrying about not having enough money to feeling like I'm almost rich."

"And then?"

"And then what?"

Really, Henry thought, sometimes I wonder why I love

this woman.

The word *love* had come into his head unbidden, and he paused to savor it. Was this a love like some of his favorite romantic songs described it? Well, maybe not the head-over-heels stuff, not like some teenaged boy. Love took many forms. He'd never stopped to analyze what love for Carrie meant. Maybe he should, especially now that they were going to be together in very close company for a week.

"I will ask Jason," he said, smiling in spite of his frustration. This was too funny—he knew she was teasing, and hadn't he already figured it out? Wasn't it something like, "The way to a man's heart is through his stomach"?

Well, everyone enjoyed good food. And Carrie's Magic Two recipe, silly as it sounded, had been very good. In fact, maybe Carrie's meatloaf recipe was even better than Eleanor's. Or was it just that, living alone, he appreciated meals cooked by any Walden Valley neighbor who invited him over to share—especially Carrie, of course, though so many of her cooking ideas bordered on the bizarre.

He was only returning her teasing now, but he did prefer straight talk. Some women seemed to have trouble with that, even his daughter Susan, though both she and Carrie had less trouble with it than most. Now his smile got broader, and, day-dreaming about Susan, he almost missed the 270 turn-off.

So of course Carrie said, "Turn, Henry, turn!" but by the time she got it out, he was already putting on the turn signal. He made the change just in time, though he'd had to brake a little harder than he liked. She'd probably noticed that, too.

But she said no more, and on impulse he took a hand off the steering wheel, reached over to squeeze her hand, and went back to thinking about love.

He guessed he'd been in love with her for almost a year now. They'd been neighbors a year longer than that, each drawn to the Ozarks by a quest, each seeking a new life and escape from darkness in their separate pasts.

He glanced at the small, round, grey-haired woman in the seat beside him. She was clever, courageous, kind, and darn cute, but she wasn't always capable of straight-out honest conversation, even when they weren't talking about anything personal.

Her head turned in response to his glance and the quick touch on her hand, and she smiled, reached out in return, and, since both his hands were now back on the wheel, gave his thigh a light pat. He was sure she meant the touch as friendly, but her hand stayed there long enough for his entire body to feel the warmth, and his senses rushed into overdrive. Whew. He needed to subdue this kind of thinking if they were going to spend a week together as friends in the same hotel room.

"We both know, Henry, that I can afford to take us to nice places now, especially if we share a room. We'll have fun here. The crystal mining, the trip on the lake, the hot baths, and the massages...ummm." Her shoulders wiggled. "And, well, you know, fun."

He gave up the stoic attempt to ignore yearnings Carrie probably hadn't a clue he was feeling and allowed his thoughts to wander where they pleased.

But he was no more than a heart-beat into a warm, cozy picture of the coming week's companionship before she yanked him back into the car by asking, "Do you suppose there are still gangsters in Hot Springs?"

His answer came immediately and without any need for thought.

"Yes, I'm sure there are."

Years in the Kansas City Police Department had ruined any long-ago imagining that there could be a city or countryside anywhere without a crime problem. That would be especially true of this city, which, from what he'd read, had once been known as the "wickedest town in North America" and deserved the title. True, there had been a massive clean-up years ago, a smashing of slot machines and gaming equipment, closing of sports books and bars and houses in the red-light district, all led by a governor too rich to be bribed. But not everything would be gone. They wouldn't see it during this coming week, but oh, yes, he was willing to bet it would still be there if people, especially men, cared to look in the right places.

Thank goodness he no longer had to deal with that sort of thing. He was out of detective work now. Well, except for when Carrie—who was drawn to humans with problems—found them and the evils that sometimes came with them. Then the two of them worked together to help solve those problems.

But this was a vacation. No possible entanglements for them this week, just fun and some sort of classroom stuff that couldn't be too bad. There would still be one big problem for him though: living in the same room with her all week long and being a gentleman every single minute!

He wished she hadn't asked about gangsters. He wished all the dark parts of law enforcement could be erased from his memory just as it had been from his life.

Carrie's next words broke into his thoughts and proved she wasn't really interested in delving into Hot Springs' crime except as intriguing history.

"I read somewhere that they once had 500 sports books in town and lots of liquor, even during prohibition, as well as many houses of ill repute. I'm not sure I understand all of it exactly, but maybe it was something like in *The Sting*? Did you see that movie?"

He nodded. "Yes."

She spoke her next words slowly as her thoughts traced the past. "Amos and I saw it together. He was never interested in movies, but someone in his law firm recommended it as a study of unique criminal activity. I think that was how he put it. Anyway, we got a baby-sitter for Rob and went one Saturday night. I loved the whole thing, the story and especially the music. Amos didn't. Said it was silly. From then until the time he was killed, if I went to a movie, I went alone."

Henry nodded again, remembering when he'd seen *The Sting*. "I went alone. Irena only goes to movies if what's showing is a highly-praised foreign film or it's some kind of benefit. At least that's how it used to be, and I don't suppose she's changed much. She attends plays, ballet, the opera. Even when we were married, she usually went to those with friends because I was so often on duty and, even when I wasn't, could count on being called out at awkward times. The people in her circle felt sorry for her—married to a common policeman. She loved the sympathy, all that stuff about being the wife of a cop who 'put his life on the line.' She always managed to make me feel like a servant to her wealthy family and friends. Being called a public servant by the mayor was okay. When Irena called me that, it wasn't okay."

He knew he'd already told Carrie the story of his role as Irena's exhibition cross-to-bear, but he couldn't keep himself from repeating it. The bitterness of Irena's aloofness, her put-downs, rather than fading, were fresher than they had been in years, so real they made a metallic taste in his mouth now. Why was that?

It was Carrie, of course. Her genuine interest in police work and obvious admiration of the way he'd faced challenges and dangers as a homicide detective were such a contrast. Not like Irena, not at all. His marriage to Irena had been a long-term habit, just "what was" until Irena finally got too bored with him and walked out. All during their marriage he'd avoided thinking about what he might be missing and concentrated fully on his work. If that had made him a better detective, well, it was some compensation.

And Susan was compensation. Thirty-two years ago his loneliness had led to a one-night-stand with her mother. A baby girl had been the unexpected result. What happened that night was wrong, and, thank goodness, Irena never found out, but after so many years and the deaths of his daughter's birth mother and the parents who'd adopted her, Susan now knew him as her father. Carrie, doing very good detective work on her own, had learned about his daughter and found a way to bring them together. Susan was worth whatever had been wrong in the past. She was...

"Penny."

"Uh, what?"

"For your thoughts. You were miles away. I think I can guess though. Come back, Henry. We agreed we'd both drop the past. My Rob and your Susan are all we're cherishing about the past."

"Sometimes that's hard."

He felt, rather than saw, her head duck, almost as if in prayer. "I know," she said softly, and his bitterness was replaced by anger, but only at himself. He'd brought her into the sadness of her past just by dwelling on his. And he could think of no words now to erase the pain.

But Carrie, God bless her, could. "Do you remember

that house in the movie—you know what kind of house I mean—where the Madam had a merry-go-round in a special inside room, and her girls could ride on it when they didn't have, um, customers? I loved that merry-go-round music and all of Scott Joplin's music. I bought the sound track recording. I still have it."

She hummed a few bars from "The Entertainer," then said, "It would be fun to see that movie again, Henry. It would be fun to see it together. Let's rent it when we get home."

Yes, God bless her. He smiled as Carrie unfolded the city map the Elderhostel coordinator had sent them and sounds of paper rattling filled the car again. But he didn't need the map. There was the expressway turn-off for Central Avenue.

They had arrived in Hot Springs.

CHAPTER II

CARRIE

She knew the descriptions by heart.

Sin City, Spa City, Fun City. A well-known resort for nearly two centuries. Once a place for pleasures and hope, whether you were a gangster from the east coast, a member of the posh aristocracy, or any person, rich or poor, seeking the curing waters.

Today the majority of visitors to Hot Springs would be ordinary tourists just as she and Henry were.

Carrie hoped the glowing descriptions in the brochures she'd collected at the Arkansas Tourist Information Center where she worked were all true. She'd sold the Elderhostel trip to Eleanor from those brochures without any trouble. Eleanor had then taken over the selling to Jason while Carrie tackled Henry.

It was Eleanor who had suggested meatloaf.

"Can't hurt," she'd said. "Meatloaf is a favorite with most men, and it's my observation that they're never more agreeable than when they've just finished a good meal. You want proof, Carrie? Well, isn't that why so many men are willing, even happy, to help with clean-up after the meal when they've had not the slightest interest in helping with the preparation, let alone getting a meal by themselves? Jason Stack always does our meal clean-up now that he's retired. But cook? He gets the shudders at the very word. You'd think we were talking about weird ingredients mixed by some bewildering scientific formula, rather than simple recipes." She'd winked a bright blue eye at Carrie. "And you know, to be honest, I'm not so sure I want him to think differently. I like Jason Stack being awed by my ability to cook.

"So you go home, make meatloaf, and invite Henry over. He'll probably be awed too. And he'll be okay about this trip to Hot Springs. You'll see."

Carrie didn't tell Eleanor, whom she considered the epitome of old-fashioned womanhood, that she felt uncomfortable using such manipulative methods to convince Henry he'd enjoy attending the Hot Springs Elderhostel with her. That was way too *feminine*. She wanted him to decide based on logic and reason, on wanting fun and the opportunity to enjoy a vacation with her. Not on meatloaf.

But...maybe, to be absolutely sure? Meatloaf would be an interesting challenge. So why not create one?

She couldn't remember having ever made meatloaf. Until her marriage to Amos McCrite when she was nearly thirty, she'd lived at home with her parents, and her mother had insisted on doing all the cooking. Becoming the wife of an already established, very busy lawyer did nothing to improve her cooking skills. Amos thought any word connected with a meal was hyphenated: business-breakfast, business-lunch, working-dinner. Except for the time when Rob was growing up, she'd eaten most meals alone, reading while she ate, barely noticing the food she chewed and swallowed.

But she had a brain, didn't she? Surely she could figure out meatloaf. Simple. Hamburger plus seasonings.

As soon as she got home she sat down at her kitchen table with pen and paper, trying to think what might have gone into the various types of meatloaf she'd eaten. The base was probably more than just ground meat. As she recalled, the loaf was pretty solid. And the seasonings? Onion, of course, salt and pepper, but what else?

Several minutes later all she had written on her piece of paper was "hamburger" and "chopped onion."

Pride wouldn't let her call Eleanor, or even another friend, and admit that meatloaf was a mystery to her. She should have kept a basic cookbook out of her garage sale when she was preparing for the move to Arkansas, but it was too late to remedy that now, and the nearest town with a bookstore was thirty miles away.

Oh, bother! What went into the confounded loaf?

Finally, in a down-to-the-wire burst of inspiration, she thought of the County Extension Service. After a long conversation with a woman who had the grace not to act astounded that her mature female caller didn't know how to make meatloaf, Carrie set out to create.

Picking up her pen again and referring every now and then to her notes, she designed a recipe for Magic Two Meatloaf.

And, for whatever reason, after dinner that night, Henry had agreed to come to this Elderhostel with her.

Now they were almost there, almost in "The Valley of the Vapors," the place with forty-seven steaming springs and a history of human use spreading back more then ten thousand years. A place to go for "The Cure" before the advent of modern medicine, and for enjoyment today.

It had better live up to its publicity. If not, well, she'd eat crow instead of meatloaf.

Right now they were passing vast parking lots, shopping centers, big-box stores, fast-food places. So far Hot Springs looked like Anyplace, U.S.A. Plain old city. The interesting part had better show up soon.

And it did. Easily recognized, with the main grandstand rising above everything around it, there was Oaklawn Park. A fancy horse racing track like this was something she certainly wouldn't see anywhere else in the state of Arkansas.

She read the lighted sign aloud. "Excitement! Simulcast racing, Wednesday through Sunday—can you slow down, Henry?—Post time 1:00. Arlington, Belmont, Louisiana Downs, Santa Anita..."

She twisted in the seat to look behind her as the car moved past the huge electronic board. "Instant Racing, umm, hard to see, Jackpot—$800. Thoroughbred Mania—$1250. Henry, I thought gambling was illegal in Arkansas except on races here. But did you see that sign? Doesn't it mean you can bet on all kinds of races?"

Before he could reply she went on, "There's the track itself. It's a lot like the race track we visited in Kentucky years ago."

Then they had passed Oaklawn and were back among the ordinary buildings. She turned to face front again. "We went to Kentucky to visit relatives when I was fourteen. I remember the green, green grass. Lots of green grass inside the fence back there too, but I didn't see any horses. I remember the horses in Kentucky. They were beautiful. I dreamed of riding..."

As she thought back to the dream her voice trailed off, and fifty years vanished. She imagined the racing horse under her and rolled her hand through the air behind her head, dipping it up and down in waves as if she were describing the sea. "Racing the wind, long hair flowing like melting gold in the sunlight.

"Long gold hair," she repeated, "not the short red kinks I had on my head then. In that dream, I was beautiful."

After a pause, Henry said, "You're beautiful now, Carrie, and I like kinks, especially when they're white."

She felt a flash of warmth zing through her body. Her hand stopped wave-making, dropped to the side of her head, and she began twisting one of the white curls around a finger. "Uh, thanks," she said, blinking her eyes rapidly, not looking at him. "But,"—and now she looked up—"you just wait until I wash my hair this week and you see it all wet. It will..."

She stopped, forgetting her hair, as a space opened up between the cars ahead of them and she could see down the street. "Oh! There's Bathhouse Row, and it looks just like the tourist brochures! How elegant! Our hotel must be a block or so farther on. I do wonder what the Downtowner Hotel and Spa will be like, don't you?"

Henry paused in front of the hotel to let Carrie out, saying he'd find a parking place while she went inside to locate a luggage cart and get started with checking in. Grateful for his awareness that she was wildly curious about the inside of this spa hotel, she bounced out of the car and rushed to climb the wide steps.

The cool, high-ceilinged lobby was dimly lit and 1965 chic. People were moving about in several directions, and a large group clustered near the registration counter, but crowd noises vanished somewhere in the oriental carpets, heavy furnishings, and air space.

Reminds me of a fancy men's club, thought Carrie, except they've got brochure racks over there like we do at the information center. She felt as if she'd shrunk to miniature size in the lobby's vastness and stood rooted to her spot inside the entry doors until a very low, very smooth voice said, "Excuse me, are we lost in thought, or just lost?" The deep tones dripped sarcasm.

Carrie jerked around, lifted her head, and looked up. The man was tall and she supposed he was smiling at her, but his smile seemed more like a sneer. Then she realized she was blocking his way into the lobby.

Paladin, she thought, her mind flashing back to the memory of a long ago gunfighter on television. "Have Gun, Will Travel." Richard Boone. The man in black.

But this man didn't look like a gunfighter. He looked exotic. And handsome. Very. Oh, my goodness, yes.

"Oh, my goodness," she said aloud, "I am sorry, I was just taking it all in. I'm, uh, we're here for the, uh..."

"Elderhostel, I'd bet," the man said. "Well, I am too, and I think we go over there." He pointed. "See the lady at that table?"

Now Carrie felt like mush, her spine turned soggy under the man's superior smile. He held a black-clad arm out toward the table, indicating that she should move now, go ahead of him.

After only a short hesitation she did, wondering if she looked as silly as she felt. White-haired women didn't go mushy over handsome men, even chillingly handsome men in black leather vests, silk shirts, and the tightest jeans she'd ever seen. He looked as if he'd just stepped out of a page in *GQ*. She knew what that was like because she'd peeked inside a copy on the supermarket magazine rack just a few weeks ago, looking around first to be sure the aisle was empty both ways, since the cover model—definitely female—seemed to be dressed only in whipped cream. She'd been searching for an idea about new male styles, maybe something up-to-date as a gift for Henry.

Huh! What she saw inside that magazine was definitely not Henry, nor any other man she knew. It had all looked so exotic and peculiar, though now this man...

The table the stranger had indicated wasn't identified, but it was stacked with red folders, and the woman standing behind it looked at them expectantly. When Carrie was about four feet from her, she purred, "Hello there. Elderhostelers? Good. Welcome to Hot Springs."

The purr continued without a break. "I'm Greta Hunt, call me Greta. Your trip here was pleasant? Good. Ready for a terrific time in Hot Springs? Good. Now, if you'll tell me your names, I have information packets and a few little gifts for you."

Carrie, who hadn't opened her mouth or even nodded her head during Ms. Hunt's speech, wondered what would happen if she didn't say anything now. Would the welcoming speech continue: "I'll bet you're Ms. McCrite. Good?"

"I'm Carrie McCrite."

"Then you must be Henry King," Ms. Hunt said, turning to the man in black. "I have your packets right here, and, uh, oh, my goodness, did you say McCrite? I think I put you down as Carrie King."

"No," said Carrie stiffly, "it's McCrite, and this is

not"—she glanced at the stranger, saw his lips press together, to stifle a laugh probably—"this is not Henry King. Mr. King is parking the car. He'll be here in a...oh, there you are, Henry. We're just, um, registering."

The stranger in black moved toward Henry, coming so close to Carrie that his body pushed against hers. He extended his hand to Henry. "I'm Everett Bogardus and I guess we're in this together for the week. Nice to meet you, King. You're lucky to be rooming with such a charming lady." He looked down at Carrie and lifted his black eyebrows as if to say "you wicked woman, you, rooming with this man."

Carrie stepped closer to Henry and wondered if Bogardus's rude shove was intentional. Henry had seen it and his response to the man's greeting seemed barely polite. She really didn't blame him; she felt more than a little frosty toward Everett Bogardus herself. Still, maybe the shove had happened because she somehow kept getting in the stranger's way.

As far as raised eyebrows about sharing a room with Henry, well, she'd expected a little of that from people in her age group, but let them think whatever they wanted. She and Henry had as much right to save money by rooming together as two female friends did. Anything else was discrimination. It would have been foolish to pay extra just for appearance's sake, and she didn't want to be paired in a room with some strange woman.

Ms. Hunt said into the silence, "A new badge is easily made for you, Carrie. I'll take care of that, but I'm afraid the list of those attending is already made up, and most everyone is here now and has picked up a packet. Oh, well," she laughed, a short burst of sound, "we'll all go by first names this week anyway. I'm Greta, remember? Good!

"Oh, I almost forgot." The purr was back, the problem of Carrie's last name evidently solved to Greta Hunt's satisfaction. "Your friends Eleanor and Jason Stack arrived about an hour ago and said to tell you they wanted to go for a walk after being in the car for so long. I suggested they try the brick walkway above Bathhouse Row. They'll see you at dinner and asked that you save places for them if you arrive in the dining room first. As you'll see in your packet, a buffet will be served for all the Elderhostelers in the hotel restaurant, entrance over there, beginning at six. Right after dinner we'll have orientation and introductions in the Crown Room. That's where we'll be meeting this week." She pointed to the stairs behind her. "Up there. It's just 3:45 now. You'll have plenty of time to get settled and freshen up. See you in the restaurant at six, then. Good?"

"Good," said Henry.

Carrie got their room keys while Henry located a luggage cart. When he opened the trunk of the car, Carrie wondered, as she had many times before, if she would really need all the clothes she'd brought. It might rain, of course, evenings could be chilly, days could be hot. And, in one of her letters, Ms. Hunt had said to include heavy work gloves, old clothing, and really old shoes or boots for going to the crystal mine. Carrie wondered how people who had flown here got all their stuff in.

Everything went on the luggage cart, thank goodness, and there were hooks at the ends of the clothes rack for tote bags and Carrie's briefcase. The briefcase was full of all the information about Hot Springs that she'd been able to gather, plus a few magazines, her Bible and Bible lesson study books, and mystery novels by Kate Cameron and Laurel Schunk. She never left home without plenty of reading material.

The room was spacious. It had two double beds, as well as glass patio doors opening on a balcony overlooking the street. After she'd unpacked, Carrie went out on the balcony to look down at Hot Springs' legendary Central Avenue. The first thing she saw was a sign above the porch of a white multi-columned building across the street. It proclaimed "Mountain Valley Water" in big green letters.

"Well, look at that," she said as Henry came up behind her, put his arms around her waist, and pulled her close. "I have a brochure about that place; I'm glad it's nearby. It was built in 1910 and has been the home of Mountain Valley Water since the 20's. The interior is supposed to be beautifully restored, and they're still in business, selling water all over the United States."

For a minute she relaxed against Henry, soaking up the luxury of his closeness. Then she patted his hands briskly, pulled loose, and turned to face him. "I want to see the inside."

"Well, not right now, I hope," Henry said. "Besides, it's Sunday, doubt they're open. For now, I'm in favor of doing nothing. Join me?" He took off his shoes and laid back on one of the beds without bothering to remove the spread.

"I should take a shower before dinner," Carrie said. "I'd feel fresher."

There was a rumbled "Umhmm" from Henry. His eyes were closed.

She looked down at him for a moment, realizing without a bit of surprise that she wanted to snuggle beside him on that bed. She knew very well Henry wouldn't complain about her presence there, unexpected though it might be.

Of course he couldn't see her shake her head. "Well,

if that's the way you feel," she said, "I guess I'll set the alarm."

After doing just that she plopped down on the other bed and shut her eyes.

CHAPTER III

HENRY

Everett Bogardus was just leaving the buffet line with his plate piled high when Henry and Carrie entered the dining room. Greta stood by the dessert table making sure her charges were not going hungry, and Bogardus stopped to say something to her. Henry heard what sounded like, "Excellent cuisine...equal to Boston's finest chefs."

"Obsequious show-off," Henry muttered under his breath. The man obviously thought he was quite the stuff. Tall, thin, all that black, and now he was going to take the last available chair at a large round table filled with women. Huh, no surprise there.

Then Henry suppressed a laugh. He'd noticed most of the women at the table looked old enough to be Bogardus's mother.

Carrie noticed it too. "Nice of Everett to be so friendly toward the single women, isn't it?" she said.

Henry didn't answer. Friendly? Carrie was a single woman, and he was still fuming about that adolescent body contact play he'd seen Bogardus make at the registration table.

He picked up a plate, frowned at it as if inspecting for dirt, and attacked the buffet.

They found an empty table for four and were beginning to eat when Jason came up, put his plate of food down, and dropped into a chair. He said nothing, just sat looking at them, bristly eyebrows lifted, lips squeezed into a furrowed circle that repeated the shape of his round face.

Silly old goat, making faces like a clown. Henry knew better than to let Jason irritate him, but why the stupid look? What was he up to, and for that matter, why couldn't he go through life more smoothly? Why the clowning, all the coy remarks? There would probably be one of those coming soon.

Now that Henry thought of it, this Hot Springs Elderhostel seemed to be bringing out the worst in more than one man.

He glared at Jason, expecting to hear something from those pursed lips at any moment. Instead, after a long silence, the only sound he heard was *"Um-hm?"* Henry raised his own eyebrows and watched for some sign of what Jason might be up to while Eleanor slipped gracefully into the last chair.

"Sure looks good," she said, glancing from her husband's face to Henry's and shifting her normal speaking voice to a tone Henry identified as *Mother, being cheerful with quarrelsome children.*

"Isn't this great? We're not used to full meals on Sunday

evening, but see my plate? You'd think I hadn't eaten all day. What you guys selected looks good too. Have you tasted anything yet, Pookie?"

Pookie? Henry suppressed a laugh and began to feel much better.

Jason ignored his wife while his gaze rolled over Carrie, then came back to Henry. Finally he said, "Carrie *King?* Did we miss a ceremony or something? What's this, what's this, big boy? Is it because you're timid about rooming with a woman you haven't honored with your name?"

There was an exasperated puff from Carrie, and renewed irritation flashed, unbidden, through Henry. What on earth? The man was a good friend, but he could sure be a jackass. The "big boy" nickname, which 5-foot-8 Jason used all too frequently, was idiotic. Put plainly, Henry, who was six feet tall and weighed two hundred-plus pounds, hated it. Jason knew that, which was probably why he used it. And where had the Carrie King come from?

Since he hadn't a clue what Jason was getting at, Henry said nothing and picked up a piece of fried chicken. Carrie, however, filled the conversation gap.

"Just a mix-up, rather natural under the circumstances. People can call me whatever they want, I'm sure not going to bother with any big explanation. Besides, everyone goes by a first name here anyway."

"What's the problem?" Henry asked. "Didn't they get your name right, Carrie?"

"Right or wrong," Jason said, "it's there on the roster of this week's participants. Carrie and Henry King. Haven't you looked in your packets?"

"Oh," said Henry. Now he was silent because he had no idea what to say. He knew Carrie too well to think she'd used his name on purpose.

"No, we haven't looked at them," Carrie said. "We took a short nap after we got here and didn't have time. Greta and I discussed the mistake when I registered, but I came in the hotel before Henry, so I guess he didn't hear our conversation."

Dismissing the subject, Carrie turned to Eleanor and asked her about their afternoon walk along the National Park's brick-paved Grand Promenade.

Effectively cut off by Carrie's unwillingness to be ruffled or goaded and by Henry's silence, Jason joined the description of what they had seen on the historic trail.

Henry chewed his food slowly, his good humor returning. *Pookie.* Oh, boy! He wondered if Eleanor had used the term intentionally. He'd noticed in the past that she was capable of tiny verbal jabs that served to pull her husband back into polite society.

After spending another moment enjoying his knowledge of Jason's cute nickname, he glanced toward the round table and, keeping his head at an angle so no one would know what he was really looking at, studied Everett Bogardus.

All that black looked ridiculous among the cluster of women in bright colors. The man was talking to a woman with outrageous yellow hair, leaning toward her, managing to make their conversation look intimate. Oily flirt. Too slick by far.

Since Bogardus seemed to have come here alone, Henry supposed he met the fifty-five or older Elderhostel age limit, but he didn't look fifty-five. Well, he probably dyed his hair, and did men get face lifts? Maybe. A tuck here and there? Henry fantasized about what that could do to a beard. Would you have to shave your temples? Would the hair grow up rather than down, demanding a whole new shaving technique?

Then his speculation turned serious as he wondered, once more, why this man was here.

Not only was he a dandy and a flirt, everything about him shouted "fake." Henry's fine-tuned danger warnings had gone up the minute he met him. That, and noticing the body rub, were probably why he'd missed any conversation about Carrie's name being wrong on some list. He'd been more interested in speculating why this person had come all the way from Massachusetts to Arkansas for an Elderhostel.

Henry couldn't help being put on the alert by people who seemed out of place in their surroundings; it was second nature after so many years in police work.

He scanned the rest of the area reserved for their group. There were quite a few couples in addition to the single women at the big round table and their attentive companion, who, Henry noticed, now had several gold chains dangling over the front of his black silk shirt. Was that supposed to impress people? Hmpf. This wasn't New York or Los Angeles. And how did the man even sit down in those jeans?

There were two more single men sitting at a table apart from the others, but if they belonged in the Elderhostel group they were probably rooming together. Bogardus must be alone. If so, he was paying extra for a private room.

Henry felt a hand on his arm. "It's almost time for the orientation meeting," Carrie said. "Better dig into that plate of food."

When the thirty-nine Elderhostel participants were seated at long tables in their assigned meeting room, Greta Hunt gave a short welcoming speech and an overview of their week's schedule. She explained that she was a native of Hot Springs and had been an Elderhostel Program Coordinator for six years. She then said, "Let's begin getting acquainted. Would each of you stand up in turn and tell us something about yourself and why you're here? We'll start with the Comptons."

Thank goodness, thought Henry, since Greta had indicated a couple at the opposite end of the room. I have time to think about why on earth I *am* here.

Why was he? He didn't mind being here, especially with Carrie, but it felt like she had pushed him into an avalanche heading this direction. He'd simply been bowled over by her enthusiasm. She often had that effect on him. Why?

Many things about civilian life were new and unfamiliar ground after his total dedication to a life in law enforcement. Communication with fellow officers was direct, forceful, easily understood. It sure wasn't that way now.

When he was alone with Carrie and wanted to say... personal things, he often felt like an awkward boy. Maybe he could convey a message to her in his talk here without having to say anything face-to-face.

He didn't know these folks, wouldn't see any of them but the Stacks after this week, so why worry about what he said? He could speak as if Carrie were the only one listening.

As each participant stood, some like professional performers, others with shy hesitation, Henry decided that Everett Bogardus might not be so out of place after all. Though he had expected most of the people to be from Arkansas or surrounding states, he, Carrie, and the Stacks seemed to be the only ones from the area. Many had come from places as far away as California, Florida, or New York, and there was one couple from Alaska. Others were from states between the Mississippi River and the Rocky Mountains, but still a distance from Arkansas. There must be more appeal to this Elderhostel thing than he imagined.

As the people talked, Henry made notes about each of them on his participant roster.

Jane and Russ Compton were from Minneapolis, both retired from the postal service. They had decided they wanted to visit all fifty states and were doing it via Elderhostel.

Tula and Edgar Waverman, from Torrance, California, had been married fifty-eight years. She was a homemaker, he a retired highway engineer. They enjoyed travel, and Edgar, who walked with a cane, explained that the wide range of Elderhostel programs each year gave them the opportunity for activity without having to be athletic.

There were two recent widows, Martha Rae Jones from Oregon and Oneida Bradley from Florida. They were cousins and had decided to meet here. Martha Rae said she loved to travel but the only way she felt safe, now that she was alone, was to be part of an Elderhostel. Oneida said simply that she'd needed to get out of the house. She got a bit teary-eyed during her short talk.

Crystal and Robert Howard, from Long Island, were youngish. Probably, other than Bogardus, they were the babies here. Robert—"Not Bob, please"—was a stock broker.

Crystal said, giggling, that her interest in crystals was natural, but she also owned a new age gift shop and was seeking knowledge and a source of crystals for her shop.

The two men Henry had seen at dinner were indeed part of the group. They were law partners from a large firm in Chicago, and both were still practicing. Marcus Trotter was divorced. Simpson Simpson—"Call me Sim, and, yes, my parents had a sense of humor"—a widower. Henry wondered if they'd come to look for new wives. Why else would they be here?

Everett Bogardus identified himself as a Boston University professor on sabbatical and said his field was history, though he also had an interest in geology. Speaking in a low voice with almost no definable Boston accent, he explained that the unique Native American presence here, as well as the crystals and hot springs, had attracted him.

In fact, most everyone mentioned a specific interest in one or more of the topics to be covered during the week. Carrie did, introducing herself as "Carrie McCrite" without saying anything about a mistake on the list. She explained that she was employed as manager of an Arkansas Tourist Information Center and that she'd read all the brochures about Hot Springs in her center. "I believed every word," she said. "Besides, I've always thought crystals were beautiful, and I'm interested in where they come from, so here I am to find out."

Eleanor rose to say she was a professional wife and mother, that she and her husband had recently moved to northwest Arkansas from Ohio, and she had come here to learn more about her new state while having a good time.

Jason got to his feet slowly and with exaggerated reluctance said, "I'm here because my wife is," which brought a laugh from some of the men. But he wasn't finished.

"I've had my nose to the grindstone for years, building a heat-resistant glass manufacturing business in Ohio, which I recently turned over to our son. Tom's been in training under me for about twenty years, I guess, and I finally decided he'd learned enough that it was okay to turn it all over to him. I'm sorry...uh, glad...to report he's doing just great without me. Now," he continued, "I guess it's time for me to slow down, take up a hobby"—a few people groaned—"but I admit to being what my wife calls a workaholic. We are going to be working, aren't we, Greta? Studying things? Digging? If there's no work, I'll go home."

That got an understanding laugh from everyone, including Greta, who promised to find lots of work for him during the week.

Henry's turn had come, and as all those faces looked at him, his mind went white-out blank. Why on earth hadn't he spent time thinking about what he was going to say rather than making notes about what others were saying?

After a pause that seemed to go on about an hour too long, he stood, cleared his throat, and looked down at Carrie. She was smiling.

He had to say something...

"One night last summer my friend and neighbor, Carrie McCrite, invited me over for a meatloaf dinner, um, to try out her new recipe, she said. After we'd eaten that meal, which was very good, by the way, she mentioned this Hot Springs Elderhostel and said she really wanted to come.

"She told me she thought I'd enjoy an Elderhostel, though I hadn't a clue yet what they were all about. She asked me to come along as her guest, said it would easily fit her budget, provided we shared a room. I'd have a chance to learn about Elderhostels, see if I'd like to go to more of them with her."

He glanced around. Everyone was still looking at him, most were smiling. Most were except for Carrie and Everett Bogardus, that is. She was studying her participant list as if memorizing it. He had his chair rocked back and was staring at the ceiling.

"Well, uh, what man could turn down an invitation like that from a lovely lady who makes good meatloaf?"

Now almost everyone laughed. Was that good?

His message, hidden in the "why I'm here" speech, had

been only for her, an acceptance of the conditions of this trip, a thank-you for offering it to him, and, maybe, a hint of how he felt about their relationship. He'd also meant it as a hands-off warning for Everett Bogardus.

He looked at Carrie again. She was still staring at the list, but her smile had come back. In a rush of confusion he sat down, his face feeling like he'd been in the sun too long.

Someone said, "Hear-hear," then the room was silent.

Had he said too much? Why had he admitted Carrie paid his way here? What he'd said had been stupid; he'd embarrassed himself, Carrie too, in front of everyone.

He took in air, let it out slowly. It was going to be a long week.

In his talk he hadn't mentioned being a retired police officer. He hadn't intended to. He knew what a damper that could be to a social relationship with some people. They might hate cops, fear them, or put them on a pedestal—he'd never figured out which was worse.

And he still wasn't all that sure about the man in black.

CHAPTER IV

HENRY

By the next morning his worries had shrunk. He was bright-eyed and bushy-tailed.

That's what his mother had called it so many years ago when he bounced out of bed on Saturday, eager to be off on adventures with his buddies.

"My, but you're bright-eyed and bushy-tailed this morning, son."

Henry remembered those eager-up Saturdays now as he sat next to Carrie at a back row table in the Downtowner's Crown Room. They had arrived early for this opening session, agreeing on a seating location without the need for a word of discussion. They could watch people so much better from the back row. Now they weren't talking; both were more interested in watching their fellow Elderhostelers.

Everyone looked wide awake, and the conversation in the room was loud enough to be called noise, at least until Greta stood at the front and waited for quiet.

Henry felt fine, just fine. Worries about being here, about rooming with Carrie, about his introductory remarks the night before, had faded, mostly because last night—after the meeting was over—had gone very well.

Carrie never mentioned his speech, though Greta had dismissed the group only minutes after he'd finished. It was painfully fresh in his memory, probably Carrie's too, as they returned to their room. But she'd seemed cheerful, hadn't said a thing about it, and had gone at once to get ready for bed in the privacy of the large bathroom. After he'd taken his turn in the bathroom, they sat against pillow-padded headboards discussing some of the more interesting members of the Elderhostel group, even debating about whether or not the Chicago lawyers would pair up with the widowed cousins.

After conversation faded they both read. Carrie put her book down and switched off her light before he did, turning on her side away from him, pulling the covers over her head.

Shutting out his light?

Feeling guilty, he'd turned the lamp off soon after and lay in bed thinking about the day's events, about the new turn his life was taking, and about Carrie. Especially about Carrie.

The women in his life had always been outskirts people, pushed away in thought because that made life less complicated. His mother and his wife, each involved in many interests that didn't include him, were outskirts people. He'd once been content to accept that, take them or leave them, do his own thing, make his career...his singular life.

But he couldn't push Carrie away. She, like the young boy he'd been and the friends he'd had back then, saw life as a series of adventures and managed to pull him into her adventure of the moment, making the two of them into a team.

She said she'd done enough living in other people's shadows before Amos died, so now, especially since she had a little money to spare, she was, by golly, going to enjoy herself. She was going to stand up for the new Carrie, and if that Carrie wanted to attend something like this Elder-hostel, if that was an adventure that interested her, then she'd do it, and—she'd added, not quite looking at him—it would be so much better if he came along.

He remembered pondering that last night, but then his memory faded into fuzziness. He must have been almost asleep when an idea had hit him, popping his eyes wide open again.

The two of them were both finding themselves, like people said teenagers did. After coming to the Ozarks on separate quests, they were building new lives.

Together?

That was the thought he'd gone to sleep with.

The next thing he remembered was coming awake this morning. If he'd snored, if Carrie had, he didn't know it.

Hot Springs National Park Interpreter Charles Hawkins was the first presenter of the day. About ten minutes into the program Henry looked over at Everett Bogardus. If he was truly interested in history and geology, he was sure getting his ear full this morning.

The man had come in late and taken the vacant seat next to Carrie, which had Henry bristling until he noticed the only other chair left was in the center of the front table. Couldn't blame the man for not wanting to go to the front when the speaker was already talking.

The talk *was* interesting. Carrie obviously thought so; she was busy scribbling in her note pad while "Hawk," as he'd said people could call him, spouted facts: "Three hundred million years ago the mountains here were as tall as the Alps are now. Springs emerged about 26,000 years ago. Our water is heated by radioactivity deep in the earth and percolates to the surface through a fault of unknown origin, coming out in various places near the base of Hot Springs Mountain. Emerging water temperature averages 143°.

"The water is amazingly pure, odorless, tasteless, colorless, and has no harmful bacteria. Water source: rain, which spends at least 4000 years being processed underground in some mysterious part of the earth before bubbling out at a rate of 850,000 gallons a day."

"That's a lot of hot water to get into," Henry whispered to Carrie, who nodded and kept writing.

"Most of the springs were covered long ago to protect the purity of the water," Hawk explained, "and the output of over half of them is now channeled to a reservoir maintained by the National Park Service. The water is dispensed to various licensed bathhouses in the city. Some of the water is also available to the public free of charge at open fountains.

"NASA has been interested in the water because nanobacteria found in it may be the same as bacteria found on Mars, indicating the historic presence of water on that planet."

And some link between Mars and Earth? Henry wondered.

On and on the story went, pushing Carrie's pen across page after page.

"Human use began around 10,000 years ago when early peoples discovered the pleasure and health benefits to be found in the valley's waters. By legend this was a place of peace, a place where warring tribes laid down weapons and bathed and communed together. The springs were possibly seen and enjoyed by members of the Hernando DeSoto party in 1541.

"Hot Springs became the first 'National Reservation' in the United States in 1832, set aside by the Federal Government to protect the natural features, especially the water. That was forty years before Yellowstone National Park was created, which is why some people insist this, not Yellowstone, was our nation's first national park.

"Early bathhouses were built, and various entertainments in town became notorious for what you might call licentious behavior. And Hot Springs remained a bawdy town, at least until the 1960's."

Every few minutes Henry glanced at Everett Bogardus. Most of the time he was leaning back in his chair looking bored, his eyes closed to mere slits. The rest of the time he seemed to be watching Marcus Trotter and Sim Simpson, who were sitting at a front table. Was he interested in them because they were the only other single men here?

Then Henry realized he hadn't thought of himself as one of the single men. Huh. He was, of course. Single and independent.

During the break Greta assigned Jason the work of helping the next speaker, who would be teaching the group how to grow herbs and use them in cooking. Jason disappeared, going to the parking lot to meet the speaker, while Henry, Carrie, and Eleanor drank coffee in the lobby and talked with fellow Elderhostelers.

"I'm a rock hound," said a bald man, reminding Henry his name was Don Rothman. "My wife Ethel is too, and we're looking forward to that crystal dig. We'd like to add some nice specimens to our collection. There's always hope you'll find a real treasure, right? Clear pieces? Good points?

"We flew here from Oregon, brought an extra bag along in case we locate crystals worth taking home, but who knows what today's airport security will make of that? We may have to ship what we find. Guess you drove from, what did you say, the Ozarks? Lucky. You can carry what you find home in your car."

He paused for breath, peered at Henry over his glasses, and asked, "Hey, you one of those Ozarks hillbillies like on TV? What is Arkansas called, the hillbilly state?"

"It's the Natural State, and I'm from Kansas City originally," Henry said, "but I know several old-time Ozarks hill people. I've found they have lots of practical knowledge I don't, to my disadvantage, I think. Good friends. Good, good people."

"Well, I didn't mean, that is..." Don said, fumbling and sputtering until Henry interrupted to ask if he was retired.

"Sort of. I'm an accountant. Keep my hand in during tax season. What about you?"

Henry realized he'd left himself open to that question by introducing the topic. Careless of him if he wanted to keep his former occupation a secret. He said only, "Retired," and took a slow sip of coffee, looking around the lobby as he did. He noticed that Carrie and Eleanor were talking with Everett, laughing at something the man had just said. He excused himself as quickly as he could and went to see what was so funny.

The joke was over by the time he got across the lobby, and the three were talking about Ranger Hawk's information, though Everett seemed to be adding facts of his own to what the park interpreter had told them.

"No, the small amount of radioactivity in the water isn't harmful," he was saying. "In fact, some think it's good for you. But in any case you get more radioactivity by standing in sunlight. Whatever you may think about that, for many years, and especially after the Civil War, people came here from all over the country for the water cure. They came for treatment of war wounds, internal and external aches and pains, female complaints, neuralgia, venereal diseases. Especially venereal diseases. The waters were said to cure them all."

He laughed, got only weak smiles from Carrie and Eleanor, and went on hurriedly. "At one time Hot Springs was a real pest hole. Of course eventually the place was cleaned up, and, on the surface at least, the town became downright classy. Newer and safer bathhouses were built. The Arlington Hotel was the place to stay if you had money. In the 1920's Al Capone came here frequently and rented a whole floor at the Arlington. I suspect he wasn't here to take over the criminal activity as some supposed, but to seek a cure for syphilis. I understand he eventually died in prison of that disease."

Everett was obviously enjoying the attention Carrie and Eleanor were giving him. But how's he know all this? Henry wondered. Then he remembered that the man's specialties were supposed to be history and geology.

Nevertheless...

"You know quite a bit about Hot Springs' past," said Henry, his tone more challenging than he'd intended.

Everett flushed and hesitated a moment before he replied, "Oh, I read a lot."

Nodding to the two women, he walked away to pour more coffee in his almost full cup.

Just then Jason came out of the elevator, helping an attractive middle-aged woman maneuver a cart stacked with small kitchen appliances, bowls, pans, boxes, green leafy things in pots, and containers filled with what looked like bunches of grass and weeds. Carrie and Eleanor, who both had herb gardens, hurried over and introduced themselves to the herb lady. Henry heard them offer to help set up, thus, he supposed, getting a head start on words of wisdom from the next presenter.

He wondered if anyone ever skipped sessions at these things. Didn't matter, he was going to. He wasn't interested in weeds and seeds or recipes for cooking with them; he'd rather go explore some of Hot Springs. Salt, pepper, mustard, ketchup, horse radish, hot sauce—all prepared and conveniently packaged in boxes or bottles—were the only seasonings he understood. Maybe onion too. Or was the onion a vegetable?

In spite of the promise of gardening hints and delicious samples of food prepared with various herbs, Henry left Carrie and the other Elderhostelers to enjoy the next session and headed down the street toward Bathhouse Row, saying he'd be back in time for lunch.

The day was hot, as mid-September could be in Arkansas, and Henry's forehead was damp under his hat by the time he reached the lush trees and grass of Arlington Lawn, a park located across the street from the Arlington Hotel. At the back side of the triangle-shaped park, steaming water cascaded down a high bluff, ending by spilling into concrete pools at the base. It looked inviting, and Henry walked that way.

He strolled past the pools, saw a shaded trail leading up, and decided to climb toward the source of the waterfall, undoubtedly one of the springs Hawk had talked about.

Black iron railings along the path guided him between luxuriant growth on the mountainside. At several locations it was possible to stand beside the steaming falls and watch them cascade over rocks, moss, and blue-green algae. He stopped at one switch-back to enjoy the water sounds and a wide-angle view into the park below.

Part of the sidewalk leading along Central from the Downtowner to Bathhouse Row was visible too. Leaning against the railing separating him from the cascade, Henry watched people strolling along. Their slow, rhythmic movement combined with the shush of the water sliding next to him would relax a clock spring. Wonderful place.

There was another herb session scheduled for tomorrow morning. He could come back here then, but he'd like Carrie to enjoy this place with him. She made most everything...he searched for a word...richer. That was it. She made everything richer by her presence. Or, at the least, she entertained him.

As he relaxed against the railing, he wondered what being married to Carrie would be like. The idea had been popping up inside his head since he'd learned about the mistake in the roster.

He said it aloud. "Carrie King."

Carrie would never go for marriage; she valued independence too highly. It was one reason for her move to the Ozarks. She'd wanted to escape from friends and family in Tulsa who kept urging her to move to a city apartment complex after the death of her husband.

"They saw me as helpless, wanted me to be taken care

of," she'd told him with a touch of sadness in her voice. "But I'm a strong person, not the weak elderly female they picture. You can understand how I feel about that, can't you, Henry? I am strong, I know I am. But it seems I have to keep proving it, and proving it, and proving it. You *do* understand, don't you?"

Maybe he had understood. During his many years as a police officer he'd needed to continually prove himself, prove his own strength. He'd succeeded very well until... until he killed a boy only thirteen years old during a convenience store robbery. Never mind that the child had looked older. Never mind that he'd just shot the store clerk and turned the gun on Henry. He was a child. He had died.

Henry made himself go talk to that boy's mother. After that, he couldn't carry a gun. His refusal led to retirement from the department and disgrace in the eyes of his former wife and her family.

But he'd come back to strength, and Carrie had been the avenue for his return. He'd learned quite a bit about strength from her.

He was even fairly comfortable carrying a gun again and had carried it twice in the past year. One of those times was to help save three lives—Carrie's, Susan's, and his own. The other was to rescue Carrie from a kidnapper.

He hadn't needed to harm anyone either time.

So his own proving was over, but it didn't ever seem to be over for Carrie. She said it was because things were very different for a woman.

That could be. But he wished she'd let him through her independence wall, would acknowledge that she needed him for something more than enjoyable partnership in their adventures. Sure, he wanted her to look to him when physical strength was required, but there was the other stuff too—ideas, plans. She wasn't the only one who could make plans, but get her to admit it...

He let go of the railing and stood erect. Everett Bogardus had appeared on the sidewalk below, striding toward Bathhouse Row. Henry looked at his watch. Bogardus must have left the herb program early, if he'd been there at all.

The man was walking with a sense of purpose, even seemed to be in a hurry. But then, people with long legs sometimes gave that impression. He was carrying a small tote bag. No wonder. Henry didn't see how he could get anything in the pockets of those jeans.

Henry leaned on the railing again and watched until Bogardus, no, Everett—they were supposed to use first names—was out of sight. He was probably headed for the Hot Springs National Park Visitor Center in the restored Fordyce Bathhouse, or maybe to the Buckstaff, the only building along the row currently open to the public as a working bathhouse.

Somehow Henry couldn't see the man luxuriating in a hot bath. He looked too intent, too focused. So it must be the Fordyce. But the whole Elderhostel group was scheduled for a guided tour there this afternoon. Why did Everett want to go there now?

Why? Well, if Everett did, Henry did too.

He started down the trail toward the sidewalk.

Chapter V

Henry

Henry climbed the wide stairs of the Fordyce Bathhouse, nodding a greeting to an older couple seated in chairs on the elegant veranda. They had been watching the activities along Central Avenue but looked up at him in unison and returned his smile. Wouldn't it be great to sit here with Carrie, enjoying this place, smiling and holding hands as these people were?

He opened one of the double entry doors and stepped through onto mosaic tile floors covered in soft light from the lobby's stained glass panels and transom windows. Wicker rocking chairs waiting along one wall were empty. Other than an attendant at the reception desk, he was the only person in sight.

Ve-ry nice. Marble walls, fountains at each end of the

lobby, intricately patterned floors. This must have been quite a posh place in its heyday.

His former wife, Irena, would love it. The style of the building reminded him of their honeymoon, something he hadn't thought of in years. They had toured Italy, a place Irena's family visited almost every summer, a place where she felt at home after the trips there with her parents. The honeymoon tour, arranged and paid for by his father-in-law, took them to elegant places and the buildings that were perfect settings for his new wife. She'd been happy, devoted to him, hanging on his arm whenever they left their room, laughing, the glowing, warm light on her face, enjoying the role of a bride.

Coming home to the United States had brought the curtain down on that act, and Irena the distant had taken over. Oh, she still played the devoted role in front of her parents, had kept up the pretense of a single bedroom, a real marriage, as long as they were alive. But it had been an act, and Henry, absorbed in his career with the Kansas City Police Department by then, had learned not to care. Ah, well...

"Welcome to the Fordyce Bathhouse," the uniformed attendant said as Henry walked toward the reception counter. "You're in the Hot Springs National Park Visitor Center, and also in a museum." She handed him a brochure and a floor plan of the building, explaining that he could walk around the four floors by himself or join a tour group leaving in about twenty minutes.

After saying he'd look on his own and thanking her, Henry asked, "Did my friend Everett, a tall man dressed in black, make it here before me?"

"Yes, he did," she said, recognizing the description immediately, "and I think you'll find him downstairs. He asked about restrooms. There's an elevator around the corner," she pointed to her right, "and the stairs are there too."

Henry headed for the carpeted stairs. The antique and undoubtedly noisy elevator would announce his arrival. He'd just as soon see Everett Bogardus before the man saw him.

He stopped on the stairs to analyze the reason for his caution. Why did he feel that way? He had as much right to be here as Bogardus did. It would be like seeing another kid when you were skipping school: they'd be sharing a silent, bonding knowledge of truancy.

He jogged down the rest of the stairs.

Once on the lower level, Henry crossed a wide hall and went into the men's room. Empty. As he was coming out, the object of his search hurried past the restroom alcove. Henry was still in the recessed area, and Bogardus didn't seem to see him, so he stayed close to the edge of the alcove and looked around the corner.

The man was pushing his way through a door marked with a sign warning: "Emergency Exit. Alarm sounds when door opens!"

Henry tensed, waiting for a reverberating siren or screech-honk, but he heard only a barely audible click from the closing door. Silent alarm?

He waited. Nothing happened. So, there was no door alarm, but an alarm was definitely going off inside his head. What ordinary, reasonable explanation could a tourist give for going through that door? And how had Bogardus known an alarm wouldn't sound?

Obvious. Either he'd been here before or someone had told him about the non-functioning alarm.

It was also possible he'd made a mistake. While waiting to see if a shamefaced man would return with some sort of "oops" explanation, Henry debated about going through the emergency exit himself. When the door had remained closed for several moments, he decided against following. If he was seen, he'd have no explanation, and anyway, Bogardus had probably left the building from whatever exit was behind the marked door. Maybe he'd suddenly felt ill or decided he wanted to hurry back to the Elderhostel group.

Why back to the group?

Whoa. Maybe he'd seen Henry here, had been watching him from a side hall, and decided he wanted to do more schmoozing with Carrie while Henry was out of the way. What if he was going back to see her?

Henry pictured that rude shove in the lobby. He had been tempted then to shove the man back, step between him and Carrie and take her arm, possessing her, showing she was his woman.

Hadn't done it though. If he had, and Carrie figured out what he was up to, she'd have pitched a fit—given him her speech about independence.

This morning dear Everett had been very friendly toward both Carrie and Eleanor, but Eleanor was married, her husband close by. Carrie, on the other hand...

Oh, cut it out, King, he told himself. This was stupid. Carrie wasn't a young woman with a roving eye and racing hormones. Everett Bogardus might act like he was some hot male, but Carrie was too sensible to respond to anything like that. Too sensible...

Wasn't she? He thought back to a time he'd held Carrie in his arms, kissed her, and how she'd responded, and...

Stop, stop it!

Henry's forehead creases deepened as he pictured Everett Bogardus in his tight jeans and the silk shirt showing off biceps to be admired. Had Carrie admired them? Did she notice things like that?

And that gaudy gold jewelry, all the fancy stuff...oh, hey now, that was something odd. Here at the Fordyce the man wore no jewelry at all, and there had been a ton of it looped around him earlier this morning.

Henry leaned against the wall, thinking. Could it all be real gold and Bogardus smart enough to know that showing it off in public made him a mark for thieves? Maybe he took the stuff off for that reason.

Maybe.

It still seemed suspicious that a posh college professor from the east would come here to learn the simple things being taught at this Elderhostel, but, so what, it was none of Henry's business. As for his actions toward Carrie, Everett Bogardus could be a harmless, if repulsive, flirt. Carrie, being a woman, probably understood that sort of thing.

What about the door? The man had walked confidently through it as if knowing the promised alarm would not ring. It was possible he'd wanted to leave the building by the quickest way he saw...but why?

The lawman's brain wouldn't shut up. There were too many *why's* floating around. Henry shook his head. The minute he'd seen Everett Bogardus, he'd suspected he might be up to something. Too slick, too sophisticated, didn't fit with the group. True, Henry's suspicions were nothing more than an itch in a mind long seasoned on suspicion.

Forget it, King, it isn't any of your business.

Okay. But since he was here, he might as well enjoy a look around. First he'd see what else was on this level, see where Bogardus had been before he rushed through that door.

Henry headed to the other end of the hallway and found himself in a small carpeted room with a glass display window labeled "Fordyce Spring." The glass protected a square, tile-framed hole in the floor. Henry looked into the hole and saw steaming water moving silently by, not even a ripple bothering its surface.

So, the Fordyce had its own hot spring.

Another glass viewing wall on the same side of the room allowed visitors to see into what must have been the original mechanical area of the building.

Henry peered through the glass. Except for several huge black water tanks, it looked pretty much like any old basement in any old building. It was probably supposed to show what the basement here had been like back in 1915, right after the Fordyce opened. He could see rough concrete floors and walls, an area floored in dirt, the black tanks, lots of pipes. There was an open set of wooden shelves not far from the window, backing up on the dirt-floored area. The shelves, once painted dark green but now peeling and splotched, were separated into box-like rectangles. Each rectangle was full of what must be pieces of the building's original plumbing fixtures.

Suddenly Henry sensed motion at the far left of the basement's visible area, and his head jerked that way as if something had pulled it, his hand automatically rushing to the place where his gun would have been, once upon a time.

Nothing.

Horrified by his quick and unthinking move toward deadly force, Henry shoved his hands into his pockets. But he still kept his eyes focused on the place where he'd sensed motion.

There! There it was again. He had seen something, a person, someone dressed in black, stooping over. Darkness swallowed details, but the movement had come from an area behind two big tanks lying close together on their sides. There was enough space back there for several people to hide.

The trained detective's suspicions were fast becoming facts, his thoughts lining up in orderly rows, all leading to one conclusion. Everett Bogardus was back there, up to no good, and there was more than one reason he went around dressed in black. Black, without the gold jewelry, would make anyone almost invisible in the dark areas of this basement.

It couldn't have been a workman, not in that get-up. Park employees wore grey and green uniforms.

So why was an ordinary tourist messing around back there among the tanks, pipes, broken concrete, odd cubby holes? Because he must be, as Henry had thought all along, much more than an ordinary tourist.

Was he hiding something? It would be a terrific place to hide an item of moderate size—like the contents of that tote bag.

Henry's mind froze on his next thought, tried to erase it, couldn't. Surely the man's intent wasn't...wasn't to plant a bomb or perhaps some incendiary device? People had cause to be antsy about things like that, but no, no, not here.

Stay out of this. Let it alone.

He was too suspicious, and he was no longer a police officer. He had no investigation or enforcement standing here. Or anywhere. He was on vacation, and even thinking about stuff like this could ruin his vacation—and Carrie's.

Bomb?

Everyone knew how many bad things were possible today and what kind of damage a bomb hidden or carried by one person could do.

It was too much. He had to take some action. If Bogardus was back there, he shouldn't be, no matter what.

Henry headed for the stairs.

A guided tour group was leaving the lobby when he got to the front desk, and Henry had an almost uncontrollable urge to tell them to leave the building immediately. But, once more, he realized he was overreacting to the police officer's instincts. As the chattering crowd moved away, Henry walked up to the reception desk, deciding as he did so to leave out any description of what the person he'd seen was wearing. He'd asked the attendant about a friend dressed in black only a few minutes ago.

"Did you find your friend?"

"Didn't make contact with him," Henry said, "but I did see something that seemed odd to me. I was in the basement, looking through that glass wall into where the black tanks are, and I thought I saw a man back there. He was acting like he wanted to stay hidden."

She was instantly alert. "Someone in the utility basement?"

"Yes. About ten minutes earlier I had seen a man, probably the same one, going through the door marked 'Emergency Exit.'"

"Was he wearing a uniform like mine?"

"No. He had on...dark street clothing, dark jeans, dark shirt."

The woman studied Henry for a moment, then said, "I'll call someone. Would you wait here please?" She picked up the phone.

The ranger who responded was in the lobby almost immediately and introduced himself as Rusty Hobbs. He asked Henry to describe what he'd seen; if he was surprised by the organized and thorough accounting, he said nothing.

"Call the Ranger Station," he told the attendant. "I'll

go check now, but get law enforcement here. I think Jake is on duty, and maybe Norman. I'll be in the basement." He headed off at a trot, with Henry right behind.

They went through the no-alarm door into a narrow hallway where Rusty swiveled to the left, going into what was obviously an employee break room. He opened a supply cabinet, took a flashlight, and returned to the hall with Henry still on his tail. When they reached the open door into the rough part of the basement, he stopped.

"Stay here while I check. I don't want your safety on my hands. Please go back to the break room. When a law enforcement ranger comes, send him along after me. He can holler, since I'll probably be out of sight. The old part of the basement is pretty big, and it's cut up into odd spaces as well as full of stuff like these tanks."

He thunked his hand against an enormous tank by the door. It was larger than any Henry had seen through the glass wall and had "Hot Springs Plumbing & Machine Company" painted on its shiny black side.

Henry stopped, reminded himself that, to this guy, he was just a civilian. He said to Rusty's back, "I'll keep an eye on the doors."

He had noticed a closed metal door at the end of the hall where he stood, probably the actual exit door named on the sign in the basement foyer. Anyone back in the mechanical area would have had plenty of time to leave that way while Henry went to get help; if the other door was an indication, no alarm would sound.

But, if Bogardus was still here, they now had him boxed in.

A dark man built like a football tackle came through the exit door, introduced himself as Law Enforcement Ranger Jake Kandler and, without any direction from Henry, hurried after Rusty.

While he waited, Henry fought a police officer's inner war between wanting to be in on the action and doing necessary sideline work. He *was* guarding doors, but he hated sitting still, he hated waiting.

After what seemed like ages, both men came back.

"Gone," said Jake, "but it looks like someone may have wanted to make a hole somewhere back there. Left this." He held up the small geologist's pick in his gloved hand. "At least I think this was left recently. Neither of us remembers seeing it before, and it has no ordinary purpose here in the Fordyce, though people sometimes take them on crystal digs. It's been used somewhere. Look here." He pointed to the head of the pick, but didn't touch its surface. "Scratches."

He thought for a moment, then said, "If someone was poking around back there, they must have seen you and left by this outside exit while you came to get us."

"Could be," Henry said, "but what about the alarm? Doesn't either door alarm sound?"

"Not during the day. Having to turn them off to come to the break room is inconvenient for the rangers and volunteers. But," he glared at Rusty, "they'll be on now."

After writing down Henry's name and his room number at the Downtowner, Jake dismissed him, saying, "Thanks for your help, but you'll be wanting to get some lunch."

Henry looked at his watch. Uh-oh! Lunch for the Elderhostelers had begun ten minutes ago, and he'd promised Carrie to be back in plenty of time for that.

Saying he'd be available all week if help was needed, Henry left the two rangers talking in the lunch room, pushed through the no-alarm door, and hurried toward the stairs.

He had more on his mind than being late for lunch. He was eager to get back and talk with Carrie about the happenings here. Of course he'd have to wait until after lunch and they were back in their room to discuss it with her. As he recalled, their schedule showed a couple of free hours between lunch and the Fordyce tour. They could come here early, he'd show her where everything had happened. She had a natural talent for detective work, and, with his help, was learning to be very good at it.

Or...should he tell her? Maybe it would be better not to mention seeing Bogardus come here, go through the door, skulk about back in the basement.

Why not? Usually they'd talk openly about something like this. Why the hesitation now? Was it because he suspected she'd defend the man or make light of his own suspicions?

Of course it was.

As he hurried out of the entry door, Henry noticed the same older couple was still sitting on the veranda, watching the crowds visiting the restaurants, gift shops, and galleries across the street.

Awareness hit him. These folks didn't look much different in age from him and Carrie, or Jason and Eleanor, and he'd automatically thought of them as "older."

Squaring his shoulders, Henry stood as tall as he could, clipped briskly down the stairs, began a parade march toward the Downtowner. Then he stopped.

A sign in the window of a rock shop across the street had shouted at him in neon words: "Crystal Dig Supplies."

Henry crossed the street.

Chapter VI

Carrie

Well, botheration! Where was Henry?

She glanced at the clock, sighed, then returned to the stack of Hot Springs tourist brochures she'd been trying to absorb. The words and photos zipped by in fast forward, a blur of color that didn't register anywhere in her brain.

She dropped the brochures on the bed beside her, stood up, went to the balcony, leaned over the railing. There was no sign of the familiar flat-brimmed khaki hat on the section of Central Avenue sidewalk that she could see.

Back inside. Now the clock said sixteen minutes past lunch time. She went to the bed and sat, fidgeted, wondered what to do next. Deciding, she stood, hurried to the desk, rummaged for a piece of paper, wrote, "Waiting for you downstairs, C.," and left the room.

Be calm was the first thought she had as she stepped into the lobby and looked at the floor marker for the second elevator. It was at the lobby level too. She figured that meant Henry hadn't been going up while she was coming down.

Now what? Ah! She'd stand by the fish tank near the restaurant entrance. She could see all directions from there. Five more minutes passed. Jason came from the restaurant to check on her, suggesting she eat with them. "You don't want to miss lunch. Besides, who knows what that rascal has gotten into," he said.

That was just it. What? She was hungry, a little bit peeved, and quite a bit worried. Henry was never late for anything.

She thanked Jason, said she'd wait a few more minutes, and went back to scanning the lobby.

Well, worrying was certainly not accomplishing anything, so it was past time to pray. She needed to erase her own rising temper and put God in charge here, especially in charge of Henry! She faced the huge tank and, pretending to watch the flashes of color flicking through the water in front of her, began a prayer with familiar verses from the 121st Psalm:

"The Lord shall preserve thee from all evil... The Lord shall preserve thy going out and thy coming in from this time forth, and even for evermore."

After a few moments she began to feel calmer, even confident that Henry, wherever he was, was under the promised preserving care she had just affirmed.

A hand fell on her shoulder. She jerked in surprise, banging her forehead on the glass wall of the fish tank.

"Oh, I am sorry, I didn't mean to startle you. I should have recognized that your thoughts were miles away. But since I'm late for lunch and it looks like you are too, I thought we might eat together."

It was Everett Bogardus, and her brand-new calmness had faded with his heavy touch and her forehead's contact with the fish tank.

Well, why not eat with him? Henry wasn't here, and he could hardly care if she went ahead and had lunch before the buffet closed.

After one last look toward the hotel entrances, she said, a little too loudly, "Yes, thank you, that would be nice."

There were no seats available at the larger tables in the area assigned to their group, but the single table for two was empty. Everett headed for it and pulled out a chair for her.

With a smile and only a twinge of regret, Carrie sat.

After a silence long enough to feel awkward he asked, "Did you enjoy the herb session?"

She'd been biting into a deviled egg and staring at the door. "Excuse me?"

"The herb session, did you enjoy it?"

She swallowed. "Uh, yes, very interesting. I have a small herb garden myself. I grow tomatoes too and use my herbs in a tomato sauce I make. I freeze pints of it every summer."

"I fear gardening isn't my interest. I live in an apartment in Cambridge."

"Oh! I know Cambridge, though it's mostly because of Legal Sea Foods and not scholarly pursuits. I go to Boston every few years to attend a church meeting, and I always spend a couple of extra days in the area playing tourist. In addition to all the other places I enjoy, I want to eat at the restaurant that has made its reputation serving fabulous lobster."

"Ah, of course, Legal Sea Foods is the place all right. In fact, I think this pen..." he reached in his pocket. "Yes, this pen was their give-away last Christmas. A good pen, actually." He held it out. "See the picture of the lobster on it? So now you know, Cambridge residents eat at Legal Sea Foods too. It isn't just for tourists."

He winked at her and returned the pen to his pocket. "We can eat there together the next time you come to Boston. Let's plan on it."

She decided it was time to change the subject. "I noticed you weren't in the herb session."

"I decided to go for a walk instead. Arlington Lawn Park is just down the block, and it has shady places where one can sit and enjoy the waterfall."

He was speaking very softly, leaning toward her. Without being conscious of it, Carrie bent toward him as she copied his soft tones. "My friend, Henry King, went for a walk too. Perhaps you saw him?"

That's when Henry appeared beside their table.

His face was flushed, and he looked cranky. His eyes bounced back and forth between her face and Everett's. After one glance at him, Carrie had to subdue not temper, but an urge to laugh. He looked so funny, like a caricature titled *Man, acting suspicious.* Was it because he was jealous?

She avoided his eyes, studying instead the lovely black hair going grey at his temples. It was mussed. For a fantasy moment she imagined herself combing it back into smooth waves...combing, letting her hand follow the comb...

Henry's words tumbled out in breathless jerks. "Well, here I am. Sorry to be late. Unavoidable. I see you're already eating. Any food left?"

It was obvious he'd been hurrying. Carrie's urge to laugh was replaced by a wild curiosity about what had made him so late.

"Oh, still plenty of food," Everett said, smiling. That's

when Carrie felt one of his legs push between hers under
the table and begin to rub up and down, up and down,
oh, so smoothly.

She slid back in her chair as far as she could and pulled
her legs to the side. Accidental touch? Oh, no. There
couldn't be any mistake about his intent this time.

"You weren't here, so I came on in," she told Henry,
working hard to keep her face calm. Her effort was wasted
because he was looking at Everett, opening a sack he'd
brought with him, pulling something out, plunking it
against the table top.

"What's tha...?" she began, stopping in mid-word as
Everett's knee slashed sideways, shoving her own knees into
the table leg and slopping water out of their glasses.

"Well, my goodness, you keep bumping into me, please
be more careful," she said, speaking as if he were a naughty
child.

Her eyes went to Henry's face to see if he'd noticed the
reaction.

He was still looking at Everett. "I found this geologist's
pick while I was out this morning," he said. "I thought we
could use it on the crystal dig."

He must have meant his words for her, but all his attention was still directed toward her table companion.

Something was very peculiar here. What about the little
pick had so unnerved Everett Bogardus?

He'd begun to mop water with his napkin, and now
Henry stared at her over the bent head and mouthed the
words, "Watch him." He looked wary, his police officer
look.

Everett was still mopping. He didn't seem to be paying
attention to either of them.

Henry put the pick in his sack and left for the sandwich

line. As soon as he was gone, Everett dropped the soggy napkin on his salad plate, excused himself, and went to the buffet table. Carrie watched as he stood there for a moment before picking up another napkin. By the time he turned back to her he'd regained his composure, but she noticed that something had happened in his eyes. They looked hard, like blue ice.

He sat down slowly, unfolded the napkin, lifted the corners of his lips in a smile. After a pause he said, "So, is there some kind of understanding between the two of you? I don't think he approves of us having lunch together."

"Goodness no, not an understanding in the way you mean it. We are good friends, and we often work as a team. I'm sure he doesn't mind about lunch. He wasn't here, after all."

She smiled back, hoping her smile didn't look as fake as his, and glanced past him to see Henry taking one of the many chairs that were now vacant. Most of the Elderhostelers had finished eating and left the restaurant, hurrying on to whatever activities they'd planned before the Fordyce tour began at three o'clock.

Well, bother. Henry wouldn't know there weren't any other seats available at the bigger tables when she and Everett came in.

"You work together? At a tourist information center?"

That's when she decided she'd try to shock him. Maybe he'd say something she could report to Henry.

"No. We're detectives."

That did it. Everett's eyes flashed surprise, and the smarmy smile vanished.

"Ahhhh. You must admit detective work seems an unusual occupation for...well, you'll excuse me, I don't want to appear insensitive, but how on earth did you get into that?"

"Oh, it was natural enough. It began with the murder of a friend of ours. Henry and I identified the killer. Turned out we made a pretty good team. There have been other things since then. Word gets around, you know."

She knew she was showing off, God forgive her, but it was for a good cause. She just hoped she'd find out what the cause was as soon as she could be alone with Henry.

"I've always been the curious type, and I enjoy doing research. A lot of that is needed in our line of work. For Henry, detective work comes quite naturally, of course. He's a retired police major. He was with the Kansas City Police Department for many years, in homicide, mostly."

Everett was watching her intently now. She could picture wheels turning inside his head. "I wouldn't have guessed," he said, "though your friend Henry does seem a bit too inquisitive."

She tried to convey an air of calm innocence, not wanting to let the man know she understood that his "too inquisitive" comment was meant to be what she would call snotty.

"Oh, yes, that's what we are, inquisitive. It's a very helpful skill in our line of work." She pasted on another fake smile, then looked at her empty plate and decided it was time to be more inquisitive about Everett Bogardus.

"Now it's your turn to tell me more about yourself. This is my first trip here, but when you were talking about some of the local history after Ranger Hawk's program, it sounded like you'd been here before, maybe even lived here. Was this trip a sort of homecoming for you?"

There was a long pause before he answered, and Carrie imagined she could see the wheels whirling again while he decided how to reply. Finally he said, "Oh, I was here once, a very long time ago. Don't remember much of it. I was pretty young." Then, turning away from her question and any follow-up, he began an account of the university classes he taught. His words sounded memorized, as if he weren't thinking about what he was saying. Carrie faced him as he talked, but she was watching Henry over his shoulder. A couple from Iowa and the two lawyers from Chicago were now sitting at Henry's table, and the Stacks had also stayed behind to keep him company.

"...university students have changed since then. More experienced sexually, of course, and in every other conceivable way as well. 'World-weary' is a term I'd use as a generality. Right now they are at least more aware of the importance of understanding our history. I applaud that, though probably world events and not my brilliant teaching brought their interest to the fore."

"Oh, I'm sure you're a brilliant teacher, Everett," Carrie said, noticing that most of his sandwich was still on his plate. He hadn't taken a bite for several minutes. Her fault? She'd kept him talking. Or was it nerves?

"Well, thank you. I do find that Middle Eastern history is drawing interest right now. Fortunately it's a specialty of mine. I have..."

Henry had finished lunch and was leaving.

"Everett, I hate to interrupt this most fascinating account, but look at your plate, you've barely touched your lunch. I've been selfish, asking you these questions. I'll leave you alone so you can finish eating, and we'll continue our conversation later. Thanks for inviting me to sit with you. Now, if you'll excuse me?" She laid her napkin on the table and stood, causing him to leap up and rush to move her chair back, dumping his own napkin on the floor.

"See you at the Fordyce," she said, not caring whether

he thought she was rude or not.

Carrie swished out of the room, following Henry toward the elevators.

He'd stopped at the brochure racks, and the minute she appeared around the corner he shoved a couple of flyers in his pocket and came to take her arm. As soon as the elevator door closed behind them, she said, "Henry, what on earth is going on? Where *were* you, and why did that geologist's pick put Everett in such a snit? He's beside himself with worry over that thing."

"He should be worried. It's a long story. I'll tell you in the room."

And he did.

"That's so weird, even fantastic," she said after he had finished. She didn't mean unbelievable. In fact, she did believe it, the whole story. For one thing, Henry wasn't given to telling lies or even stretching the truth. For another, right now she'd believe almost anything of Everett Bogardus. Including something like this? Yes, most certainly.

"Henry," she said, thinking out loud, "you said you and the rangers suspected Everett had gone in that basement to hide something. But, especially if that pick was his, doesn't it seem more likely that he was there to find something?"

He sat down on his bed. "Find something? In a bathhouse? You mean some wealthy matron from Detroit left her jewels behind in a dressing room locker, or Al Capone dropped his diamond cuff links in the spring?"

"No, of course not, or at least I hadn't thought of anything like that. But the Fordyce is an old building. It was open as an active bathhouse for years and years."

She sat on her own bed now, her eyes seeing nothing

as she tried to think herself into the past. "We've got to learn more, find out when the Fordyce Bathhouse closed, for one thing. And we need to look more carefully at that basement, see if a pick could be used to dig something up, or break into something."

"Sounds fantastic, just like you said. And, what dif..."

Her words swept over his. "But then, when it closed wouldn't matter, would it? The building was always there, empty or not, and probably empty would be even better for people who needed to hide something. A lot of gambling money and payment for, uh, illegal services floated around Hot Springs all the time, at least until sometime in the '60s when Winthrop Rockefeller became governor. Then the Arkansas State Police moved in, smashed it all, closed down the open gambling, the bawdy houses.

"Tell me, Henry, where did all those illegal profits go when that happened? Wouldn't most transactions have been in cash? Don't you suppose at least a few people got away with gobs of money?"

"Well...if things were chaotic and the bosses couldn't keep tabs on all of it, I suppose..."

"No suppose about it. There *must* have been loose money up for grabs if you had half a brain and were crafty enough. It's easy to imagine what could have happened. And, some of that money must have been hidden in the Fordyce! There would have been chaos everywhere like you said, maybe people grabbing up wads of money when the police broke in, some of them needing to hide it and get away until the raids were over. What do you think? Maybe the person who hid money in the Fordyce was going to be searched, couldn't be found with the money."

"You're letting your imagination run away on a wild theory, Carrie. You're remembering *The Sting*."

"Humpf, may be, but you've got to admit it could have happened like that. If even one person hid money in the Fordyce, well, of course, it would have to be enough money to make it worth hiding, and that might mean a fortune, even today. It would be worth going to some trouble to find it."

"But why didn't that person come back to get your hypothetical fortune long ago? And since then the building's been restored and used constantly by the Park Service, with lots of workers going through it and people around all the time. Besides, if someone tried to spend really old paper money today, it would raise red flags in the banking system."

She could tell he was playing devil's advocate, but that only made excitement bubble higher inside her. "Trust me, Henry, Everett Bogardus was not trying to *hide* something! He was trying to *find* something that's probably still there. Undoubtedly the person who hid the money couldn't get back and, somehow, Everett learned about it. It's actually kind of romantic. And finding money like that isn't really illegal, is it? It doesn't belong to anyone now. Wouldn't it be 'finders keepers'?"

She saw Henry wince at her use of the word *romantic*. Maybe she should have chosen another word.

He said, "If illegally gained assets were subject to seizure by the state back in the '60s, they'd be subject to seizure now. They're still illegally gained assets. Time doesn't change that. Of course, nothing about this would be all black and white. It's the sort of case that could be argued in court for years, and ownership by the state might be hard to prove. Someone could claim that the money was from a family fortune and was hidden to keep it out of the wrong hands."

"So what he's doing, though a little shady, might not be

all that criminal. It could be his family's money."

"I'd bet it's stealing, no matter what," he said. "And here's another thing to think about. If there is hidden money, how did Bogardus learn about this supposed treasure? I guess we need to find out more about him and his past."

"Eleanor and I noticed this morning that he knows a lot about Hot Springs' history, and during lunch I asked him about it. He admitted to being here before, said he was very young at the time. He wouldn't say more and avoided revealing whether he came here as a visitor or lived here. He changed the subject completely, as a matter of fact. I wonder where we could check on his past?"

She picked up the phone book, turned pages. "Hm... no Bogardus listed. Well, it was a thought."

Henry pulled two brochures out of his pocket and handed them to her. "Here's another possibility. I found these in the racks in the lobby. They're from the Garland County Historical Society. How about checking with them and seeing what material they have? We might find information on the raids you're talking about, maybe get an idea how much money was recovered and whether law officers, the IRS, state treasurer, or anybody else thought a quantity of money was unaccounted for. And maybe they have school records. We could check those for Everett Bogardus's name."

"That's a brilliant idea, Henry. He might have actually lived here during the '60s. I'd guess he would have been somewhere between fifteen and twenty-five years old back then. If he didn't hide the money himself, it could have been hidden by his father, or some other family member."

She cut off her speculation and jumped up from the bed where she'd been sitting. "Let's go to the Garland County Historical Society after lunch tomorrow. There's a continuation of the herb class in the morning, but the afternoon session doesn't begin until 3:00. Won't we have time to check up on the history stuff after lunch? Right now, though, I'd sure like to go to the Fordyce. We have at least an hour and a half before our scheduled tour begins, and I can't wait to see that basement.

"Let's wear dark colors, just in case. Maybe we'll have a chance to get into the mechanical area like Everett did.

"Hand me the geologist's pick. I think I can fit it in my purse."

"*What?* Carrie, I do hope you're joking!"

Chapter VII

Henry

The trouble was, she hadn't been joking. Henry knew that quite well.

But reason prevailed. When she'd hefted the weight of the pick inside her purse, Carrie agreed it was best to leave the thing behind. He saw her put it on the night table shelf.

She did insist that he take his small flashlight, and he went to get it from the car before they left.

Now they were standing at the glass viewing wall in the public area of the Fordyce basement staring at rough concrete, black tanks, mysterious spaces, dark shadows.

"It's a perfect place to hide something," Carrie said. "Look at all those irregular walls and dark corners." She pointed. "I can see at least one hole broken into that wall over there. Some of the walls must be made of hollow clay blocks. See where those terra-cotta colored chunks have fallen in a heap on the floor? The entire area looks like a hidey-hole paradise.

"I wonder if some special marking says where the money is hidden, or if you have to measure, or count tiles, or something? Maybe there's a map or drawing—I sure wish we knew. If I thought it would get the truth out of him, I'd almost cozy up to Everett, or," she looked up at Henry and grinned, "I mean *act* like I am, of course, though, truth be told, I'll bet an approach like that would scare the man to death!"

It was too much. She was going beyond reason on this hidden treasure thing, though he had to admit her theory was at least possible. But offering to... Well, now she *was* joking, of course, but it was still too much.

"Carrie, this isn't like you at all. You're more reasonable and intelligent than to even think such thoughts. Come on, let's get out of this basement. I've had enough of it and enough of Everett Bogardus. We're on vacation, remember?"

She looked up at him quizzically, then turned toward the glass again. "But the idea of a treasure hunt is such fun. Why can't we sneak a peek back there? We could stay away from this viewing area—look at all those concealing walls and hiding places where we could duck out of sight.

"I haven't seen or heard any rangers go through the exit door recently, and the woman who came out when we first got here didn't push any buttons or even slow down. I'll bet you they never turned that alarm on. If it's been off for years, why would workers be willing now to fool with disabling it every time they want a cup of coffee?"

"Still doesn't matter, my dear girl. Alarm or not, that

area is off-limits to the public. The rangers know *I* know that! I wouldn't dare get caught back there, and we would be caught. Count on it!"

"Oh, pooh, Henry. Standing here looking into that basement is just like looking at your grandchild through the hospital nursery window and not getting to hold him!"

He didn't comment on that. He knew how badly Carrie wanted her son Rob to marry and present her with a grandchild.

"Never mind. Why don't we go look at the rest of the building? Who knows, there may be lots of possible hiding places on the other floors too."

"But..."

"Carrie, please think more clearly. You must understand that we absolutely cannot go back there. It would be trespassing, and it would be stupid."

Her silence lasted at least thirty seconds before he heard a reluctant "okay."

She looked at the building guide the receptionist had given her. "It seems the only public restrooms are on this floor. They call them 'Comfort Stations.' How quaint. I should visit the comfort station before we go upstairs, so why don't you go on up and wait for me in the gift shop? We need to pick out post cards. I promised the Booths I'd send them one, and I also want to send cards to Rob and Susan."

"Later. I'll go in the men's comfort station while we're here."

The hall was empty when he returned. He sat on the bench outside the restrooms and waited. Several minutes passed. Finally, when no female had appeared to check inside

"Women's" for him, he went to the room's entry alcove
and listened. Total silence. He said, "Carrie?" More silence.
"Carrie, you okay?" Still quiet.

Moving quickly, he headed around the corner, looked
long enough to see that the room was empty, and hurried
back out into the hallway. Thank goodness there were still
no people around to see where he had come from.

Confound the woman! He hadn't believed she'd do it,
but it seemed she would.

He went to the exit door at the end of the hall and
pushed it open. He knew the alarm wouldn't ring. It hadn't
rung, after all, when Carrie opened it.

No one was in the break room or locker room, and
no voice or hand stopped him when he passed through
the open doorway into the mechanical area. Enough bare
light bulbs were glowing to make walking fairly easy, and
he went forward as quickly as he could, stopping several
times to listen and look around.

Nothing but silence. Where was she? Maybe he was
wrong. Maybe she had gone on to the gift shop.

Then he heard what sounded like the scrape of a shoe
on rough flooring.

"Carrie?" He didn't dare say it too loudly.

"Henry? Thank God you've come. I'm in the little room.
Go through the broken wall we saw from the other side.
There's a man in here...he's hurt. He's..."

Her voice faded away, but Henry had located the sound.
Heedless of the fact that he would be visible from the glass
viewing area for a few moments, he rushed ahead, finding
a small doorway that had been cut into the concrete and
clay block wall. Stooping, he went through.

Carrie was on her knees next to a rough concrete
platform in the back corner of the room. Her hand, show-

ing up lighter than the surrounding darkness, seemed to be against the forehead of a man lying crumpled on the platform. Henry snatched the miniature flashlight from his pants pocket, switched it on. The man wore a park ranger's uniform.

Her face looked unnaturally pale as she squinted into the blueish light, and tears on her cheeks sparkled and danced when the flashlight moved.

The words stumbled out. "I wanted to see...just look around a bit, and...after I got to the basement door, I...I... heard funny sounds, scraping, some sort of a clunk. Then I heard him moan. How could I not come here, Henry? How could I not?" She bowed her head, was silent.

Henry knelt and put his left arm around her as the flashlight in his right hand swept over the man on the floor. Rusty Hobbs!

There was blood. It had come from a wound on the side of the ranger's head. A geologist's pick, probably the same one he'd seen here this morning, and all too exactly like the one he'd bought later in the shop across the street, lay in the concrete crumbs and dust beside Hobbs. Small pieces of floor litter were stuck in blood on the head of the pick.

Carrie lifted her hand from the man's forehead, glanced at the blood on it, looked up at Henry. "He's breathing," she said, "and I felt a pulse."

She bowed her head again, and Henry heard, "The Lord bless you and keep you safe." The rest of her words disappeared into a silent prayer.

Well, it was too darn late to worry about who should be back here and who shouldn't. The important thing now was to get help.

But, as much as he hated to leave Rusty Hobbs alone, he knew he couldn't leave Carrie with him. What if the person...what if Everett Bogardus was still hiding somewhere in the basement and came back to hurt her? It was a terrible decision, but he couldn't leave her here.

He pulled at her shirt, tugging her into a crouch and then back through the rough doorway. At first she resisted, but then she was moving with him, up and down over half walls and broken concrete, around black tanks, and, at last, into the light, bright employee break room.

A startled park volunteer gaped at them, took one look at the blood on Carrie's hand, and asked, "How did she get hurt? I'll call for help."

"Yes, please," Henry said. "Call 911 and park security. Rusty Hobbs has been attacked. He's back in the mechanical area of the basement, in that little room near the viewing wall. We're going back now to stay with him until help comes."

The woman began talking into the phone, no longer paying attention to them. Henry wondered how long it would be before she realized they were strangers in the wrong place, might even be the ones who'd attacked Hobbs.

He said to Carrie, very quietly, "Wash your hands thoroughly. You don't have any cuts or scrapes on them, do you? You haven't touched your face, bare skin, or clothing? No? Good. Then when you're through washing, dampen one of those towels and we'll take it back with us, maybe use it to help stop the bleeding if it hasn't stopped already. I'll take this dry towel to slip under his head."

Her hands were already under the water and she nodded briskly. Thank goodness she'd returned to her sensible, quick-thinking self. They were about to face a whirlwind of questions and would need to give clear, well-reasoned answers.

As they hurried back to Hobbs he was hoping they'd have a minute alone to talk about those answers before the ambulance or anyone from law enforcement came.

But they didn't get that minute. Carrie was just handing him her damp towel when the voice of Law Enforcement Ranger Jake Kandler echoed through the basement, asking where they were.

CHAPTER VIII

CARRIE

"Henry, please be quiet. Let me talk first."

She had no idea what this law enforcement ranger thought of her bossiness, but it didn't matter. She had to get her story out before Henry could open his mouth and mess things up. It would be so like him to be chivalrous and try to protect her. Ever since they became friends, she'd been trying to make it clear she didn't want or need protecting, but, too often, he couldn't get around his image of the strong male who took care of everything. Especially her. Well, phooey!

Thank goodness this bear of a park ranger hadn't tried to separate them, not yet at least. He was keeping them with him, seated on the irregular, dirty basement floor, waiting for the EMT's and, evidently, for both the FBI and the

Hot Springs Police. She didn't dare think about that now, as intimidating as it might be. She must tell her story where Henry could hear it since this man had shown up before they could coordinate what they were going to say.

She rushed words out, not looking at either Henry or the big ranger. Instead, she watched the barely perceptible rise and fall of Ranger Hobbs' chest. It was easier to keep an eye on him now since the new ranger—what had he said his name was?—since he had brought a battery lantern.

"After Henry, uh, Mr. King, told me about what happened when he was here this morning, about the man hiding in the basement, I wanted to see the place."

Would a nervous laugh sound right at this point? Even if it would, she couldn't manage it.

"So, since we had time, we decided to come here before our guided tour started." She looked at her watch. "That begins in forty-five minutes with Ranger Hawkins. And when I said I wanted to look around back here in the rough basement, Mr. King made it very clear this area was off-limits to tourists. He said we couldn't look around, couldn't leave the public area."

Now she glanced at the ranger's face. Hadn't he said his name was Jake something? Jake Candle, that was it!

"So, Ranger Candle, I..."

"It's Kandler."

"Oh. Excuse me, Ranger Kandler, of course. Well, anyway, I didn't see what harm just a little look around could do. It was as if I were *compelled* to come back here. Do you understand? So when Henry went in the men's room, I came through that door in the hall he'd told me about. And," she said, trying now to show the piety she honestly felt, "it's a very good thing I did. I think God led me here so this man would get the help he needed. We all should be grateful to God for His guidance."

Surely the ranger wouldn't quarrel with that statement. No matter what his religious beliefs, he wouldn't dare quarrel with God. And, for that matter, neither would Henry Jensen King.

"Of course, Henr...Mr. King, came to find me, to get me out. But, instead..." She gestured toward Rusty Hobbs and fell silent, as if awareness of the injured man said it all. She looked past the ranger at Henry's face. It was impassive, but after a moment he pursed his lips, almost as if blowing her a kiss. Well, at least he'd heard her story and would have no choice now but to agree with it. There would be no hiding of what had been, after all, her decision. What she spoke was the truth.

"It was a good thing I came here," she repeated.

Kandler looked at her briefly, then back at Hobbs. Keeping his eyes on his friend, he asked, "Anything to add to that, sir?"

"No, except that we did leave him long enough to get help."

"Both of you?"

"Yes. Because of the circumstances I didn't want to leave Ms. McCrite or send her through the basement alone. I thought the person who attacked Hobbs could still be back here and that her presence had cut off his only avenue of anonymous escape. She said when she first came through the door, she heard a scraping sound and some sort of clunk, then a moan. It's possible she heard the actual attack. I also thought it possible that the perpetrator supposed Hobbs was dead, and because of that he would be doubly frantic to get away—whether Ms. McCrite was in the way or not.

"So we went to get help together and returned here as soon as we'd asked the park volunteer to call 911. We were gone less than five minutes, and during that time I didn't see or hear anyone opening the exterior door."

Kandler nodded. "We'll search the basement more thoroughly as soon as extra help comes. In the meantime Shirley is keeping an eye on the exit doors."

For a moment he was silent, then he shook his head and came back to Carrie and Henry. "Did either of you touch anything here? That pick, maybe?"

"Just Ranger Hobbs," they said in unison.

And that was the end of the conversation. Loud voices and scraping feet were headed their way. Henry and Law Enforcement Ranger Kandler went to the cubby hole opening to direct the emergency team. Carrie, still seated on the floor next to Rusty Hobbs, noticed Henry had left his little flashlight in the dirt beside her. She picked it up and stuck it in her pocket.

Real FBI agents, it seemed, looked and acted just like those who mimicked them in movies and on television.

Or at least this one does, Carrie thought, as she stared at Agent Colin Bell's perfectly aligned burgundy tie. She was also getting a definitely non-TV impression, and she sniffed to be sure. Yes, the man smelled like soap. He smelled just-out-of-the-shower clean.

Agent Bell had been writing, but at the sniff he looked up. She reached in her pocket for a tissue and wiped it across her nose. Satisfied, he went back to writing.

They were seated at a table in the Fordyce employee break room. As she understood it, Jake Kandler and Henry had gone to offices on the third floor of the building to await the arrival of a second FBI agent. Meanwhile park employees and one Hot Springs police officer were searching the basement. Their voices, accented by occasional clunks, scrapes, and pings, carried down the hall. But, here in the break room, she and Agent Bell were alone.

A second Hot Springs police officer, who'd appeared with the ambulance, hadn't stayed. Agent Bell explained that the two officers were responding only to see if they could be of any assistance and to accompany the ambulance. City police, it seemed, had no jurisdiction in a national park.

Her eyes went back to the burgundy tie. It lay against a perfectly ironed white shirt and was framed by the jacket of a dark grey suit. Agent Bell looked downright crisp. Carrie wondered if he had just come on duty. She also wondered if he or his wife had pressed the smooth white shirt minutes before he put it on.

Was there a wife? Children? She was beginning to imagine two children, a boy about ten, and a girl who was fourteen, maybe, and the apple of her father's eye, when Bell stopped writing and looked at her.

"So that's it? Mr. King told you about seeing a person, probably male, in the mechanical area of the basement earlier today. He said this person was dressed all in black and was trying to stay hidden. When rangers searched the area after Mr. King reported the presence of this person, the only unusual thing they found was a geologist's pick, unknown source. And when you heard this, you decided that money left from the '60s raids might be hidden here and the person King saw was looking for it?"

He paused, as if for emphasis, before he asked the next question. "You wanted to search for the money yourself?"

"I said *nothing* to you about wanting to find the money myself. I was just curious about the incident and, as you say, reasoned that a search for hidden money would be one good explanation for what happened. I believe that might be a natural conclusion for most people who know anything about Hot Springs' history."

She was seated facing the room's refrigerator and wondered what the agent would do if she got up, went to look inside, maybe found cans of pop and snacks. She could offer him a drink and something to eat. She could have something herself. What might he do about that? Would anything that folksy and casual unnerve him?

Whatever. Agent Colin Bell had begun talking again.

"I see. You also say you knew that the area of the basement we're concerned with here is off limits to the public. There's a sign of notification on the door."

"Oh, yes, I know all about that sign. But I also know the alarm doesn't ring."

"I see," he said again. There was a long pause while the agent looked down at his notes. What was he thinking?

Carrie shifted in her chair, moving it slightly so it would scrape on the floor while, with her foot, she pushed her purse farther under the table.

"Agent Bell?"

He looked up. "Ma'am?"

"The Elderhostel group we're part of is taking a tour of this building right now. It began at 3:00. We have friends in the group who will wonder where we are, and the coordinator will be keeping track of any missing people. Wouldn't it be best if I went to join them, especially if Mr. King will be tied up for a while? Our absence might cause a stir and an effort to find us. Henry or I should be there to explain."

"I'd rather you didn't explain. No one here, outside the staff, knows about the attack on Hobbs yet. Ranger Hawkins knows, but he will not mention it to your group. Perhaps he's already given some simple reason for your absence. I'd like to avoid any public agitation or alarm, and I also want to find out more about your interest in the off-limits area of this building. It seems odd."

"Not odd when you consider the circumstances."

She paused, thinking about those circumstances and wondering whether or not she should mention suspicions about Everett Bogardus to this man.

It was sure unhandy, being separated from Henry. What was he saying, and would their stories mesh? Would he mention Everett?

Agent Bell's light blue eyes studied her, and he waited without speaking. The silent treatment.

"One of the circumstances is the unique history of this place as I said, plus the fact that Henry and I have recently had some success as private detectives. We notice mysteries. We take an interest in them, and this was certainly something out of the ordinary. A mystery."

The blue eyes widened just a bit. Of course he couldn't show emotion, he wouldn't dare unbend and be informal. But his look said, "Detectives? Aw, come off it."

She might be exaggerating her role as a detective, but it was no exaggeration to say that Eleanor and Jason, and probably Greta, would be concerned about their absence from a planned Elderhostel activity, whether Ranger Hawkins had given any explanation or not. But, in spite of that, her main interest in joining the tour was to find out if Everett Bogardus was there.

She wished she knew if Henry had mentioned him. Well, no matter, if Ranger Kandler or Agent Bell saw a man dressed all in black, they'd make a connection since Henry had told them the person hiding behind the tanks was wearing black. That was assuming they believed Henry, of course.

She decided he probably hadn't said anything more

than that. Everything about Everett's involvement was still speculation, and Henry was a stickler for facts. Therefore, at this point, he would not be likely to implicate Everett Bogardus.

Agent Bell put down his pen. "You're *detectives?*" The two words, full of scorn, spoke worlds.

"Yes. We don't do it for pay, but in a small way Henry and I have been able to help people in trouble more than once. We fell into it easily enough after a friend of ours was murdered and we discovered who had killed her. Henry, you know, is a retired police officer. He was a major in the Kansas City Police Department."

That ought to take the agent down a peg or two.

It didn't. "Yes, we learned that from Ranger Kandler. He confirmed Major King's background after the incident this morning. There was no need to look up any record for you at the time. We didn't know you were involved."

Carrie shifted into her grandmotherly mode. "I haven't got a record, Agent Bell, unless it's a record of the Social Security payments I get or the taxes I pay. As I told you, I do work for the State of Arkansas, but only as manager of a Tourist Information Center. And I think you must be through asking me questions now. I simply haven't any more to tell you. Besides, we'll be in Hot Springs the rest of the week if you need us. We're just two senior citizens who came here to enjoy an Elderhostel and, because of my, uhhh, excessive curiosity, we were able to get quick help for an injured park ranger. That's it. I may be overly curious, but you must admit that connecting the turbulent circumstances of the '60s with the presence of an unknown person back in the basement who was carrying a geologist's pick isn't all that unusual. The whole sequence of events, added to the town's history, made me curious. It should make you curious. In fact, I would think you'd want to look for that money yourself."

I can probably outstare you, she thought as Agent Bell met her eyes again. *You'll blink first.*

And he did.

"All right, go find your tour group. Do not mention the circumstances that delayed you or anything about the injury to Ranger Hobbs. I suggest you tell the coordinator and your friends that you and Mr. King got involved in a conversation with rangers about various events in the park, or something of that sort. I'm going upstairs after I check with the searchers, and I'll tell Major King you're with the Elderhostel group."

"Thank you. And would you please keep us informed about Ranger Hobbs' condition? You have our room number at the hotel. We are praying for his full recovery."

The agent inclined his head as Carrie reached under the table, tugged at her purse, and hefted the strap across her shoulder. That accomplished, she got up to hurry out of the room.

"Ms. McCrite!"

Her heart almost stopped. "Yes?"

"There's dirt from the basement floor on the back of your slacks. Before you join the group, you may want to brush it off."

He would notice dirt on clothing. "Thanks for telling me, Agent Bell. I'll take care of it."

"And, Ms. McCrite, under no circumstances are you to return to this area of the building. Is that clear?"

"Perfectly clear."

Only a few more steps now, and she'd be safely away.

In her rush she almost missed it. Although the floor in the employee area hallway was clean, and bright with fluorescent lighting, the background color of the pen matched the baseboard paint. It was hard to see, lying there in the angle between the floor and wall. It could be missed if you were agitated, as she—as they all—had been earlier.

But now she could see it clearly, even the tiny red lobster on its side.

She hesitated only a moment, then, holding her purse securely, turned back into the break room. "Ever been to Boston, Agent Bell?"

He gaped at her, probably deciding she was even more loony than he'd supposed.

"Nice place to visit, Boston. Cambridge too, just across the Charles River. I've been there several times. One of the best places to eat in the area is Legal Sea Foods in Cambridge. They're known for their lobster.

"And you know, that's quite a coincidence, because one of our Elderhostel group, Everett Bogardus, is from Boston. I happened to mention Legal Sea Foods to him at lunch today, and he said he eats there sometimes. He even showed me a pen they'd given him last Christmas. Had a red lobster on it.

"If you ever go to Boston, you really should try that restaurant. Everett knows all about it if you want to find out more. The address is probably on his pen."

She smiled at the agent, whose expression now could only be described as blank.

"Just a word to the wise, you know. Never can tell when you might need odd information.

"Well, good-by again, Agent Bell."

She pushed out the door and hurried toward the ladies' to brush off her pants. She was thinking, *I wonder what Henry would have done about that pen?*

CHAPTER IX

CARRIE

Drat! The restroom mirrors were placed too high to show dirt on the backside of a 5'2" woman. After craning her neck fruitlessly and making a few ineffective swats at her behind, Carrie took off her slacks so she could see where to brush. Now she stood bare-legged in the middle of the restroom floor, thinking about what to do next.

Not all the dirt she'd sat in on the basement floor would come off with brushing. That, however, was not her main concern at the moment.

Her main concern was the geologist's pick weighing heavily in her purse. She needed to get rid of it before one of those law enforcement people decided to investigate the contents of her purse or Henry discovered what a fool she'd been.

Not that her original idea had been wrong, actually. In fact, she still thought it a rather good idea. After hearing Henry's report of his morning adventure, she'd decided a quick survey of the basement here would reveal possible places money could be hidden. Never mind that no one had found anything in over forty years. They weren't really looking.

She imagined herself finding it. It wouldn't be difficult in a basement like Henry described. All it took was a bit of informed reasoning, and any possible hiding places should be obvious. Then a few taps of the pick; mystery solved, treasure revealed, Everett Bogardus thwarted.

So when, at her insistence, Henry had gone to the car to get the miniature flashlight she'd given him for his birthday, she'd stuck the pick in her purse. Why not?

She didn't want to speculate now about what might have happened to her if Ranger Kandler or Agent Bell had looked in her purse and found a geologist's pick like the one used in the attack on Ranger Hobbs. After finding the injured ranger with the bloody pick beside him, she never wanted to see a geologist's pick again—in her purse or anywhere else. She could still picture the one lying on the dirty floor, dust and darkening blood in a messy...

No! Carrie shook her head, trying to erase the image, and forced her thoughts back to things at hand.

The little bit of dirt that wouldn't come off her slacks gave her a good excuse to go to the hotel and dump the pick. Then she'd change clothes and come back to join the Elderhostel group. Even if Agent Bell found out she'd left the building, her dirty slacks offered excuse enough. He, after all, had been the one to point out the dirt.

She tugged the slacks back on, thankful for an elastic waist, and rushed toward the stairs, intent on getting up to the lobby, out of the building, and down the street.

But at the top of the stairs, she ran smack dab into a swarm of Elderhostelers coming out of the Fordyce theater.

"Oh, there you are, Carrie," Jason called out. "We missed you and Henry at the movies. Did the two of you get involved in some private activity of your own?" And of course he snickered, causing the few who hadn't already noticed her abrupt arrival to look her way.

Someday, Carrie thought, in a flash of temper, *I'm going to throttle that man.*

Greta's voice broke into the awkward silence. "I'm sorry you missed the informational film, Carrie, but you'll have time to catch it later. We've divided into two groups for the building tour so everyone can be close enough to their guide to hear explanations. Why don't you and Henry go with Rina Jenkins? Her group is smaller. Or," she looked around, "isn't Henry coming?"

Carrie shrugged, at a loss as to what she should say.

"He's okay, isn't he?" At Carrie's affirmative nod, Greta continued, "Good. He can join us later. All right, we're ready. Ranger Hawkins will begin on this floor, volunteer guide Jenkins and her group on the third floor. Shall we get started?

"Gather around, gang," Rina Jenkins said. "You can walk up to the third floor, or you can take the elevator. Even if you choose the stairs this time, I suggest at least one experience riding in our elevator. It looks antique and it is, but it's been completely re-vamped and is quite safe. We'll divide into smaller groups to ride it."

Surrounded by fellow Elderhostelers, Carrie was swept through the elevator's grillwork door; accompanied by interesting mechanical clanks and clicks, she rose up and away from the lobby exit she'd been intent on reaching.

Oh, well, so what? If anyone saw the pick in her purse, she could say she purchased it in preparation for the crystal dig. They wouldn't know the difference.

Of course Henry would know, but surely she'd have a chance to slip it out of her purse and back onto the night stand shelf after they returned to their room. He'd spend time in the bathroom while they were getting dressed for supper. She could put the pick back then.

Besides, she'd decided she really didn't want to miss the tour. She was genuinely interested in learning more about this beautiful and fascinating old building. And Henry said there might be possible hiding places for money on the other floors too. He could be right. She'd check that out.

Their group stopped first at the viewing rail in the third-floor music room. The room glowed with golden light coming through its stained glass ceiling. Airy wicker furniture invited relaxing, writing, card playing, and reading. She saw a grand piano in the women's lounge at one end and a pool table and smoking area for men at the opposite end. The floors were covered in elaborately patterned mosaic tile. Beautiful, Carrie thought, how very beautiful.

"Beautiful," came an audible echo of her thoughts in a masculine voice.

He'd startled her because she hadn't noticed him anywhere in the group. When she turned around she knew why. Clothes sure did make the man! He no longer wore black. Everett Bogardus had changed into green slacks and a grey guayabera shirt. He looked ordinary, almost lost-in-a-crowd invisible.

"Don't you find the ceiling breathtaking?"

"Well...yes, yes, I do."

"Wait until you see the ceiling in the men's bath hall."

His voice was low, purring. "It has over eight thousand pieces of colored glass and depicts three people swimming: a mermaid, a man, and a woman. All nude, of course. Lovely, lovely." His thigh touched her hip, and he took her arm. "We're going to the gymnasium next."

"Oh?" Her voice squeaked, and she cleared her throat. "I didn't hear the guide say."

But he was right. They moved down a long hall to the building's elaborate wood-paneled gymnasium. It showcased leather punching bags, mats, various ladders and rings suspended from the ceiling on ropes, and racks with evil-looking Indian clubs in graduated sizes. There was a long horse, bars to climb and swing on, lumpy leather medicine balls. *It's a kind of 1920's torture chamber,* Carrie thought as she looked around.

Their guide was just beginning to tell about the use of all these items by both men and women when a smiling newcomer approached the group. He asked Rina for permission to tag along and listen. "I couldn't help overhearing your explanations. I'd like to learn more too," he said.

No one offered a spoken objection, and Rina welcomed him cordially, but objections began banging inside Carrie's head as soon as she saw the man.

He was casually dressed in a polo shirt and jeans, but she recognized him immediately. It was one of the police officers who had responded to the 911 alarm call for Rusty Hobbs. As far as she was concerned, his effort to look like an ordinary tourist didn't work. He needed to slouch more and should have put on a ball cap, or maybe even a hair piece. His bristly haircut and erect bearing were stereotypical, if not for law enforcement, then the military. He looked too stiff in the company of all these "I'm for comfort first" senior adults.

She felt the throb of her heart increasing. He'd been sent to keep an eye on her! Oh, golly, it was time to get away from Everett and out of here.

Beside her the soft, insistent contact of Everett's body suddenly changed to steel as his grip on her arm tightened. Oh, my! He must have recognized the law officer too. Maybe he'd been concealed someplace, watching, when people began responding to the emergency calls on behalf of Rusty Hobbs.

An awful thought hit her, and she almost wept when she realized she and Henry should have thought of it before. It was possible Rusty could identify his attacker, and that Everett knew he could.

Even if this police officer didn't have any idea yet that Everett Bogardus might have been the one who attacked Rusty, then Everett wasn't aware he didn't know. She could hear the quickened breathing, feel the steel-spring tension in his too-close body.

Her thoughts were racing back, once more trying to remember exactly what she and Henry had told various law officers that might point to Everett. She was sure all Henry said was that the man he saw wore black. They wouldn't know more than that unless Agent Bell had found the lobster pen and made the connections she'd hoped her remarks would initiate.

But the man in black was no longer wearing black. There would be no similarities for the police officer to observe.

Everett squeezed her arm harder. She looked up, said, "Stop that, it hurts," loudly enough for a few in their group to hear. With a small grunt she supposed was meant to be an apology, he dropped her arm and turned back toward Rina.

Good. Now she could get away. She started to slide backwards toward the door of the gymnasium. Her thoughts were moving more swiftly than she dared move her feet. First she needed to find Henry and warn him that Rusty might be able to identify his attacker. Henry and the law enforcement people should know Rusty required a guard.

Where was Henry? Where were the offices? Agent Bell said Henry was in a third floor office. She'd put the building floor plan in her purse but didn't dare take time to search it out now.

At last she was out of sight of the group, so she turned to run on tiptoe toward the main hall at the front of the building. She'd seen only open doors and public display areas on this side of the third floor. Offices must be on the opposite end.

She'd just reached the corner of the hall when, coming from nowhere, Everett shoved against her. Before her thoughts could grasp what was happening, his left arm circled her neck, cutting off her breathing. Something sharp pricked at her throat.

She heard the familiar purr through a ringing in her ears. "I have a knife. I can slit your throat and kill you faster than anyone could with a gun. You're going to be quiet, and you're going to do what I say. Walk to that doorway straight ahead of us. Quickly now, Carrie."

Oh, God, dear God!

Her heartbeat added its heavy thrum-thrum to the ringing in her head. She couldn't catch her breath, gagged, and the vise-like hold on her throat was removed. His fingers dug into her upper arm. She started to twist away, and the knife pricked her side.

"Now, now, Carrie, none of that."

Dear God! Think. Pray. "*He that dwelleth in the secret*

*place of the most High...under the shadow of the Almighty... he
shall give his angels charge over thee...* " The 91st Psalm, her
companion in emergency now as it had been many times
before. *Help me, help me, God.* Her mind couldn't seem to
manage anything more coherent. Terror buried any other
words, all other thoughts.

Step-stop, step-stop, step-stop. "Keep going," he said
as he pushed his legs against hers, left-right, left-right, forc-
ing her to move. "Now open that door. It's not locked, no
matter what the sign says."

It wasn't locked, and it led to a stairway that probably
offered access to all floors.

Down they went through the empty stairwell. Everett
shoved at her with a knee whenever she slowed down, and
she felt the prick of his knife point each time. They came
to a wide landing area stacked with file boxes and, only
after they'd squeezed past, she wondered if she should have
tripped, falling away from the knife and sending boxes
crashing down the stairs.

Her thoughts had calmed, and she began to evaluate
her situation. Surely Everett didn't plan to kill her. He
could have done that easily as soon as they entered this
empty stairwell. He might hurt her badly, but reason now
suggested Everett Bogardus had no stomach for outright
killing. He was too...fastidious. He could not cause violent
death with his own two hands, he could not watch it happen. The attack on Rusty Hobbs must have come in reaction
to surprise. Everett had not meant to kill.

They'd started the descent in silence, but now he began
talking, more to himself than to her. Her panic bubbled
up again as she realized the familiar purr had changed to
a twisting whine. He sounded like a small child totally focused on himself. Was the man deranged? If so, what did

that mean for her?

"Meddling witch, should have known the boyfriend saw me...wasn't sure...and he told this meddling witch, and someone said something to the police, probably this mouthy witch right here. Getting the rest of the money will have to wait. But the old man was right. It's been here all along.

"Fah, all those years of doing without, working nights, going to school days, and the money was here, right *here.* I should have had it, he knew how hard it was, said the struggle was *good.* Good for who? Him and his righteous religion, him the upstanding preacher? But it's here like he said, even though I wondered if he was off his head that day he died. *Baking powder tins!* The fool, why not use bigger cans? So much easier. Only two cans so far, but I will have it all. Just a short setback now because of this witch."

Everett's voice changed again, the whine becoming a raspy sing-song. "If only he'd told me...too bad for me he got religion. Sin of my father, his sin punishing me. Too bad."

Maybe he was so absorbed he wasn't paying attention to her. She started to twist away from the knife. A sharp stab in her side stopped the motion.

The sing-song voice went on without a break. "No, no, you can't stop me now, *can't!*"

His last word was a shriek. Carrie prayed someone had heard him.

They reached the bottom of the steps. Everett pushed her under a rope barrier hooked across the open doorway, and they came out into the hall next to Fordyce Spring. No one was there, no one to hear his shout or any cry she might make.

Where were all those crowds of tourists, where was Agent Bell? Where was Henry?

There, oh, there at last, thank God! A woman from the Elderhostel group came from the elevator and headed toward the restroom. Carrie took a deep breath to cry out, but the knife ripped sharply into her blouse and, she was sure, into her skin.

The voice, quiet and purring again, said, "Smile. Say hello only. Be afraid for yourself, Carrie, be afraid for that woman."

She murmured, "Hello," and heard a second, purring, "Hello," from behind her right ear. Would the woman—Diane, that was her name, Diane from Iowa—notice anything wrong? Could she see the terror on Carrie's face? Could she see the mouthed word, *Help*?

Carrie realized her best move would be to break away from Everett right this minute. "Women should never go with an abductor without a fight," Henry had told her. "The first moments are the time to break away, especially if people are in the area, because what's coming is usually going to be much worse than those first moments."

But Everett's hand held her arm so tightly it was cutting circulation off. She couldn't pull free. The knife pressed a hot line into her flesh, pricking her, again and again. He seemed to enjoy using it to torment her, hurt her, cut her skin. Could she risk large, vicious slices into her body? Did she have enough courage, expecting knife wounds, to twist and yank, to make a defensive move, to kick Everett as Henry had said she should kick any man trying to hurt her?

She didn't, she couldn't. Fear had obliterated courage, and she couldn't muster the strength to defeat that personal enemy.

Carrie wanted to weep, to wail out her grief to the skies. She was a coward, a coward after all.

Since she'd come to the Ozarks, she'd finally begun to believe in her own strength, and Henry had praised her bravery. But the fear of being hurt held her prisoner now as much as Everett himself did.

In front of them, intent only on her mission, Diane barely glanced their way and disappeared inside the ladies' restroom.

Oh, no. Oh, dear God. Diane, remember, remember seeing us here.

Everett pushed Carrie ahead of him through the "Alarm will ring" door. No alarm rang, no people came. Break room? Empty. Locker room? Empty. The Legal Sea Foods pen was gone from the floor. On to a third door Carrie hadn't paid any attention to earlier. The door was closed, but Everett said, "Open it," and she did, flipping a light switch at his command. A storage room. The door thudded shut behind them.

Now what? Would Everett lock her in here? Would he...*Please, God, abide with me, cover me with angels' wings. Help, oh, help me.*

A plain room, used for storage. A few folded tables and chairs. Boxes. Everett was dragging her across the floor toward a steel square...trap door...ring handle.

He shoved a box off the metal square and reached for the ring, almost pulling her over sideways as he bent to lift the door without losing his hold on her. Finally the heavy metal square banged back against the wall.

Black-black-hole.

Oh, God, oh, please...

It wasn't like her to beg, but she was so scared. Tears blinded her now, and she sobbed, pleaded, "Please, Everett, please, oh, no, no, please, no," as he pushed her toward the black hole.

She heard him laugh. "Let's see you escape from this one, detective lady. You...won't...get...my...money."

Still laughing, he shoved, and shoved, and she could cry no more, it was too much to bear.

The knife...

A final shove. The solid floor became space. Space, and nothing, and blackness.

God with me...

Silence. Falling. Harsh and painful against the buzzing in her head, fighting the silence, a metal door clanged shut, and she heard a woman's long, undulating scream.

Chapter X

Henry

Agent Colin Bell pushed between the chairs and shoved aside a stack of papers on the desk top with no apparent concern for their order. Park Curator Shirley Sandemann, whose desk it was, began a protest that was cut off mid-squawk by a warning glance from Superintendent Adahy Hinton.

Guess the FBI is boss, even here, Henry thought, as he sent a sympathetic look toward Sandemann. Her tiny office had been chosen for the meeting of park personnel and law officers because—no matter how crowded—it had more floor space than the other cubicles built into the area formerly occupied by bathhouse state rooms. The park service obviously hadn't wanted to disrupt any more of the original Fordyce floor plan than necessary.

Agent Bell laid a white square of paper on the cleared area of the desk, tipped up the paper bag he was carrying, and slid a cheap-looking plastic pen onto the white surface.

It's obvious that pen has great significance in Bell's mind, Henry thought. *He's treating it as if it were a diamond bracelet.*

The agent squeezed his way to a corner, placed his feet carefully on either side of a waste basket, and leaned against the wall, surveying them. Those already seated in the room—Henry, the superintendent, Curator Sandemann, Law Enforcement Ranger Kandler, and FBI Agent Willard Brooks—stared back.

Henry, who was closest to the agent, watched him for not more than three seconds. He wasn't going to risk a crick in his neck just to stare at an FBI agent's face. Instead he glanced around at the others in the office to see how they were reacting to the plastic pen.

Agent Brooks as well as Sandemann, Hinton, and Kandler—all looked blank.

"Significance?" said Agent Brooks, who, Henry had already observed, was a man of few words.

"How about the significance of this pen, Major King?" asked Bell. "Ever seen it before?" He took an elegant silver pen out of his pocket and used it to poke at the plastic pen. It rolled over to reveal a lobster printed on the barrel.

"No. I don't remember seeing it."

"The printing on the side says it came from a restaurant called Legal Sea Foods. Have you ever eaten there?"

"I've never heard of the place. Where is it?"

"Boston. It's a chain in and around the Boston area."

"I haven't been in Boston for more than thirty years."

"Do you know anyone connected to Boston who's here

in Hot Springs at this time?"

Ahhhh. Henry looked down, worked one fingernail under another as if chasing an annoying piece of dirt, and decided it was time to talk about Everett Bogardus.

"Yes, a man in our Elderhostel group is from there. His name is Everett Bogardus."

"Interesting. Just before she left to join that same Elderhostel group, Ms. McCrite mentioned a pen like this, described it fully, said she'd seen Mr. Bogardus with such a pen. And what do you know, on my way up here I found the pen she'd described lying in the hall just outside the break room. Can you think of a reason she might have put it there?"

He paused, but Henry said nothing.

"Ms. McCrite also told me she's been to Legal Sea Foods more than once on visits to Boston. So she, as well as Bogardus, could have a pen like this."

Outwardly Henry looked no different than he had when Agent Bell joined their group, but now his senses were zinging. Did this idiot think Carrie was involved in the attack on Ranger Hobbs or the search of the basement?

He decided to copy Agent Brooks's conversational style.

"Why?"

"Why what?"

"Why would you assume she had a pen like that and perhaps dropped it in the hallway for you to find? To what purpose?"

Henry spoke the words in a low growl, and everyone in the small room leaned forward, straining to hear him.

After a pause he continued, managing to make his more normal tones sound condescending. He ignored the inner voice warning him not to antagonize any law officer, especially an FBI agent.

"I find it amazingly easy to understand how that pen got where it was, and why she told you about it. Neither she nor I have wanted to implicate Everett Bogardus in the attack on Ranger Hobbs when we had no proof, but now I will say that we both believe he was the person hiding in the basement this morning and also the person who attacked Hobbs. She was evidently trying to lead you to think about that issue yourself. She must have seen the pen in the hall, remembered seeing it earlier in the possession of Bogardus, and realized the significance of it being in the employee area. You notice she was smart enough not to pick it up herself and bring it to you? This is no rocking-chair granny you're dealing with, Bell. She's smart, she's intuitive, and she's a darn good detective."

Agent Bell's steel-blue eyes froze on Henry's face for just an instant, though he had to twist his neck down and sideways to manage it.

"I never suggested anything different, did I?" said Bell as he moved his head up and glanced around at the group, smiling as if all of them but Henry were in on some secret. "And I would like to hear why you and Ms. McCrite think this man is involved in the incidents here. But first, I suggest we all go down to the employee break room. These offices are far too small to allow for efficient work."

Even Adahy Hinton flinched at that remark.

Just then a man with military bearing stuck his head into the office, and Henry recognized him as one of the two Hot Springs Police Officers who'd responded to the emergency call for Rusty Hobbs.

"Excuse me," the man said, "but I need help here. I joined the Elderhostel tour to keep an eye on Ms. McCrite as you"—he nodded at Bell—"requested. Ms. McCrite was with the tour when I caught up with them, but now she, and a man whose name is Everett Bogardus, have both disappeared. I've already searched this floor, which is the last place all but one of the group remembers seeing either of them. One woman says she left the tour to visit the restroom facilities and saw them together in the basement hallway. Says she paid little attention because of the urgency of her errand, but does recall they were standing very close together and both looked serious, as she puts it. So, don't we need to do a building search at once?"

Carrie...missing? Henry leaped to his feet and, giving no one time to object, said, "Agent Brooks and I will go directly to the basement since I think that's the most likely place to find them if they're still in the building. I suggest the rest of you divide into two teams and sweep the floors downward to the basement. Be sure someone is watching the exterior doors. And I think you should consider Bogardus dangerous."

Before Agent Bell or anyone else could say a word, Henry and Agent Brooks had rushed out of the office and were running for the stairs.

It only took a couple of minutes to check the public areas in the basement, then Henry led the way through the no-alarm door. He glanced into the empty employee break and locker rooms and was heading for the mechanical area with Agent Brooks right behind when a third door stopped him. It was probably the door to a closet but, whatever it concealed, he wanted to see inside.

The door wasn't locked. He opened it, felt for the light switch, clicked it on, and froze in place, hand still on the switch.

Agent Brooks pushed past him, then began swearing—the most words Henry had heard him say at one time.

"Know who it is?" asked Brooks.

"Everett Bogardus," Henry said as he stared at the sprawled body, the knife, and the pool of blood.

Oh, Carrie...

Chapter XI

Carrie

Gu-gu-uck!

Warm. Floating. Couldn't focus...drowning?

Carrie tested that, concentrating. In-whoosh, out-whoosh. In-whoosh, out-whoosh. Breathing air. Not drowning. Another sniff. Wet dirt.

She moved her hands and felt mud. Warm mud, cradling her head, wrapping gently around her body, supporting her back. Never had mud bath...nice, but why...dark? Maybe dark...part of mud bath...

She floated away again, cushioned in mud.

When she awakened the second time, the pleasant feeling, and some of the moisture, had evaporated. There were drying, itchy patches of clay behind her ears, around her neck, along her arms.

Something tickled her face. She scratched at the tickle with dripping, mud-coated fingers, and a small creature scuttled away.

Carrie opened her mouth to suck in air for an involuntary scream, then spat sandy goo. *Oh, uck, UCK.* She hoped what she tasted was clean mud.

There was a soft, sucking sound as she rolled sideways, hoping to distance herself from the creature. She pushed up on one elbow, then on into a sitting position, extending her legs straight out and thinking of...messy diapers.

The thin edges of the mud that encased the back of her body were drying, but there was still plenty of warm, wet mud under her. When she wiggled, she could hear squishes and feel the suck of mud against her slacks.

Guh-thump, guh-thump.

Funny noise.

She tried to focus, to remember, until memory rushed at her, bringing a wave of terror and shaking her so violently that dried chunks of mud cracked off her upper body and fell silently into the wet muck she was sitting in.

Knife! Everett...shoving at her...grabbing for knife. Pushed down to...

Here? Oh, dear heaven, where was she? She reached one arm out and felt a wall, concrete, maybe. She scooted back, felt another wall. Sideways, and there was more concrete. A concrete septic tank?

No, of course not, couldn't be. Catch basin of some sort? What?

It was too dark to see the trap door, but it had to be above her. Everett was above her...had to get away...

Another shudder. She was in the place where she was meant to die.

Tears washed into the mud on her face, and for several

seconds all she could say to herself, over and over and over, was "God, God, God, oh, God."

Guh-thump, guh-thump.

Carrie turned her head in the direction of the noise, then inched forward, expecting to bump into another wall. The wall was there, but the noise clearly came from beyond it. Moving her quivering hands up the wall, she came to the edge of a large hole; getting on her knees to look through, she saw a faint patch of daylight. Reacting only to the stimulus of light, she pushed up and through the rough hole, down onto rocks, and began crawling toward the overhead glow.

Her knees hurt. She was in warm water moving over bare rocks. Scent of something...exhaust from a badly-tuned car?

When she was under the light source, she sat in the water, looked up, and saw the bars of an iron grate. Tires rolled over it while she watched—*guh-thump, guh-thump.*

Daylight! A busy street. Sewer drains. What did that mean? Her thoughts were still scrambled. Think, think. "Oh, dear, all-knowing God, help me think."

Central Avenue! She had gone through a trap door in the basement of the Fordyce, the Fordyce fronted on Central, and Central was built over...OH. *She was sitting in Hot Springs Creek.*

Everett had shoved her through the trap door into a concrete room that opened on the creek.

Her mind began to search through what she could remember of Ranger Hawk's program on Hot Springs' history. The creek, which carried away storm run-off and extra water from the hot springs, had been open until 1884, when the Department of the Interior ordered it covered with a masonry arch topped by a roadway. Instead of the creek bed that cut the downtown area in half and had become a stinking open sewer hosting rooting pigs, Hot Springs gained broad, fashionable Central Avenue. Many people—from then until now—didn't realize they were walking or driving over a covered creek when they were in front of Bathhouse Row.

Now that she sat in the flowing creek, Carrie was grateful for mud. She had no idea how far she had fallen before landing, but the mud provided a cushion. Here in the creek bed there were rocks everywhere.

Had Everett known there was mud under the Fordyce?

Her body began to shake again, but this time with fury, because logic told her he hadn't known. He would have expected her to be hurt or killed by a fall on concrete or bare rocks, and he was the only one who knew where she was. That was a death sentence. No one would come to help; he had not meant for her to get out of this alive. He couldn't allow that after letting her hear him talk about his treasure.

What was she going to do? Do? She didn't even know what to think.

Calm...calm.

She vaguely remembered hearing someone say that the best time to be grateful to God is during the worst challenge. Be grateful?

Well, yes, she could do that. There was mud to be grateful for, the mud that had protected her from rocks. How funny it would sound when she got out and told Henry she was grateful for mud.

When she got out—when she got out. When she saw Henry, told him about her experience down here. When...

Oh, God, help me.

She was alive, able to move around. That was something else to be grateful for. And if God could part the Red Sea, guide Noah in making an ark, bring the ark through the flood, He could help her now, help her here in nothing more than a little underground creek.

She ignored the tears streaming down her face and looked up at the grate. Too thick and heavy. And anyway, it was far above her, she couldn't reach it.

Well, she could holler, there would be many people walking by on the sidewalk, probably heading for restaurants at this time of day. Someone would hear.

Carrie stood slowly and balanced on the rocks, taking time to be grateful she was wearing her rubber-soled walking shoes. She lifted her head and began to shout, "Help! Help me!" She listened for breaks in traffic before shouting each time, then cried out as loudly as she could manage.

Long minutes went by as Carrie shouted, cried, and pleaded. After a forever in time her neck was getting stiff, her voice was nothing but a croak, and not one person had come to look through the grate. No one had answered, no one had heard.

There would be no help, no one would come.

She slumped back into the water and looked around her prison. In spite of light coming through the grate, it was too dark to see more than a few feet into the tunnel. She lifted her arms in supplication, stretching them toward the grate as if it were some god offering salvation.

She shut her eyes to stop more of the futile tears and saw herself in Mrs. Hicks' Sunday School class, sitting on one of the little wooden chairs, all those years ago. She wore her yellow Easter dress with the rows of ruffles. It had panties that matched, and she remembered that the panty ruffles made sitting feel funny—slidey and lumpy—kind of like sitting on these wet, slimy rocks.

She and the rest of the class were stretching their arms up, up, like she was now, then moving them around, saying with Mrs. Hicks: "God is up here, God is out here, God is down here, God is ev-e-ry-where."

Ev-e-ry-where. Everywhere.

She needed more light, and evening was coming. She needed...

Oh, OH! Her hand went to the pocket of her slacks. The cloth was wet, of course, and her cotton underpants were soaked, but, as she recalled, the card behind the little flashlight's bubble pack had said water-resistant. She'd read the card in the store when she bought the flashlight as a gift for Henry.

Maybe... She stopped breathing, clicked the switch, and now the tears signaled yet another reason for gratitude as Henry's tiny flashlight, picked up off the floor of the Fordyce basement this afternoon, glowed. The beam was too newly bright in the darkness, and she blinked, imagining she saw things moving.

They *were* moving. Roaches scuttled away in every direction, and Carrie sighed. Roaches were such a small problem right now.

What next? She had light, but...

"Shepherd, show me how to go..."*

So, dear Shepherd of us all, where to go? She shone the flashlight back and forth in the creek bed. The light-sparkled water was flowing to her left. Go that way, she thought, almost as if hearing a directing voice. It was reasonable, there must be an outlet of some kind. For all she knew, the only

* From a poem, "Feed My Sheep," by Mary Baker Eddy

inlets were storm drains and pipes running from springs and bath houses. So—go with the flow. She began moving with the water, picking her way carefully over rocks that were clearly revealed in the flashlight's beam, though the sides of the tunnel were still hidden in shadows. Armies of roaches retreated, bodies piling on bodies in the haste to get away. She hoped they were the only creatures living in the tunnel.

She passed around a curve, under more overhead grates. It looked like the daylight was less bright now. What time was it? She hadn't the faintest idea and, unlike the flashlight, her watch had not survived the drenching. Its hands were stuck on 4:15.

She began to hear a rush of falling water as she moved forward. Waterfall? Surely that couldn't be, not in here. Ranger Hawk hadn't said anything about a waterfall. She lifted the flashlight and peered into the tunnel ahead of her, seeing only haze.

Carrie walked more slowly as she came closer to the sound. No, not a waterfall. Through the haze, which was becoming very warm, she saw a torrent of water spraying into the tunnel from a drain pipe. It was moving with such force that spray almost reached the curved wall across from the pipe. The water in the creek bed churned and boiled, and she could no longer see the bottom. Probably the force of the spray was digging away the rocks and silt.

Now haze drifted all around her, and intense heat beat against her face. The haze was steam, and not only was the creek becoming uncomfortably hot, it was getting much deeper, rising to her waist. She had started to push backward, away from the heat, when she slipped on a mossy rock and was suddenly in water up to her chin, water hot enough to make her want to scream with pain.

As she fought to get out of the pool, her foot struck a protruding rock, stopping her forward slide into the churning water. Skin tingling, she stumbled away from the heat, splashing back into the creek bed where she had been walking. There the incoming water was only moderately warm and not more than a foot deep.

Carrie sank, panting, into the cooler water. She began to splash it over her arms and blouse as she stared at the steaming torrent.

The water ahead of her was too deep to walk in, too hot for swimming.

She was trapped.

CHAPTER XII

HENRY

They couldn't do this to him, *they couldn't.*

But Henry knew they could. He was no longer Major Henry King of the Kansas City Police Department, he was a civilian. They were doing exactly the right thing, the legal thing, what he would have done back in Kansas City under the same circumstances.

As soon as Agent Bell arrived in the storage room, he ordered Henry to leave the area. After a discussion that had become more heated than Henry intended, Bell amended his order and allowed Henry to stay in the employee break room, warning him not to leave without an escort, and not to touch anything but his chair and the table.

Being in the break room, however, was turning out to be almost worse than exile to the hotel. He knew too much—and too little—about what was going on. FBI agents, park rangers, uniformed police officers and detectives had been coming and going in the hallway for some time. Henry could hear few actual words from the storage room, but he understood most of the procedure from his years of police experience. Jurisdiction here was different though, because the crime had happened in a national park. The FBI, with Colin Bell as case agent, was in charge.

As soon as he'd viewed the body and the crime scene, Bell began calling in his teams of experts. He'd escorted Henry to the break room, pointed him into a chair, and made several phone calls, not seeming to care if Henry heard his end of the conversations.

An FBI evidence recovery team from Little Rock would be on the scene within two hours. In the meantime, the park's law enforcement rangers were securing the area, and, with assistance from the Hot Springs Police Department, had begun a wide-ranging search for Carrie throughout the park and the city. Early on, Henry had heard one detective say that a thorough search of the building, including the elevator maintenance room, roof, and, Henry supposed, even the long-unused dressing rooms, private bathing areas, and steam cabinets, had proved Ms. McCrite wasn't anywhere inside the Fordyce.

At one point Henry saw lights flash in the hall and knew that crime scene photographs, and probably a video, were recording visual evidence. An emergency medical team and the coroner came soon after that. Bell also requested a K-9 tracking unit, and a police officer accompanied Henry back to his hotel room to get Carrie's dirty shirt for scent-identification. The officer suggested, very firmly, that Henry remain at the hotel. He refused and returned to the Fordyce with his escort.

Now the waiting was driving him nuts. Everyone working in the basement rooms had a purpose, something definite to do. Everyone but Henry. All he had was too much half-knowledge and too many thoughts, thoughts that were rapidly sinking into helpless rage and a boiling worry. He was able to control those only by searching his memory over and over for clues that Bell and the others might miss. His information—and Carrie's—together with their fresh viewpoint were going to be of great importance in this case. To begin with, why had Bogardus abducted Carrie? No one seemed to be asking that question yet.

After another hour they carried the body out through the exit at the opposite end of the hall while Henry watched from the break room doorway. Almost immediately they brought in a ladder, working it into the storage room through the narrow spaces and sharp turns.

A ladder? What...? Oh! That blasted trap door!

God, make her be okay, take care of her. He wished he knew more about praying, understood more of what Carrie believed in and trusted.

He had paced the small room then, going around and around, bumping chairs aside. Finally, using a spoon he found in the sink, he began opening cabinet doors, pushing the spoon through the handle loops so his fingers wouldn't touch them. He peered inside every cabinet, saw nothing out of the ordinary, and pulled the spoon out quickly, allowing the doors to bang shut. He hoped someone would come to see what the noise was so he could ask a question or two. But no one had paid any attention to him, no one came.

He sat at the table chewing on stale restaurant crackers he'd found in one of the cabinets. Well, why not? The crackers were too old for anyone to enjoy. At least opening the little packets gave his fingers something to do while his well-trained mind searched through all he'd observed since coming to Hot Springs. For one thing, it was possible that Bogardus wasn't the only one here under false pretenses. An Elderhostel could provide a convenient cover for anyone over fifty-five. Henry wished he'd picked up his attendance list when he was in the room getting Carrie's shirt.

After finishing the crackers, he took a paper cup from a stack on the counter and got a drink of water. The heck with Bell, he knew what to touch and what to leave alone!

He played with cracker wrappers for a while, trying to fold them into smooth little squares. Then, in a frustrated burst of energy, he swept the wrappers off the table and watched them scatter as if they were trying to escape from his impotent fury.

After a space of time he knelt on the floor to pick the wrappers up, wadded them tightly inside a clenched fist, and dumped them in the trash basket.

Back at the table, he let his fingers drum the slick surface. Tap, tappity tap-tap. Tap, tappity tap. He knew what Brooks and Bell and the others were thinking—that, in panic or rage, Carrie stabbed out at Everett Bogardus and, after realizing what she'd done, had fled.

In this special situation they should let him help with the investigation. Henry had offered to help as soon as Bell arrived on the scene, reminding the agent of his years of law-enforcement experience. "And after all," he'd *almost* said, "Carrie's my wife." He caught himself in time, wondering where that thought came from, realizing he could only say, "She's my lady-friend," or "my special friend," and those connections sounded so weak, almost like there was no important connection at all.

His appeal had done no good. So be it. They didn't

understand.

God, keep her safe.

Whoa, that was it. Carrie believed in God, in His Commandments, "Thou shalt not kill," and all the rest. She could not kill anyone, not even a man who threatened her with some unspeakable evil. She couldn't...

He sighed. Yes, she could, under some circumstances, he knew she could.

Henry folded his hands, shut his eyes, and tried to think a prayer.

All that came were images of Carrie hurt, frightened, lying someplace unable to get up. The pictures rushed around and around inside his head like a horrible silent movie.

He heard the break room refrigerator motor click off. In the silence, Henry noticed it was also very quiet down the hallway. Now there was only an occasional voice murmur, a few muted thumps. What was going on?

If only he'd stayed with her, hadn't been willing to leave her alone with Bell. He should have been with her when she joined the tour group or, at least, kept her with him. He should have...should have...there was so much he should have done differently. He'd had that gut feeling about Bogardus, he should have paid more attention.

There was a step in the hall and he opened his eyes to see Agent Brooks standing in the doorway. Henry said nothing, waiting in the awkward silence, and, for a moment, Brooks didn't speak either. This agent had never appeared tough, but now, as he looked at Henry, his cocoa brown features softened even further and his eyes radiated sympathy and understanding.

He came over to the table, lifted a large plastic bag, put it down in front of Henry. It made a squishing sound and sagged with the weight of something large and lumpy.

Whatever it contained was wet. Brooks pulled the top apart. The translucent latex gloves he wore made his hands look purple.

"Identify this?"

Henry looked. Globs of mud covered it, but he knew the item too well. "It's Carrie's," he said, "her purse. Where did...?" His eyes misted over then, and he had to stop talking. Blast, oh blast! What was he going to do?

Brooks studied his face for a moment, then looked away, concentrating on a careful inspection of the refrigerator door. He said, still looking at the refrigerator, "Heavy. Getting warrant to look. Any idea about that weight? Concealed weapon?"

"Certainly not," Henry answered, knowing Brooks meant a gun. But Henry had already pictured something else. If a geologist's pick was a weapon—and they all knew now it could be—it was likely there was a concealed weapon in that purse.

He coughed, cleared his throat, and asked, "Why is it wet? Where did you find it?" He thought his words sounded hesitant and unsteady, almost as if he were about to cry.

"Oh, come with me then, man, I'll show you," Brooks said, stringing a surprising number of words together and speaking as if Henry were a child who had begged to go with Daddy on a forbidden trip.

Henry knew the body was gone, of course; he didn't expect to see it there, but its presence lingered in the room. It always took a while...

Agent Bell was kneeling beside the open trap door when Brooks and Henry came in. He looked up, noticed Henry, scowled, but said nothing, and made no objection when Henry looked over his shoulder into the hole. An electric cord snaked across the floor and dropped into the opening.

It ended in a light socket holding a strong bulb.

At the bottom of the hole two men wearing hip boots were moving around in what looked like a pit full of mud. Was Carrie somewhere down there?

Henry's voice sounded unnaturally high in his ears. "Is she...?"

Bell said, "No, she's not there, just the purse. Nothing else has been found. We think Bogardus had opened the trap door, was pushing her toward it when she managed to grab his knife, struck out, stabbing him fatally. Then she ran, leaving the building by that outside door at the end of the hall. Her purse must have fallen over the edge while she and Bogardus struggled."

"What is that place?"

"It's an old water storage tank for the Fordyce, not used for years. Has a hole broken in one side now, only about two or three feet across. If you went out the hole and down fifty feet or so of a rocky slope, you'd be in the creek."

"Creek?"

"Hot Springs Creek runs beneath Central Avenue through the downtown area. The creek was covered with an arched tunnel in the nineteenth century and Central Avenue built over it. Comes to daylight at Transportation Plaza." Bell waved his hand to indicate a direction. "Creek's still active with storm run-off and excess water from the springs."

"Ah, yes. I remember the ranger telling us that." Henry paused, staring at the floor. Finally he said, "So you're still searching for Carrie." It wasn't a question.

"Of course. The Hot Springs P.D. and Park Rangers are helping. They're combing the area around here for a couple of miles as well as watching for her at your hotel, and the K-9 tracking unit will arrive soon. I'd strongly suggest you go to the hotel now. We'll report to you when we have her in custody. I know you'll call us if we miss her and she returns to the room and that you would hold her there."

Henry's face burned with sudden heat. In custody? Hold her if she comes back to the room? Did he think Henry cared more for law enforcement than he did for Carrie's welfare? Did he dare think…?

He controlled the urge to spit angry words at Bell and kept his head lowered to conceal the expression on his face.

After a silence, Henry said, "All right then, I'll go back to the hotel. Be sure and call me if anything happens… ah, when you find her. I am strongly concerned about her welfare."

Agent Bell didn't answer. He had already turned back toward the hole in the floor and was telling the men to come up.

As far as he's concerned, thought Henry, *I am of no consequence right now. But,* he reminded himself, *these men are just doing their jobs.*

As Henry rose to his feet, Agent Brooks, standing above Bell's back, gave Henry a thumbs-up and winked at him.

Henry had the unsettling feeling that Brooks could read his mind. He also felt sure that, even if Brooks guessed what he planned, the man wasn't going to say anything about it to anyone else yet, including Agent Bell.

He climbed the stairs to the Fordyce lobby and, as he crossed the porch, noticed the chairs were all empty. Probably everyone has gone to dinner, Henry thought. He stuck his hand in his pocket, feeling for the flashlight Carrie had insisted he bring with him this afternoon.

Gone!

Then he remembered. He'd used it in the basement of

the Fordyce after Carrie found Rusty Hobbs. He'd probably dropped it there, but Agent Bell and the others sure
wouldn't let him back in the basement to look for it now.
Besides, he didn't want them to know he had any interest
in a flashlight.

So, once more, Henry headed across the street toward
the Central Avenue shops.

The feeling of urgency that drove him also dictated
his purchase of the first flashlight he found, even though
it was bright purple and had a picture of Winnie the Pooh
on one side. Never mind, it made light. He paid for it, a
set of extra batteries, and, sack in hand, headed toward the
Downtowner.

Instead of walking to the lobby, however, he turned off
into an alley near the hotel. He had no idea where police
officers were, and, at least in the hotel lobby, they'd be in
plain clothes anyway. He doubted that the FBI had reported
he was on his way back to the hotel or had given out his
description, at least not yet, but still he had no intention
of risking a return to the room.

When he was behind the hotel, he inspected the fence
around the overflow parking lot. He'd climbed more than
one fence in his life, and it was obvious several people had
already climbed this one. Broken-out places offered foot-
holds, and the potentially sharp wires across the top were
bent down in several places. He just hoped no one was out
on a hotel balcony right now.

There were no alarmed shouts as he climbed or after
he had dropped inside. Looking around, he saw no one at
all, let alone anyone who might be guarding the area or
searching for Carrie. Probably they assumed she would have
no interest in locked cars. They certainly knew she wasn't
carrying a purse with car keys inside.

When he reached his car, Henry looked around again before unlocking the door to slide in. Even in the fading daylight there was a possibility he might be seen and recognized when he went past the unloading area at the side of the hotel, but he had to chance it. He was counting on the fact that no one, with the possible exception of Agent Brooks, suspected what he planned, and they would therefore have no interest in his car. Ducking his head as low as he dared, he headed toward Central Avenue. He didn't look around as he passed the glass wall of the hotel lobby.

After he was well beyond Bathhouse Row, Henry wondered where to go next and watched for signs that might give a clue to where he was. Finally he saw a sign announcing a city information center; turning left, he pulled into the parking lot. Now, if only the place was still open and there were no law enforcement watchers around. Nothing looked out of the ordinary, so he got out of the car and joined a group of tourists going through the open door of the building. The tourists stopped to look over offerings in a post card rack, so the attendant was available, and in just a couple of minutes Henry was back out with a clearly marked map of the area. He started the car and headed for Transportation Plaza.

He wanted Carrie found as quickly as possible, but he still hoped it hadn't occurred to anyone, except maybe Brooks, that Carrie could be in the creek.

Interesting. Agent Brooks seemed willing to respect him as a fellow law-enforcement professional, retired or not, and also to honor his special interest in this case. Had something happened in Brooks' own law-enforcement career that was coloring his judgment? Henry knew Brooks would have had the right, even the duty, to question him about his plans in front of Bell, especially if he'd guessed what Henry was about to do.

It was a good thing he hadn't asked those questions. Henry would have had to answer them with lies. But both intuition and logic—or something of that sort—told him Bogardus shoved Carrie through the trap door, and then she'd probably made her way out of the mud pit and into Hot Springs Creek, seeing it as her only avenue of escape. She wouldn't even know Bogardus was dead. She'd gotten away from the trap door and from what she would see as a continuing threat from Everett Bogardus. That was logical.

Henry had also realized, after some thought, that Carrie Culpeper McCrite would not have stabbed Everett Bogardus and run away. Oh, it was possible that, to save her own life, she had stabbed the man, not intending to kill him. But she wouldn't have run away, she'd have run for help.

He tried to picture the scene, the struggle with Bogardus as he pushed her toward the opening, Carrie and her purse going over the edge, dropping into the deep mud below. That fit the circumstances as Henry figured them.

But how could a fatally wounded man shut that heavy iron trap door? In his quick look around the room before Bell removed him, Henry had seen no blood anywhere but on and under the body, no bloody hand prints on the trap door. Did that mean someone else had been there after Carrie and shut the door?

Maybe Carrie could answer that question when he found her. Maybe she could answer a lot of his questions.

CHAPTER XIII

CARRIE

She'd made it this far, and now she was trapped.

Carrie's shoulders slumped. She bowed her head, shut off the flashlight, shut her eyes. Maybe she should just lie down in the water and go to sleep.

"Hold thou me up, and I shall be safe..."

Psalms? Yes, it was the long one, the 119th, verse 117. She remembered because of the high numbers. *"I shall be safe."*

Well, get busy proving it, girl.

Carrie opened her eyes, switched the flashlight back on, looked around again. Now she paid full attention to a sewer pipe that had been running along the side wall of the tunnel for some time. It looked about fifteen inches across, and if she could climb up and crawl along the top, it would get her past the hot water pool. The gush of water coming into the creek splashed on the pipe too, but it was only a little splash. If she crawled fast and could endure a few moments of the heated water, she'd make it.

The pipe was above her. She stood as tall as she could and reached up…no, not quite. She stretched, jumped, and her arms went around the pipe, holding tight while her toes dangled in the water.

Now what? Remembering long-ago days on monkey bars she tried swinging her feet up and, after several tries, got one leg over the pipe. She lifted the other leg, wrapped it around too, and hung there, wondering how to climb to the top. The pipe's surface was slippery; she couldn't move up and didn't have the strength to scoot along hanging from the bottom.

If only Henry were here, he could give her a boost.

But "if only" got you nowhere. So, it was *Carry on, Carrie,* just as it had been for as long as she could remember. Still, if Henry came… Ah, well, he wasn't here, couldn't be.

She unwrapped her legs from the pipe, hung for a moment, then splashed down and sat in the creek again. The water felt warm and comfortable here above the torrent, and she was getting very used to being fish-wet.

Since she'd met Henry, there had been fewer of those *Carry on, Carrie* experiences. She'd gotten into trouble a few times in the line of their detective work, but when he was beside her, even the bad things seemed less severe and nightmare memories vanished quickly.

Wasn't that good? It seemed good, felt good. He was so dependable, like a great rock in a weary land.

Great rock. That was from the Bible too, but for the life of her she couldn't remember where she'd read it—not that it mattered now. She'd look it up and tell him about it when they got back home to Blackberry Hollow. When...

She sat there for several minutes, thinking about Henry. It seemed a good time to let her thoughts about him fly free. Certainly no one was going to interrupt.

Was she a weaker person because Henry had stood beside her through some bad experiences? Not really—no, she wasn't, and her almost instant awareness of that surprised her. In fact, things were quite the opposite. She felt stronger.

How confusing. A year ago she would have said she mustn't ever get too close to anyone, especially a man, if she wanted to remain independent. She needed to be strong on her own in order to survive. Somehow things seemed different now. Why? Because of Henry?

Her mind searched back over the year since she'd met him, seeing for the first time that he'd come to treat her as a dependable friend and ally. He made her feel like his strong partner, standing with him just as he stood with her. They worked together very well, and he didn't make a big deal of that. It just...was. She hadn't thought about the nature of their partnership until now. He simply accepted her strength, accepted it, not as a goal, but as a present reality.

He'd once told her, "People need people sometimes."

She'd argued with him about that, saying independence and strength were qualities women had to prove constantly and prove on their own if they were going to get along in the world.

But maybe, if she wanted to be able to help other people—and she did want it; that was one reason detective work suited her—then she needed to be more open to accepting help herself.

It could be that having Henry as her friend and partner made her stronger, not weaker, though at the moment
she couldn't for the life of her settle on exactly how that
worked.

Henry, her great rock.

"Henry King, I love you."

She'd said it aloud. What made those words pop out
of her mouth?

Love...

She sighed. Not now. Better get on with the job, girl.
Get out of here and find Henry.

Would she tell him her thoughts? No, she couldn't,
he wouldn't understand. Besides, her feelings might have
come because of the stress of this situation, or maybe they
were only imagination. Hopeful imagining? She couldn't
answer that.

Back to the business of the moment. She ran the flashlight beam along the sewer pipe. A few feet behind her there
were support brackets around the pipe, and the wall was
rough in spots, offering places where her feet might grab
hold. Maybe if she could hang onto a bracket? She stretched
up again, touched a bracket and pulled away. She needed
gloves to protect her hands from its sharp metal edges.

Then she thought of something. Well, why not?

Carrie pushed her arms out of her soggy shirt, unfas-
tened her bra and took it off, wringing water out of the
soft cup linings. Then she pulled the shirt back on, nested
the bra cups in her palm and reached again, grabbing hold
of the bracket. Bracing each foot against the wall in turn,
holding tight and pulling her weight up with her padded
hand, she inched higher until, at last, she was sitting on the
pipe, her legs straddling it on either side.

Yes!

After returning the torn bra to its normal usage, ineffective though that might be now, she got on her hands and knees and, holding the flashlight in her teeth, began to crawl, steeling herself against the sting of the hot water when it began to splash on her face and neck. As the water hit, her head jerked reflexively, but she kept her mouth clamped on the flashlight and forced herself to go forward.

Only a little farther...keep moving...keep moving forward, Carrie...and she was on the other side of the steaming torrent.

Her light showed that the water in the creek still looked deep, the bottom was invisible, so she stayed on the pipe and continued to crawl.

The tunnel was darker now; there was less daylight coming through the grates, though headlight beams occasionally flashed as she passed under one. Must be suppertime. She was hungry, hungry enough to eat almost anything. Well, not roaches, though goodness knew there were plenty of those here.

She almost laughed, knowing she'd make it, she would, she would, even if she had to eat roaches. She could do it on her own!

She crawled along the pipe for what seemed like dozens of blocks as the creek swirled below her, filling the bottom of the tunnel. She had passed several spouting drain pipes, and they undoubtedly added to the depth of the water, though none of the water sprays were as hot or large as the first one. Was the water over her head? She was afraid to test it.

Then she came to the end of her sewer pipe highway. It angled off and disappeared through a hole in the wall of the tunnel.

Carrie sat on the pipe, both legs dangling over the water, and stared down. Nothing to do but jump in; there was nowhere else to go. She held the flashlight as high as she could in her raised right hand, pinched her nose with the fingers of her left hand in the classic jump-in-the-pool pose, and prepared to drop, praying that the water wasn't over her head. She was just too tired to swim—she'd never been very good at it anyway.

Then she took her fingers away from her nose and let her arms drop. The water swirled and swirled below, rolling in waves against the tunnel sides. Its constant motion was almost hypnotic.

She was so tired. How deep was that water?

She imagined Henry below her, reaching arms up to catch her, reaching...

So tired, so very tired. If only...

"Carry on." She said the words like some chain-gang rhythm shout. "Carry on, carry on!" But first she was going to rest here a few more minutes.

She thought back over the day, all the terrible events. She deserved a rest. Besides, maybe Henry would come, her great rock.

What? What did she hear, far away? A new sound? An echo? Or did she hear unfamiliar splashes?

She shut off the light and peered down the tunnel. Yes! Another faint light flickered far away. Henry was coming!

No. Oh, no, it could be someone else. Maybe someone else was searching for her. Maybe Everett Bogardus...was he coming after her? No, no, please, no. Had he seen the light?

Where in this place could she hide? Was there room for her in the sewer pipe's exit hole?

Chapter XIV

Henry

In the glow from a line of old-fashioned street lamps Henry could see the grinning face of Winnie the Pooh. He wished he felt as cheerful as the molded plastic bear on the side of his flashlight case.

He pushed the switch and the flashlight winked on, glaring into green-tinted water rushing over rocks as big as bowling balls. Whew, he hadn't expected a cheap flashlight to be so bright. He clicked the switch off, looked around, saw no one. If somebody noticed him climbing into the creek they would probably call the police.

At least the water didn't appear to be deep. Wading would be much easier than swimming upstream against the force of that current, and moving with the flow of the shallow creek coming toward this opening, as Carrie surely must be, would be even easier. It was good the creek wasn't deep. Carrie wasn't much of a swimmer.

Henry looked around again. The plaza remained empty, though there were several cars parked next to a building that looked like a restored train station. All the windows in the station were lighted—something must be going on there, a meeting, maybe. He hoped the people inside the building would stay put until he was out of sight.

He turned the light back on, let it wander over the creek bank. Steep, grass-covered. He'd slide on that grass the minute he started down the slope. Henry moved the flashlight beam up the bank toward the white concrete arch at the tunnel opening. There was a metal mat lying on the ground there that looked like chain-link fencing, and he walked closer to inspect it. It appeared to be very sturdy and went all the way down the bank to the rocks along the edge of the water. Good. It was probably put there to stabilize the bank when the park was built. He'd climb down right here, even though the bank was much steeper at this point. He could hold onto the chain link mat to keep from sliding.

Henry shut the flashlight off as shuddering doubts hit him like the shock of a highly charged stun gun. Was she really in there? On re-consideration his idea sounded un-believably far-fetched, and he—with the possible exception of Agent Brooks—was the only one who'd thought of it at all. Why were they the only ones? Because it was a crazy idea? After all, he knew nothing about this tunnel. Maybe humans couldn't get through it and that's why no one else was looking for Carrie here. Maybe Willard Brooks was new to this area and didn't know what was in the tunnel either.

Was he about to walk into unknown danger, ruin a good pair of slacks and new leather walking shoes on some cockamamie, ridiculous, crazy, dreamed-up fool's adventure?

He pulled in air, puffed out his cheeks, blew the air out. No! His plan was logical. Carrie must be in this creek. Where else could she be?

He knew she hadn't run away from an injured or dead man; she wouldn't do that. That meant Bogardus had shoved her through the trap door and, whether he'd been fatally injured by then or not, had slammed the door shut after her.

Or someone else had. Henry shook his head. Maybe Carrie could clear up that mystery too.

Since there would be no escape for her through the trap door, she must have crawled out of the hole in the wall and found her way into the creek. She was a fighter, and, unless badly hurt or, or...dead...*no*, maybe not even hurt, she would be fighting to make her way out right now. She'd see the flow of the water and understand that following the flow was the most likely way to freedom, and...

She would see? No, blast it, how could she see without any light? Again there was that stun gun feeling, turning his bones to cooked spaghetti.

Carrie wouldn't be able to see where she was, let alone see her way out.

That meant he *had* to get into the creek and go through the tunnel. She was probably huddled someplace back there near the Fordyce, hiding. She'd be terrified, of course, hurt, maybe. She must have been unconscious when the FBI team was searching the mud-filled room, didn't even know anyone had been down in that room looking for her. He had to get to her as quickly as possible.

Henry looked around once more, saw no one, and forced his rubbery body to carry him to the edge of the slope. He sat more quickly than he'd planned when his feet slipped out from under him on the grass, then rolled over on his stomach and slid until he could grab the chain-link mesh. Down he went, holding onto the fencing all the way into the water. He was glad he had on his walking shoes after all. The rocks were going to be tricky.

Switching on the flashlight again, he got to his feet and, picking his way over the rocks, headed into the tunnel. It was good to be doing something; he couldn't have stood the wait in his hotel room, his room and Carrie's.

He began sloshing his way along the creek bed—hey, piece of cake. He'd find Carrie in minutes.

The feeling this was going to be easy changed as soon as he was in the tunnel. The water, now confined between walls, was suddenly much deeper. He had to move each foot carefully, trying to avoid unseen hazards, big rocks, whatever else might be at the bottom of the creek. His shoulders jerked in frustration because the going was so slow. If he hurried he might slip and fall, and there could be two casualties lying in the tunnel. Given Bell's mind-set when Henry last saw him, neither of them would be found until it was too late, unless Brooks spoke up, of course.

Stop it! He was fantasizing in the worst possible way. He *would* find her and take her back to...

Blast! Back to the hotel? How was he going to get both of them back there without being seen? They would be wet, she'd be dirty from the mud. They'd want to shower, change clothes. She'd probably need time to rest too and have something to eat. Where could he find food without attracting attention? It wouldn't be fair or smart to subject her to aggressive questioning by Bell or anyone else before she'd had a chance to clean up, rest, and eat.

There was also the terrifying possibility she wouldn't be in any condition to answer questions. Henry shook his head violently at that idea, slipped on a rock, and almost fell. She had to be all right, had to.

The water was getting steadily deeper. He tried to swish his legs and feet against the current more quickly until he almost fell again, so he slowed back down. A walking stick sure would help.

The flashlight beam roamed ahead and then over the concrete walls on each side and above him. There was a large pipe running along the side of the tunnel now. He hadn't noticed it before. Big enough for a small person to crawl on, but probably too high for Carrie to reach.

He turned the flashlight straight ahead again and pulled his legs forward against the current. *Dratted rocks, they...* One foot slid sideways, and this time he couldn't recover. Arms flailing, he splashed backwards and disappeared under the water. The light went out. Winnie the Pooh was gone.

Henry came up into total darkness, sputtering, cussing even Winnie the Pooh, saying words he thought he'd put behind him forever. He certainly wouldn't have used them if he thought anyone was around to hear. Carrie would be giving him the dickens if she...he choked and gagged, coughing up water and gasping for breath.

He was blind, helpless. Helpless...couldn't find her. How could he find her when everything was black?

Had to find her. *Oh, God, oh, my God.*

Was he crying? Shouting, choking, hot tears on his already wet face blinding him in the awful blindness of total darkness.

"Carrie, Cara." His words, his sobs, would be humiliating if anyone could hear him. "What am I going to do, oh, what, what..." *No one else would hear him, no one!*

And it was his fault he was alone.

He couldn't get to her now. He had to find his way out of here, ask that pompous Bell for help...convince him to have a team search the tunnel. Plead, do anything so he'd act quickly enough... Hurry, hurry, follow the flow of water, get to Bell.

Why had he been too proud to ask for help before? Why had he come here alone? He knew better. Law enforcement was about teamwork.

He was still gasping, fighting for control, pushing deep, jerky breaths in and out. At last, breathing more smoothly, he heard the bubbling and shushing of the creek in the new silence.

Then, "Henry?"

It was a small sound. Hallucination?

"Huh?"

A light winked on somewhere behind him.

"What you are going to do, Henry, is come back here and help me out. I think I'm stuck—like Pooh Bear in Rabbit's hole."

Chapter XV

Carrie

She wasn't stuck after all, because the minute Henry got to her she slid easily into his arms, and then they were in the water together, hugging and laughing and babbling, saying nothing sensible, just making noises, mingling tears and creek water and forgetting everything about them that was damaged.

The first words she understood out of the babble of declared love and the repeats of "Thank God, thank God," were "Cara, why were you in that hole?"

"Because I thought you were Everett, of course, coming after me, and I was trying to hide. Henry, that man is crazy, and he is after money hidden in the Fordyce. He kept mumbling about his father hiding it there all the while he was taking me down the stairs to...to push me through that trap door. I guess he thought we knew about it and that I...we, were trying to get the money away from him... or something."

She stopped, remembering. "He called me a meddling witch, and...other stuff, and Henry, he had a knife. At the last, I remember trying to grab it. I don't...don't know what happened after that. Did he get away? Did you catch him?"

"He didn't get away. Little love, you're safe."

Then he was hugging her again and thanking God, maybe crying just a little, and saying her name over and over.

Suddenly she was too weary to react to all the emotion, so she listened in silence, holding tight to him, waiting, while he thanked and thanked and hugged and kept kissing the top of her head.

She hadn't heard Henry mention God this many times during the entire year since the two of them met. That alone could cancel out the swearing she'd heard, the wonderful swearing in Henry's familiar voice. It was a good thing she hadn't been able to see him—splashing around in the creek and spitting water as well as spouting those perfectly awful words. She'd probably have laughed at him, no matter what he was saying.

Finally she began to wiggle, lifting her head away from his chest to say—interrupting yet another round of hugs and kisses—"Henry, can we go? I'd like to get out of the water. I've had enough being wet and being underground. Is it far to the end of this tunnel?"

He laughed and with one more hug released her. Hooking arms to help keep each other upright in the uneven creek bed, they walked with the flow of the water, moving so quickly now that it felt like running. In minutes they were out in the glow of street lamps under a huge, open night sky littered with stars that twinkled at her, even through city lights. The air smelled wonderful, and Carrie took huge breaths, remembering to do it quietly so Henry wouldn't worry that she was gasping.

Then she said, "The sky is beautiful, and I'm so grateful to be able to see it again."

The sudden blast of light was such a shock that she shrieked, and Henry swore. Movie-set bright, lights flashed on from everywhere, and Agent Bell's voice shouted, "King, Ms. McCrite, wait right there, we're coming for you."

Henry said, his voice low and urgent, "Carrie, I'm picking you up. You've been through a terrible ordeal. They won't bother you now if you're hurt or weak. We need time to talk and plan before they come at us. There are things you need to know."

It would be tempting to nestle in Henry's arms, to act weaker than she felt, but then they'd probably end up shoving her in some emergency room and she wasn't about to let that happen. She had to be strong.

"No, I'm okay," she said, but still he reached for her, bending to put his arm under her legs. She yanked away in an action that was more instinctive than reasoned, and, off balance, Henry stumbled past her and fell, landing with his shoulder wedged between two huge rocks in the now-shallow creek bed.

Carrie watched in horror as he attempted to pull free, made an awful yelling sound that burned in her brain, and sank back into the water.

She knelt, no longer conscious of wetness, unable to speak as two creatures in black wet suits sloshed toward them and bent over Henry. "Looks like his shoulder. Probably dislocated it," one of them said.

Then arms were tugging at her and, somehow, they were on the bank, and she was dimly aware that Henry had been carried up on a stretcher. She knelt beside him, and Agent Bell was there too, taking off his grey suit jacket, pushing it around her shoulders, fumbling to button it across her front without giving her a chance to put her arms in the sleeves.

He was making her a prisoner inside his coat! She cried aloud, only an incoherent wail, and looked down to shove his hands away. Then she saw that her shirt was slit where Everett's knife had pushed through it. Wet and clinging, the shirt had twisted around to catch on flesh and expose... Oh! Bell's move was one of chivalry, not imprisonment. She knew her bra had been cut open when she used it to pad her hands against the sharp pipe brackets, but now the only thing left, exposed to the world, was her own rounded flesh, pinkish and wet in the glare of light.

She put on his jacket and rolled up the sleeves.

Everything whirled, there were sirens, the lights were too bright...so many people. She remained on her knees by Henry's side, even pushing away someone in uniform who tried to lift her as a female voice murmured soothing words. She wanted to shove everyone away, wanted peace somewhere else, wanted to somehow take this all back. "Oh, I'm so sorry, all my fault," she whispered and tried to pray.

Henry finally opened his eyes, and though his face was twisted with pain, he attempted a smile as he spoke to her. She noticed he stopped for a breath between every few words.

"Cara, car keys in right pocket. Get them. Need my

billfold. In the trunk. You know where. I put it away before coming, didn't want it wet.

"Going to hospital now. Shoulder. Sorry, can't help it. Could you drive my car and come? Are you okay? Can you do that?"

She nodded. "Of course I will, don't worry." She bent to kiss him on the cheek, dripping tears there too. She felt in his pocket for the keys, moving her hand slowly and carefully, and was warmed by even that small, intimate contact. Then she became unimportant, feeling invisible as ambulance attendants hurried up and attention focused on Henry.

She must get to the car quickly. But she stood there, alone in the crowd, stuck to her spot on the pavement, frozen by panic and despair.

Hurry, she thought, *hurry,* and still couldn't seem to move. She must follow the ambulance. She had no idea where they were taking him, didn't know where the hospital was, and at night, even with a city map, how could she find it? As she pondered this, the ambulance pulled away, going she knew not where. She was alone and had never felt so completely lost.

Maybe Jason and Eleanor...but they would be asleep, she couldn't...

She deserved this agony. What had happened to Henry was her fault: she'd jerked away, causing him to fall. *Why, Carrie, oh, why?*

She bowed her head, drowning in a self-focused remorse, asking God to give her the words for a prayer. Her reaction to Henry's attempt to pick her up hadn't been a conscious one. She'd simply pulled back, resisting him, resisting his idea of help. What was *wrong* with her?

That's when the police officer touched her arm, a

woman. She must have been close by all along, must have been the one murmuring words of comfort earlier. Carrie hadn't heard or felt anyone walking toward her now, there had been no sound of steps on concrete.

The officer said, her voice soft, gentled by sympathy, "Hey, there, you okay? We'll go to the hospital now. You need to be with him and have someone check you over too. I can drive his car if you like." So the woman had been there, had heard their conversation.

Carrie caught herself before the automatic words shot out of her mouth: "No need, I'm fine." After a pause she said only "thank you," and the two of them turned toward the car.

Under a street lamp Carrie looked down and began to laugh hysterically, alarming her companion, who took her arm, shook her lightly, and said, "Hey, now, it's gonna be okay."

"No," Carrie said, "no, it's not that, not hysterics, or maybe not, but look at me, just *look* at me!"

They both looked. From mud-stained shoes, up the legs of once pristine khaki slacks that now looked like baggy camouflage pajama bottoms, and above those, Agent Bell's rumpled jacket with the sleeves rolled up. The police officer made a muffled whooshing sound, then she was laughing too as her eyes went higher, up to Carrie's face and hair. "I have a comb in my shoulder bag," she said, "and damp towelettes. Those will help...some."

Carrie retrieved Henry's wallet and also pulled out his insulated food carrier. She handed the car keys to the officer and, when the doors were open, put the soft-sided bag on the passenger seat before she got in the car. No need to mess up Henry's upholstery in addition to messing up everything else in his life.

And she was crying again. There had been many years in her life when she hadn't cried at all, hadn't been able to. She'd lived inside herself, as insulated against the outside world as this food bag insulated ice cream from the heat. Then she met Henry, and when JoAnne was killed,* Henry brought comfort by putting his arms around her, hugging her until the tears came easily. Too easily, as if a dam had broken. Now crying was more a problem of too much than not enough. *Stop, stop it!*

She snuffled, hiccuped, fastened her seat belt, and said, "Sorry. I'm ready now and I really do appreciate this. I don't know where the hospital is."

"No problem. Actually you're my assignment tonight anyway. I'm Officer Gwen Talbot; you can call me Gwen."

Gwen reached into her shoulder bag before she fastened her own seat belt, then held her hand out toward Carrie. "Here's a package of fairly fresh peanut butter crackers and my comb and the wipes. I'd bet you're hungry, and you sure do need the comb and something to scrub the dirt off your face. You might wipe one of those things over your hair too. Is there a mirror on the back of that visor? Probably you can see enough in the city lights to clean up a bit and comb your hair."

She faced front, clicked the seat belt, and turned the car key. "We're on our way."

After a pause Gwen continued. "Everyone sort of overlooked you after your friend got hurt, but seems to me you've had a pretty awful night yourself. Weren't you in that tunnel for several hours? I went all the way through there as part of my training when I joined the department. Very wet, very dark."

---

* As told in *A Valley to Die For*

"Yes, but I'm okay, really...it's Henry..."

"All right, but here's how it is. Though the National Park itself is under FBI jurisdiction, Hot Springs Creek and the tunnel is ours, so that's one reason we were at the tunnel exit with the FBI agents when you came out. I'm sure you had quite a time in that creek, not to mention being abducted by a man with a knife. I'm not clear on all the details, you know more than I do about it, but I want you to realize that no one really blames you for what happened. In fact, I think it's good work you got the knife away from him before he stabbed you. I always say we women have to protect ourselves with every tool at hand."

Her words came slowly into Carrie's head and fizzed around. "Everett?"

"Well, yes, him of course, though everyone understands you killed him in self-defense, so they aren't going to arrest you, not exactly. We're all sympathetic, even Agent Bell, who seems a cold sort, but he's okay, really. After all, he sees that you're a tiny woman.

"There will be some court stuff though. You'll need legal advice—after you've seen to your friend, that is."

Carrie's voice wavered as she grabbed at Officer Talbot's words. "Everett is *dead?*"

Gwen Talbot looked away from the traffic to stare at her for a long second. "Oh, golly, didn't you know? You stabbed him to get away, and, uh..." Finally, eyes back on the traffic, she said, very softly, "Didn't you?"

Carrie slumped back in her seat, and a huge "Ohhhh" wavered out. "I don't know," she said, "I just don't know. Surely I couldn't have." There was a long pause. "But right now I don't, I can't remember."

"You poor thing," Gwen said, as she pulled up by the hospital's emergency entrance.

More bright lights, more bustling people; Henry, lying on a gurney in an exam room; attendants waiting to take him away somewhere.

"I'll be right back," Officer Talbot said. "I need to check in with my captain."

Carrie bent close to Henry, brushing her lips against his forehead, touching his right hand, getting no response from him. He was frighteningly quiet, eyes tightly shut, wrinkled into slits. She didn't say "I'm sorry." It wasn't the time for that. It was, over and over, time for murmurs of assurance, and love, and still—no response. Oh, God, oh, why, why? There was more guilt throbbing inside her than she could take in or process.

"We've given him medication for pain and the resulting nausea," an attendant told her, "and we're getting ready to x-ray his shoulder." At her blank look the man said, "Demerol and Phenergan."

He waited. She said nothing.

"X-ray to see what's wrong, though we think he's dislocated his shoulder. Do you understand?"

"Oh." Her head buzzed and she swayed. *All my fault* was throbbing around and around inside her head like some stuck recording.

The man took her arm, looked into her face; then his eyes worked down, all the way to the still-wet shoes. Maybe he was looking at her that funny way because of how she was dressed—the dirt, the clown-like get-up—though they were probably used to seeing peculiar clothing combinations here. Surely he wasn't holding her arm because he knew what was going on inside her head.

"We want to check you too. Why don't you sit down right here? Someone will be with you soon."

"No, no, I don't need anything, I'm fine, it's just that..." She shoved his hand away, and as soon as she had, almost stamped her foot, thinking she'd been shoving people away all night. She wished she could take back her reaction to his touch. He was only being kind.

And oh, if she could take back that other reaction, the jerking away from Henry, if she could erase it out of existence. If...

Officer Talbot was beside her again, and a nurse directed them to a counter at one end of the room. Carrie found cards in Henry's wallet that seemed to satisfy the woman behind the counter, who didn't look up as she asked, "Wife? Name?"

Carrie could manage nothing but a blank stare. Wife? Where?

After a long silence Gwen's head came close and she whispered, "She's asking if you're married to him."

"Oh! Oh, no," Carrie said, speaking loudly, too loudly she realized, because several heads turned toward her. "Um, not married, good friends." Now she was whispering as softly as Gwen had a moment earlier, and the attendant leaned forward to hear her, still typing on computer keys.

After handing Henry's cards back, the woman explained that he was undergoing something that sounded like "reduction of dislocation" and pointed to a door down the hall. It seemed that Carrie, with Officer Gwen shadowing her, was free to find Henry.

And free to wish she hadn't.

When Gwen opened the door and they went in the room indicated, two large men were attending Henry, their actions other-world bizarre. The treatment, if that's what they called it, was nothing like any hospital activity Carrie had ever seen or imagined. She wished she had some place to sit down as the process unfolded and her legs felt increasingly spongy.

First they tied a rope-like rolled sheet around one man's waist, a nurse, Gwen said, and the other end of the same sheet was tied to Henry's waist. The male nurse held tightly to Henry as another nurse helped the second man—"Doctor Abrams, good man," Gwen whispered—wrap a second rolled sheet around Henry's left forearm. That arm was raised at a right angle to his body, and Henry grunted while the second sheet was tied to the doctor's waist.

What on earth were they doing? It looked like a bizarre kind of torture. Carrie wanted to shut her eyes but forced herself to keep them open. *God, give Henry the strength to get through this, give me the strength to keep from falling on the floor or screaming.*

There was a count-down, "One, two, three," a fierce pull from the man holding Henry's arm while the nurse held Henry's body. Carrie heard a click and a cry of pain from Henry. She discovered she was holding her hand tightly over her mouth, and that suppressed the yelp that wanted to surge out. Had they broken a bone, had something gone horribly wrong?

But the sheets were being untied, the two big men, nurse and doctor, seemed satisfied by what had happened. Now Carrie did close her eyes.

Gwen slipped her arm around Carrie's waist, steadying her. "They'll do another x-ray now," she whispered, "to be sure everything went back together okay. Then they'll secure the arm and shoulder and probably let you take him back to the hotel. Don't worry about finding the way. I can drive you while another officer follows in the police car."

Carrie blinked her eyes open. She and Gwen and a female nurse tidying up were the only ones left in the room.

"That's it?" asked Carrie.

"That's it," said Gwen. "Now, while we wait, let's go sit down and talk. Are you ready to answer a few questions?"

Carrie shrugged and said, "Why not, since I would like to sit down." She didn't mind speaking her feelings aloud to this woman, and she had to wait for Henry anyway.

"We could talk in the morning."

"No, no. I want to think about something else besides this." She swept her arm around the room. "Wouldn't you if you were me?"

"Yep," said Gwen, "I sure would. So, shall we visit the Ladies' and then go back to the waiting room and have a chat?"

There was another uniformed police officer in the waiting room when they got there, but he stayed where he was as Carrie and Gwen took seats in a relatively quiet corner. Then two men in suits got up from chairs against the wall and came over. They each pulled up a chair, giving Carrie names and titles she barely grasped, other than comprehending one was a Hot Springs Police detective and the other an agent from the FBI office in Little Rock. She didn't catch which was which. After the few words of explanation neither man said anything more. One took notes, the other just watched and listened. Gwen and Carrie did all the talking.

"Since you and I have already been getting to know each other," Gwen said, "I'm the one chosen to ask about what happened to you this afternoon and tonight. I thought you'd be more comfortable with that. Most of what you'll tell me did take place in property that's under the jurisdiction of the National Park Service and the FBI, as we've discussed, but Agent Denby will be their ears here. If he has any questions about something I don't cover, he'll break in. Okay?"

"'Kay," said Carrie, who was beginning to relax and, as a result, felt sleepy.

"First, could you describe what happened from the time Everett Bogardus took you away from the tour group until you went through the trap door in the Fordyce?"

Carrie described it all, her voice droning on and on in her ears as she forced herself to think back, and to tell Gwen about it.

"Then he opened the trap door. I was so scared, things got blurry. I...I don't remember anything more until I woke up lying in mud."

"And the knife?" Gwen asked. "Where was it?"

When Carrie frowned and didn't answer, Gwen said, "Before you went through the trap door, did you struggle with Everett Bogardus? Did you attempt to get the knife away from him?"

Carrie worked on finding a clear memory of that terrible moment. She answered slowly, pushing through horror to try to re-create what had happened.

"I was crying. I think I screamed when he shoved me over the edge. I remember trying to grab his hand, the one with the knife. I wanted to get the blade away from me. I did touch the blade, here," she held her hand out to show a thin slice across two fingers and noticed that the marks were already very faint. "After that, I don't remember a thing until I woke up in the mud."

CHAPTER XVI

HENRY

His shoulder hurt like fury, but throbbing pain no longer wiped out everything in his head. Still, he wasn't sure he was thinking clearly enough to consider problems like murder and what to do about Carrie.

They'd given him pain killers, probably other stuff too, and how would he know if his head was working sensibly? He'd been in enough emergency rooms during his many years with the Kansas City Police Department to know that sometimes, even when you thought your head was working well, it wasn't. Kind of like being drunk, something else he'd known a lot about, once upon a time.

One picture in his mind was way too clear. Through all the ordeal at the hospital he hadn't been able to erase the image of Carrie kneeling beside him on the creek bank—wet, scared, looking like a pitiful puppy someone had tried to drown. Drugs or no drugs, he could still see the image very clearly and understand that he had caused it.

His fault. He'd planned for her to lie, pretend she was incapacitated when she wasn't. Why? Some of his reasons were noble, but not all of them. Sure, Carrie deserved time to clean up, get a bite to eat, rest. They both did. But he had to admit he'd wanted to hear the full story of her abduction before the FBI messed with her head—something they could do without any planning before the fact, or regret after. Maybe they wouldn't do it intentionally, but even with the most benign motivation, they would do it.

There would be nuances in the questioner's expression, voice tone, the way questions were worded, and in reactions to answers. Even the most stoic trained law officer couldn't help transmitting something. The first questioning period in a criminal case often changed the perceptions of the person being questioned, provided they were alert enough to notice.

Carrie would certainly notice.

Plain and simple. He'd wanted to debrief her before anyone else did. Then, together, he and Carrie could plan what to say, telling the truth of course, but maybe an organized truth.

And look what had happened! She said no, he didn't pay any attention and tried to pick her up as if she couldn't make it on her own. When she resisted, he'd ended up dumping himself on the rocks.

Served him right.

Carrie knew very well that he was a stickler for telling the truth. He had been all during his career in law-enforcement, even when a slight alteration in the truth might have helped bring justice. So, when he wanted her to pretend she was too weak to talk with anyone, he'd probably confused her, maybe even made her angry at him. More than once in the past he'd chided her about telling "helpful fibs," said they were nothing but lies, no matter what she called them. Now he'd been the one urging her to join him in creating a lie.

He grunted without realizing he'd done it as Dr. Abrams continued the job of securing his arm to his body. The doctor murmured soothingly, "Just another minute and you're on your way."

Blast! He was going to have to face her now. Would he be able to tell if she was angry? Who knew?

They insisted on putting a loose hospital shirt around him because his own shirt wouldn't fit over the bound arm. They also insisted on the wheel chair, so he sat, listened to a long list of instructions and "don'ts," stuck the bottles of pills a nurse handed him in his shirt pocket, and rode off to face Carrie. At least the hospital corridor was long. That gave him a chance to think about what he was going to do and say when he saw her.

By the time they got to the waiting room, he'd worked out a plan.

Uh-oh. She was sitting with the uniformed police officer he'd been dimly aware of before and...two suits.

Henry's appearance broke up whatever discussion had been going on between Carrie and her companions. He wished he knew what she'd told them and how the police and FBI were viewing the murder of Everett Bogardus.

Everyone stood when the nurse wheeled Henry into their circle.

The uniformed officer spoke first. "Hello, Mr. King, glad to see they put you back together again. I'm Officer Gwen Talbot of the Hot Springs Police Department." She waved an arm toward the two men. "This is Agent Kaylor Denby from the Little Rock office of the FBI and Detective Hunt Wilkinson with our department. While we waited for you, we were asking Carrie...Ms. McCrite...to tell us about the unfortunate events of this afternoon and evening."

She smiled at him. "If you're ready to check out, I'll drive you and Carrie back to the hotel in your car. My partner"—another sweep of her arm, indicating a uniformed officer who seemed to be dozing in a chair near the emergency entrance—"will drive the police car and follow us."

Henry nodded at each person in turn as introductions were made, then looked at Carrie. She'd combed her hair and her face was cleaner, but his heart twisted uncomfortably as he saw that she still had the pitiful puppy look in her eyes.

Watching her face carefully, he said, "Carrie, could you find a phone and call Jason and Eleanor? I know they'll be asleep, but under the circumstances, I think we need their help, and we need it before morning. I'd like Jason to come stay with me in our room. He knows about this kind of thing." He waved his right arm toward the bulge under the hospital shirt. "He dislocated his own shoulder a few years back when he was painting their house and fell off a ladder." Henry didn't give his other reason. *And besides, he's a man.*

"It would be good for me to have him close enough to help for a day or two. The doctor said I could take this binding off after twenty-four hours, but until then things will be awkward, and I'm not used to operating with one arm. Could you stay with Eleanor until I'm not quite so helpless?"

She started to open her mouth, stopped, swallowed, looked at him, nodded, and left to make the phone call.

He wanted to rush after her and, even in front of all these people, yank her into his arms...arm, hold her. He wanted to assure her that this was just a temporary rough patch and everything would soon be all right. The very fact she was making no protest about changing rooms and letting Jason take her place told him worlds. She didn't like it, he knew her well enough to read that in her carefully expressionless face, but she'd complied without a word.

Where was his feisty Carrie?

Henry straightened in the chair, winced, and heard a murmur of sympathy from Officer Talbot. He turned his head away to avoid looking at her or the other people crowded around him.

Maybe it was just as well that he couldn't manage to hug Carrie. He couldn't manage to tell her everything would soon be all right either.

CHAPTER XVII

CARRIE

Eleanor's "hello" sounded way too perky. How could she manage it, this time of night? Carrie's phone response under the same circumstances would have been a grunt. Suddenly Carrie was angry at her friend, even as she realized how stupid and unfair that flash of anger was. But Eleanor was safe in bed at the hotel, whereas Carrie...

"Hello? Hello? Who's calling?"

"Oh, Eleanor, I am sorry to wake you, but Henry and I are in a bit of a pickle and, uh..."

"Carrie, for goodness sake, where did you and Henry get to? There are rumors going around—have you heard anything about what happened to Everett Bogardus? We know something happened, he's missing, along with you two of course, and there have been police here at the Downtowner, not to mention the Fordyce. Greta would only say there had been a bit of trouble and it wouldn't affect our activities, we weren't to worry. Not worry? Well, I guess you can tell it didn't exactly keep us awake, but still...oh, sorry, Carrie, I'm chattering. Where did you say you were? Are you okay? Is Henry with you? What do you need? We can dress in ten minutes and be there."

"Whoa, Eleanor, we're at the hospital here in Hot Springs..."

"*Hospital?*"

"...where Henry's just had a dislocated shoulder, uh, fixed. We'll tell you about it later. Now we're on our way back to the hotel and because of, of, his shoulder, you know, Henry wondered if Jason could move in with him in our room and I, well, would you mind if...you see, he needs extra help and..."

"Dislocated shoulder, how on earth? Well, bless your hearts. And of course that's the sensible thing to do, change partners, so to speak. Oh, wait a minute, Carrie.

"Yes, Jason, that's what I said, change partners, but it's Henry, not Carrie, who has the dislocated shoulder. He's going to need you. Well, just a minute, dear, I am finding out more.

"Carrie, I was telling Jason about it. He had a dislocated shoulder a few years back, you know, and Henry will need help, as I remember all too well. Jason was cranky as...oh, sorry, there I go again. Is it right or left?"

"Left shoulder, I..."

"Left shoulder, well, good for that at least, but still, unzipping pants and all the other, and you're not even married and, well, of course Jason will switch with you. That's only proper. Yes, he's nodding his head right now. I remember how awkward everything was when he...it was the left one too, but still..."

"I..."

"So, Carrie, listen to me. I think the sensible thing to do is for me to go get your room key and begin changing things around right away so Henry, and you too, can go to bed as soon as you get here. Call the hotel desk now and authorize them to give me a copy of your key. Then I'll call down there in a few minutes to be sure everything is okay. How soon will you be back here?"

"I haven't a clue where we are in this city in relation to the hotel, so I don't know a time, but we're ready to leave the hospital and it shouldn't take long; we'll have a police escort."

"Oh, my goodness. Police there too? Why? Well, never mind. How about something to eat? I think hot soup helps any bad situation. I always bring some of those packages of soup to mix in hot water, and tea and crackers and other things. I have bananas too. We use the coffee pot in the room to heat the water."

"Oh, Eleanor," Carrie was close to tears again, "I'd love some soup. I don't know about Henry, what with all the medication and other stuff he's been through. I don't know how he feels about food right now."

"Then we'll just ask him when you get here, won't we? Now hang up and call the hotel about your key. Do you have the number? No, of course you don't. Let's see, here it is, got a pencil and paper?"

There was a pause, and then Eleanor was reading numbers into the phone. "See you in a bit, and Carrie, quit that sputtering. Don't you worry, we're glad to help. You know Henry will be okay soon. Jason recovered and so will he."

She hung up.

Carrie sighed. She was going to have to do something

really, really nice for Eleanor and Jason. Maybe it was because she'd raised three children, but her friend was so "take charge capable." Right now that was very comforting. Carrie, in spite of everything, was beginning to feel better.

Then she wondered if she'd have felt as comforted if the person taking over had been male. Had been Henry.

Oh, dear.

The hotel staff must have known something unusual was going on because they made no objection when, with very little explanation, Carrie asked them to give Eleanor an extra key. So far, so good, and at least she had something positive to tell Henry while they waited for Gwen and her fellow officer to bring the cars to the emergency room door.

Jason and Eleanor met them in the hotel lobby, gave their uniformed companions only a brief glance, and said the room changes were all taken care of. Without delay Jason and the male police officer began helping Henry toward the elevator.

Carrie had known they were going to have to account for Henry's injury somehow, so she said he had fallen in the creek when both of them were at Transportation Plaza. She knew that sounded incredible to Eleanor and Jason, who had never heard of the place, but there would be time for a more complete explanation later.

While they were walking to the elevators, Eleanor asked Henry if he'd like anything to drink or eat, and he agreed to hot chicken broth, which Jason said he could make without Eleanor's help, thank you. Then the three men were in an elevator, not waiting for the women to join them. The doors slid shut and Henry was gone. Carrie's shoulders slumped.

She obviously wasn't needed.

As they waited for a second elevator, it was also obvious that Gwen was making no move to leave, so Carrie introduced her to Eleanor, who began at once to ask questions about women in police work.

Carrie turned away to look around the quiet lobby. She studied the casually dressed man seated in a chair near the brochure racks. Could he be some kind of law officer? He seemed to be paying no attention to them as he read a paper, but why would anyone be sitting in a hotel lobby reading a newspaper in the middle of the night? Gwen and her companion had ignored the man. Would they have done that if they didn't already know who he was?

Oh, what did it matter? He wasn't bothering her, not yet at least.

As the elevator rose, she wondered if Gwen planned to spend the night with them in their room or, perhaps, outside it?

Outside, it seemed. After looking around, Gwen said, "Don't worry about being disturbed tonight. Someone will be guarding the hall at all times. There are no hotel guests on this floor other than Elderhostel people and no reason for them—or you—to be out and about until breakfast. Anyone coming from the elevators or stairway will be stopped."

"So," Carrie said aloud, "does that mean Henry and I are being protected from some unknown evil or that I'm under guard?" Eleanor looked startled by the question but said nothing.

Gwen was silent for a moment, looking from Carrie to Eleanor and back.

"A little of both. We still have a lot of unexplained stuff to account for. Maybe now you'll remember more about what happened before you went through that trap door, since there's less stress and all."

"I've already arranged for room service breakfasts for the four of us," Eleanor said, still bright and cheery though it was after two a.m. "They'll be delivered about ten, so should I add one for you, Gwen...uh, Ms...Officer Talbot?"

"No, I'll be gone by then, but I'll probably see you ladies again tomorrow evening."

She said a quick goodnight and left the room.

Carrie looked at Eleanor. "I'd better explain all this."

Her friend held up a hand and sighed. "Not now. We'll have time in the morning. For now, just get out of those awful clothes and into the tub. Be sure and wash your hair. It's a mess.

"I'll see about laundry in the morning and dry cleaning for whatever needs it, including that jacket you're wearing. Whoever loaned it to you will hardly want it back like it is.

"Oh, my goodness, your shirt and bra are all torn, and look at those scratches. How...well, never mind, just get in the tub. I'll take care of your clothes in the morning, though it looks like some of them are fit for nothing but the trash."

"Oh, Eleanor, the morning session is more from that herb lady. You can't miss that. I hate this, hate it. You're doing so much."

"Hush, we'll catch up later if we think we missed any-thing important. A trip to the herb farm is planned for later in the week, and the presenter said she sells growing instructions and recipe books there."

"I'll buy you all the books she has," said Carrie as she slipped into the tub and Eleanor put a cup of soup in her hands.

In spite of the fact she'd been in more than enough hot water only a few hours earlier, Carrie enjoyed the bath, the clean feeling, and, at last, snuggling under the covers.

Eleanor went to sleep quickly, but Carrie stayed awake for another hour, trying to recall all of her last minutes with Everett and praying very, very hard. What had happened in that basement room? And, even more important to her now, why did she push people away when they tried to help her?

She cried out as loudly as she could, "Help me, oh, no, no, no." She screamed at Everett to stop. Someone had to hear her, Henry...someone...had to come and pull Everett away.

No one came, and he shoved and shoved and she tried to grab at him, at anything, to keep from falling into that awful blackness, but all she touched was the knife blade! Not ever the handle, the blade!

Then she heard herself repeating Henry's name until Eleanor was there, holding her and rocking her back and forth, murmuring, "There-there, there-there, you're safe now, it was a nightmare, wake up now, you're safe, the bad things are gone, wake up, Carrie, open your eyes and look at me."

With a last gasped cry Carrie opened her eyes and stared at Eleanor, feeling dazed and hoarse. She swallowed, pushed back. "Oh, my."

"It was a nightmare. You can wake up from nightmares, they aren't real. But I think it's time you got everything that happened yesterday out in the open—put the light on it and got it out and over with.

"Here, take a drink of water, then tell me all about

it."

"Eleanor, *fingerprints!* They should check for fingerprints if they haven't already. My fingerprints cannot be
on that knife handle, only on the blade. This is how it
happened..."

Carrie was trying not to cry again as she finished, tired of
it all, tired of the emotional roller coaster. After a space of
silence she went back and repeated something she'd said
just a few moments earlier. "I jerked away from Henry. I
jerked away, and that was why he fell. It was my fault he
got hurt."

Eleanor sat quietly on the edge of the bed looking down
at her hands, and Carrie copied her pose, too disturbed and
embarrassed by her own confession to lift her eyes.

"I don't want to be that way, to shove everyone away,
but if I'm to remain independent and strong, I can't always
depend on others, not even Henry."

Eleanor didn't speak for a long time. Then she moved,
and Carrie could tell she had looked up—was probably
studying Carrie's bowed head. Finally she said, "You know,
one of the reasons we women are strong is because we're
willing to ask for help when we need it! You've heard the
old joke about men refusing to ask for highway directions
when they're unable to find where they're going, so they end
up wasting minutes and sometimes hours being incredibly
lost? Well, a women would *ask*. We use all the resources we
have at hand and it adds to our strength.

"No, Carrie, hear me out. I understand your need to feel
you can depend on yourself, but you know the Bible even
better than I do. Where in the Bible does it say 'Trust in
Carrie McCrite' or even 'Trust in human strength?' What it

says is—here, I brought your Bible with your other things; look at Proverbs 3, verse 5—'Trust in the Lord with all thine heart; and lean not unto thine own understanding.'" She laid the open book on the bed and her finger pointed at the page. "You must put trust for strength where it belongs."

Now she used her finger to lift Carrie's chin until their eyes were on a level. Eleanor's eyes were bright and glaring, her own chin set at a high angle. That look of defiance was something Carrie had never seen on her friend's face before, and it silenced any response she might have made.

Carrie bowed her head again. Eleanor was right, of course. Carrie yearned to make the words real, have them motivate her rather than knee-jerk reactions to any offered help from outside. Could she do it? She wasn't sure. But, simply put, she had to if she wanted to save her friendship with Henry.

Now she heard his voice repeating what he'd said to her last fall at a time of sadness: *People need people, sometimes.* He'd meant they both needed other people, sometimes. Why couldn't she fully accept that?

Eleanor broke into her reverie. "Okay, shall we go back to bed? Scoot under the covers; I'll tuck you in."

And Carrie let her do it. She went to sleep repeating the words *Trust in the Lord* to herself, over and over.

Chapter XVIII

Henry

The best Henry had been able to manage for a clean up was a wet washcloth wipe-around. Wet was the operative word. He couldn't do a good job wringing out a washcloth one-handed and wasn't in the mood to ask Jason for help.

At least he didn't have to deal with mud like he'd seen on Carrie. He started to smile, remembering her stained and splattered appearance, then sobered as he thought of what she'd endured. And he could have prevented all of it. If only he'd stayed with her in the Fordyce. If only he hadn't wanted her to lie about being hurt. If only, *if only.*

Right now she'd be confused, even angry at him for reversing his usual staunch position against lying. Well, that made two angry people. He was angry at himself, though, blast it, he couldn't think how else he might have handled the situation. She had no idea how important it was that she be protected from invasive questioning—he'd only been thinking of her, he...he...no. That, too, was a lie. There was something about Carrie that...

Huh, what was he going to say to himself next? *She made me do it?* Come off it, King. Whose fault is this?

Well, he couldn't change what had happened. Time to forget it. Carrie had probably just gotten on with what she had to do, scrubbed the mud away, was in bed asleep by now.

Time for him to be asleep too. All he had to do after he finished his tea was swallow the pills Jason had set out on the night table and pull up the covers.

He'd noticed that Jason was being surprisingly restrained. He hadn't asked about Carrie and Henry's mis-adventures, just made a joke about rolling in the creek instead of the hay as he hung Henry's clothes to finish drying.

Now Jason was sitting up in his bed, his voice droning on and on as he described the Elderhostel tour of the Fordyce. Henry figured Jason was trying to be helpful, trying to take his mind off his troubles, help him relax, but he had tuned out the actual words a long time ago.

Then he realized the room was quiet. He looked over and saw Jason staring at him. "Don't you want to turn in now, big boy? Take those pills and..."

This time Henry was not in a tolerant mood, and his feelings exploded, cutting Jason off. "I swear, if you call me big boy one more time, I'll put a second arm out of joint socking you. I..."

He choked off the remainder of his sentence when he saw the look on Jason's face, a mixture of surprise, and what? Sadness? Of all the reactions he had expected—belligerence, jokes—this wasn't one of them. Henry started to shrug, forgetting present circumstances, and was stopped by his painfully immobilized shoulder. So he just sat, stewing in confusion, wondering what to say next.

After a long silence Jason solved the problem. "Well, then, I won't." There was another long silence before Jason spoke again. "It's a compliment, you know. You are taller than I am—bigger. In school I was usually the shortest, especially in the early years. No good at sports. Got beat up a few times because of it. Couldn't defend myself."

His eyes looked beyond the walls of the room into some unknown distance and the usually booming tones were soft, almost dreamy. "Guess that's one reason I made good grades; I learned to keep to myself and spend my time studying. Nose in school books all the time. It was a form of protection. Hated being called 'runt' by the other guys, figured I might as well be called 'teacher's pet' or some equally dumb thing. You know how kids are. Don't tell me you never called a smaller kid 'runt.'"

Now he looked over at Henry, squinting. Was it because he didn't have his glasses on?

"Well..."

"See there. I feel sorry for the kid you called...that, and you should too."

Jason looked away again and ducked his head.

Maybe it was the hour, the drugs, whatever, but Henry felt tears behind his eyes. How many people had he hurt in his lifetime? And how about today? No, yesterday. Especially yesterday. How about Carrie?

Kids could be cruel and so could adults. What next, King? He guessed he could always say something nasty and sarcastic to Eleanor about her simpering attentions to her husband and friends. That would complete the circle.

Blast, oh, blast!

Still, Jason came out on top. He had a good brain, a good education. Ended up as head of his own manufacturing company. Retired rich. Very rich.

Henry knew it was a dumb reaction, but he envied Jason's wealth. And now Carrie had money too, while he... A cop's retirement was adequate, but that was all. Oh, what the heck. Life was just what came.

He heard a sputter from the other bed. It seemed Jason was back to normal and now found this funny. He looked over at Henry again and said, "Well, *big boy*, let's turn in."

Henry picked up his extra pillow and threw it at Jason. Even put off balance by the bound arm, his aim was accurate. Jason toppled sideways in an exaggerated fall, then he pitched the pillow back, aiming, not for Henry's torso, but his knees.

"Okay, *big boy two*," Henry said as Jason reached for the light switch.

He didn't take the pills. He needed to think, not sleep.

The knife. Carrie could not have been the one to use it on Bogardus. How would she get behind him, reach around, slit his throat? It was logistically impossible. For one thing, she didn't have the upper body strength. The man would have had to sit still and wait for her attack. What he'd seen and absorbed during the one quick look the FBI agents allowed him in that basement room said Everett Bogardus's throat had been cut by someone reaching around him from behind.

Besides, Carrie was forced through the trap door by a man strong enough to shove her as she resisted, fought for her life. Conclusion? Bogardus was still uninjured when she went over the edge and the trap door was shut behind her.

That meant someone else had to be involved.

But *why?* Was someone else after a Fordyce treasure? Could it simply be coincidence that two people knew about possible hidden money and, after all these years, had come to claim it at the same time? Why now? Why during this Elderhostel? For whatever reason, Henry was beginning to believe that Carrie had been right: there really was money involved. That meant a killer was still out there somewhere, and logically it would be a member of the Elderhostel group, someone sleeping on this floor of the hotel right now.

He was suddenly very glad the police were guarding Carrie through the night.

There had been a few bad dreams, and twinges when he tried to turn the wrong way, but Henry was sound asleep when someone knocked on the door at ten o'clock.

Jason had obviously been awake. As he opened his eyes, Henry saw his roommate put aside a magazine and pop out of bed to let Eleanor in.

As usual she radiated cheer. She said a bouncy "good morning" as she carried one large tray into the room. A uniformed police officer—male, someone Henry hadn't seen before—followed her, carrying another tray. Where was Carrie? Wasn't someone guarding the door to her room?

"Well, look at you two lazy lords of the realm. And here we are, your humble servants, laying your breakfast before you." She put a tray in front of Henry and directed her helper to do the same for Jason. Then she thanked the man and told him he could go back to doing boring things like guarding their door.

"Oh, do sit still, Jason! We don't want you dumping

coffee on the bed. Henry, I had no idea what you might want for breakfast, so I ordered some of everything, sort of a personal buffet. Let's put your tray on top of this folded blanket and you can use your good hand to eat. So, what will it be? Eggs, bacon, muffins, toast, biscuits and gravy, cereal?"

"All of it," said Henry.

He didn't finish quite all of it, but he came close enough.

While the men ate, Eleanor told them Carrie seemed fine this morning and had been studying her Bible lesson when Eleanor left. They'd breakfasted earlier so Eleanor could see that the men were fed. "The police are still standing guard in the hall," she said, "and an FBI agent—Bell, I think the officer said his name was—will be here in about thirty minutes to talk with you. Henry, did you tell Jason what happened last night?"

"We haven't gotten around to that yet."

"Well, never mind now. You eat, and I'll bring Jason up to speed while the FBI man is with you and Carrie. I think he expects to see you right here, so Jason and I will head back to our room as soon as he's dressed, and I'll send Carrie along to you. Then maybe I'll go down to the meeting room and catch the last part of the morning session.

"Oh, guys, I've sent out a suit jacket someone loaned to Carrie for dry cleaning and some laundry too, so if you happen to be here when it's returned, take care of it, please.

"I went down to that boutique in the lobby as soon as it opened this morning and picked out a button-front shirt for you, Henry. Sorry to take the liberty, but didn't think you'd want to go shopping, and I knew none of your other shirts would fit around that bound arm. Anything's better than a hospital shirt, I say. So, here it is, and I admit they had a somewhat limited selection." She went to the door, and the police officer on duty outside handed her a sack.

She opened the top, put her hand in, and with a "Ta-da" yanked out a huge white shirt with blue bath tubs and bright red words printed all over it. She spread the shirt out, and Jason read aloud, "I came clean in the Hot Springs baths."

After a shocked second or two, Henry laughed. There was nothing else he could do.

"Well, aren't you colorful," Carrie said, eyeing the shirt as she came in the room. "Eleanor hadn't much choice when it came to extra large shirts, so I guess one can't complain, can one? Thank goodness it's just for today. I remember the doctor said you could have a sling after twenty-four hours."

He didn't have time to reply because Agent Bell was right behind her. Since Henry was already sitting on his bed, Carrie smoothed the spread out on Jason's, kicked off her shoes, and sat, leaning against the headboard. Bell took the desk chair, turning it to face them.

He spoke to Carrie first. "Remember anything more about what happened in the storage room at the Fordyce?"

"Excuse me," said Henry, earning an irritated glance from Bell, "may I ask a couple of questions before you begin?"

Without waiting for an answer he went on.

"How did you know we were in the tunnel?"

Bell might have been angry at Henry for breaking into his questioning routine, but he answered readily enough. "The dogs. No scent of Ms. McCrite anywhere except between the Fordyce and the Downtowner, where she'd walked, and in both buildings. Nothing anywhere else. No trace of her from searching otherwise. The creek was all that was left unless she got in a car, and we pretty much ruled that out."

"Ah, I see. And you knew I was with her because...?"

"Because we identified your car in the parking lot at Transportation Plaza. Even with limited knowledge about you, Major King, I could see your concern for her and had little problem figuring out your goals and probable actions. Now, Ms. McCrite..."

"Just one more question. Have you been able to check the knife for fingerprints?"

"Yes. The Hot Springs Police Department has excellent fingerprint identification ability."

"And?" Henry felt he was dragging the words out of Agent Bell.

"No fingerprints." He cleared his throat. "*Now*, Ms. McCrite, have you remembered anything more about what happened while you were with Everett Bogardus?"

"Yes. The only time I touched his knife was when I was trying to push it away from me. My hand brushed the blade then. See, it made a little cut on these two fingers." She held her palm toward him. "I never touched the handle. And if you're wondering, I didn't see anyone else in the room. But then, all of my attention was certainly on Everett, as his was on me. I don't know if either of us would have noticed someone else coming in the room. Everett was between me and the entry door, his back to it. I was lying down or kneeling most of the time, hitting at him, trying to shove the knife away."

"Did you hear or see the trap door go shut?"

"I heard a bang, so, yes, I guess I did. Then I don't recall anything more until I woke up lying in mud. It was dark, of course. I hadn't remembered that I had the flashlight yet, so I couldn't see where I was."

"Ever notice whether the storage room door was open or closed while you were struggling with Mr. Bogardus?"

"Everett closed it as soon as we were inside the room." She shuddered.

Henry saw the shudder and said, "This is distressing Ms. McCrite, Agent Bell. Can't you stop?"

Bell looked at him. "How will we clear her of suspicion in this matter if we don't have her part of the story?"

"Easy. For one thing you know Ms. McCrite was not wearing gloves and certainly wouldn't have had the ability to wipe the knife handle, so..."

"King, you understand the procedure. We have to confirm evidence, get as much information as we can. I would prefer that you keep out of this."

"Right," Henry said, and Bell, after looking at him sternly for a moment, went back to Carrie.

"What did Everett Bogardus say during the time you were with him? Begin when he came close to you in the Fordyce gym. The police officer who joined the group just before you left noticed you two were close together, and later a couple of the participants told us they heard you say, 'Stop, you're hurting me,' or something like that.

"By the way, when it comes to the Elderhostelers, we've only done simple questioning about who saw you and where. If you talk with any of them, the coordinator is requesting, at least for the present, that you don't tell them what really happened. I suggest you say you went off with Bogardus to see something else in the building and didn't realize anyone was looking for you. No need to alarm folks. They will know Bogardus has died, but the circumstances won't be given yet. We hope everyone will assume it was from some pre-existing condition."

Carrie said, "You do realize that the arrival of the police officer was the very thing that set Everett off? I recognized the man; I'm sure now that he did too. Maybe he was somewhere around the Fordyce when the two officers from the Hot Springs PD came in response to the injury of Ranger Hobbs. By the way, can you tell us how the ranger is doing?"

"Out of danger. They say he'll be fine, no permanent damage. He's in the hospital you went to last night. I talked with him for a short time while King was being treated. Had a giant headache, but the damage wasn't as deep as it looked. He was hit with the side of the pick head, not the pointed end, thank God."

"Did he see who hit him?"

Bell sighed, looking frustrated, but he wasn't refusing to answer Carrie's questions. Henry gave him grudging admiration. At least he was now willing to treat them as intelligent adults.

"He didn't see the attacker. He said he heard a noise behind him and had started to turn when he was hit. He caught a glimpse of an arm swinging the pick, that was all."

Henry said, "The presence of someone in the basement with a pick may mean you're right about hidden money, Carrie. The attack on Hobbs indicates that person is—or was—willing to kill to get to it. But the murder of Bogardus suggests either someone hated or feared him for a reason unconnected to the Fordyce, which seems unlikely, or that more than one person knows about the money and was also willing to kill Bogardus to get to it. He, she—or they—may think you're after their treasure too. Or maybe they suspect something nearer to the real truth, that you're trying to stop them from getting it. You could still be in danger."

Carrie looked thoughtful and murmured, "Hmmm." Perhaps she was going to listen to him this time, take precautions.

She finally said, "Yes, but the danger would include you, Henry. Everett said he thought *both* of us were after his money. So if I'm seen as a threat to this other person, then you are too.

"Everett's conversation while he was dragging me down the stairs tells me he had found at least some money in the basement. He said it was hidden in baking powder tins and was ranting on about how his father had 'got religion' and hadn't told him about the money until he was dying. He said nothing that indicated he thought another person might know about it; he only mentioned us. So," she turned to Bell, "did you find money and baking powder tins in his room?"

Bell had been listening, lips curved. Was the man smiling? "We found no tins. If there were any, they probably went out in the trash. We'll check with the housekeeping staff about that. But there *was* a surprising amount of money, printed no later than the '60s, in a Priority Mail package stuck in the bottom of his suitcase. The package was addressed to Bogardus in Cambridge. You've explained the money's presence, and your conversation has been enlightening, to say the least, but can we go back to the beginning of your time with him? You said he was hurting you there in the gymnasium. What happened next?"

Carrie told them the whole story then, speaking slowly, frowning, obviously re-living the terrible events as she spoke. Henry, who, like Bell, was hearing all of it for the first time, struggled to control his rising anger. He had the urge to hurt a man who was beyond hurt—a man who was already dead.

"...and the next thing I remember is waking up in mud. Pretty soon I heard cars passing over the grate covering a storm drain on Central. It clanks, doesn't fit well. I followed the noise and found the creek, just where Ranger Hawk said it would be. Then I remembered I'd picked up Henry's flashlight on the basement floor near Ranger Hobbs, and it still worked, so I was able to wade downstream. After a time, there was Henry, come to get me."

She turned toward Henry then, and her face was so full of tenderness and—maybe it was love, or warmth and friendship at least—that he almost forgot the present circumstances. He wanted to bound off his bed and go to her.

Instead, he said, "Carrie, tell Agent Bell why you were hiding when you heard me in the tunnel."

"Oh, because I thought you were Everett, of course, coming after me."

"So she didn't have any idea he was dead," Henry said for Bell's benefit.

"I get the point. Now, Major King, how did you decide Ms. McCrite was in the creek tunnel?"

"Only place she could be. I know her well enough to realize she wouldn't leave a human who was mortally wounded, even if she did the wounding herself. The wound didn't look like something she could have caused, but *if* she'd stabbed Bogardus and had the ability, she would have gone for help, not run away. Therefore she wasn't where you were looking. She hadn't been on foot, escaping from the Fordyce above ground. That left the creek. When I understood the concrete basin below that trap door gave access to the creek, I was sure she was down there somewhere, fighting to get out. And I was very concerned that she might be hurt."

He looked at Carrie. "I didn't know she had the flash-light, and in addition to my concern over her physical condition, I was afraid she was trapped there because of the dark. As you know, I couldn't get into the area from the Fordyce, and I didn't know the lay of the land well enough to find the creek any other way than through the tunnel opening. So there's where I went."

"Actually, Agent Brooks said you'd do exactly that," Bell conceded. "Seems he was right."

"So now what?"

"Because of the Elderhostel that you're part of, as well as your professional ability, I'm going to trust both of you to help us more than I would under ordinary circumstances. Putting together what you've said with what little we've learned so far, I believe we need someone inside the group to observe everyone there. I'm going to put a police officer in with you. I think we'll call the man your nephew, King. He'll be from Little Rock, come to join you as a surprise.

"As I understand it, individuals who are under fifty-five can be part of an Elderhostel group as long as they're with a family member who qualifies. He'll be your family member; we've already made arrangements with Ms. Hunt. I know you and Ms. McCrite have been sharing a room, and we'll have to move you to connecting rooms on this same floor, not difficult since the members of your group don't take up quite all the available rooms here. The officer, Brad Jorgenson, will sleep with you, King. Ms. McCrite will be next door, with access through an interior door. If you, uh, want to visit her during the night, I don't expect Officer Jorgenson to object."

Carrie said, "That won't be a problem," and Henry noticed the agent was actually blushing. He didn't look at

Carrie. She never blushed anyway.

Bell was keeping his eyes on Henry. "And since you are without the use of one arm at this time, Officer Jorgenson will be able to assist you where needed. That's the plan. Any questions?"

Henry said, "I notice you didn't ask us if we wanted to cooperate."

When Bell didn't answer, he went on. "When will we meet Officer Jorgenson? If he's my nephew, we need to figure out a story...relationships, all that."

"Give me an hour. He'll be here. Now, are you carrying?"

"No. This was supposed to be a peaceful vacation, remember? No gun."

"Just as well," Bell said. "You'll probably be safer without it, and the officer will be armed."

"And what are you going to be doing?" Henry asked. "Do you have a line of investigation in mind in addition to this surveillance of the Elderhostel?"

"Well..." Bell grinned, the first time Henry had seen him do that. "Guess we could search the Fordyce basement for baking powder cans."

Henry said, "I don't think so. Those cans, if they exist, are bait for the killer. I even think you should continue to leave that door alarm into the basement area turned off, unless you can work it as a silent alarm, but do turn on the one going outdoors from that area, and then..."

"Yes, yes, I know." Bell grinned again. "We don't plan to search the basement for money, not yet at least."

"How about undercover? Are you going to keep people on watch at the Fordyce?"

"Law enforcement rangers are already taking care of that for the most part. Ranger Kandler is in charge, and all the park personnel, even the volunteers, will be alerted. After what Ms. McCrite has said, I'm going to suggest they cut down on time off and have more people on duty. Maybe we can add a few police officers dressed as tourists to help keep watch. And I'll also suggest that no one except law enforcement personnel go to the break room alone. Not that they would. Kandler says since yesterday coffee breaks have decreased considerably, and he thinks most of the staff will choose to eat lunch outside on one of the park benches rather than in the break room. All of them know what happened back there yesterday afternoon."

"How do we find you if we need you?" Carrie asked.

"You have a cell phone?"

"Yes, but it's in Henry's car."

"We'll bring it to you. Here's my number. You can reach me through this number at any time."

"What about my purse?"

"Under the circumstances you can have it back, but it's quite a mess. We haven't looked at the contents yet—no warrant—so I don't know how well things inside survived. I'll send it over with Officer Jorgenson.

"I think that's all for now. If you have no more questions, I'll let myself out."

Carrie said, "Agent Bell, your suit coat is being dry-cleaned. I'll get it back to you, and, thank you...for that, for everything."

He nodded. "Doing my duty, Ms. McCrite, doing my duty."

The door clicked shut behind him.

The room was silent for a minute before Henry got off his bed, took the two steps that brought him to the second bed, sat down next to Carrie, and put his good

arm around her.
     This time she didn't pull away.

Chapter XIX

Carrie

Carrie's eyes were shut, her head resting against the portion of Henry's chest not covered by arm bindings. She knew she looked peaceful, but inside her head thoughts and emotions were jumping every which way.

Henry was talking softly, apologizing to her because— he said—he'd caused his disastrous fall against the rocks!

Even before he'd come to sit next to her on the bed, offering one arm for a hug and a warm snuggle against his chest, she'd been ready to speak her own words of contrition. She was eager to get it all out in the open, to say what she'd been rehearsing silently all morning:

Henry, I was so wrong, so willful, and seeing you hurt is the worst punishment possible.

But now those words were gone, scrambled by confusion over Henry's apology for the very same thing.

His fault? How? She was the one who had jerked away, had caused him to fall. How could his wish to protect her, which he was proclaiming over and over, erase that?

She could hear his heart beating, bumpa-bumpa.

She could hear her heart too, vibrating in her ears.

Surely he knew it was her fault, not his. Did he think he was being chivalrous? She hated that. How could he possibly believe she'd fall for it?

The word *fall* stuck in her head, and with it came new waves of remorse.

"Carrie, little Cara," he was saying, his voice vibrating against her ear along with the rhythmic motion of his heart. "I was trying to save you from being bothered by Bell until we could rest, have something to eat, clean up. I admit I was also reacting to feelings stemming from past experiences with the Bureau back in Kansas City. See what that got me?"

"Henry, *don't*, not your fault."

"You are very dear to me, and I'm so sorry I caused this. Oh, heck, I'm not good with words, but I do want you to know how much I love you."

The words stopped every leaping thought in her head. "Love?"

He kissed her forehead and, as she tilted her face up, her mouth.

That's when the leaping thoughts came back again, centering, not on Henry's closeness now, not even on the kiss, but on how well she'd been getting along by herself since moving to the Ozarks.

She'd mastered a lot of skills, everything from mowing the cleared space around her house and getting leaves out of the gutters, to balancing checkbooks and doing book-keeping. She was proud of her accomplishments.

If she...Henry's mouth was soft against hers...so warm, she felt so warm...

If she ever married again, would the man...would Henry take over those things, the things she had learned to do by herself? Would he clean the gutters?

Warm...

New thoughts were exploding behind the old ones, thoughts about being lonely and about how good it felt to be this close to Henry. She was sheltered here. Cared for. Sheltered. Something she wasn't used to.

Finally she stopped trying to sort out the emotions tearing around inside her and gave in to enjoyment of Henry's body as she nestled against him. She let her arms circle around, holding tight, remembering to avoid the damaged shoulder that had begun this conversation.

After several minutes he pulled back and rested his cheek against the top of her head, saying nothing, thank goodness.

It took her a long time to remember the importance of sensible, responsible thinking and action.

Too much emotion, that was it. So many awful things had happened to them the last few hours, they were just overcome by emotions. That was what it must be.

He began murmuring again. "Love, my little love. Jason hates being called little, but you don't mind, do you?"

Jason? What did he have to do with this? Had he put Henry up to...?

She pushed away and asked, "What *about* Jason?"

Now Henry looked puzzled and spoke slowly, his thoughts obviously drifting somewhere in the past. "You know how he calls me 'big boy'? Well, I've always hated that and I finally told him so last night. He said he thinks of *big boy* as a compliment. Seems kids called him a runt when he was in school, and it hurt him. Carrie, I called a kid in my class the same thing, so it must have hurt that boy too. I've hurt a lot of people since then, and now I've hurt you."

"Henry, stop it, you haven't hurt me; you were the one who fell on the rocks." She pointed to his shoulder. "No matter what you say, that was my fault, not yours. I jerked away."

He continued talking as if she hadn't spoken. "I didn't take steps to protect you from a man I sensed might be dangerous, and, in the creek, I wanted you to lie about being hurt."

She said, very slowly and clearly, "Stop trying to take over *my* responsibilities!"

He kept talking. "If I'd stayed with you there in the Fordyce, none of this would have happened."

"Henry King, you couldn't help it. Agent Bell wanted to talk with me alone, remember? *It wasn't your fault.*"

They stared at each other. Then Henry pulled her to him again, holding her close while her unwilling mind fell into the past. She thought about men in her life, the ones who'd needed to feel big and powerful and sometimes took that need out on weaker women. Her own father had been about Jason's size, and he could sure bluster. He'd never struck her or her mother, but there were some who controlled with words. People gave in because it was easier. She'd given in.

She thought about her husband, Amos. He was shorter than most of his colleagues, but forceful in the courtroom, forceful in a different way at home. Amos never doubted that his ideas and plans were the only ones they should live by. Again, she'd given in. But that was the past. Today she knew how to be strong.

As far as Jason was concerned, Carrie had observed that Eleanor was as capable of bullying as he was. In fact they both seemed to enjoy it. It was like they were taking part in a game only the two of them could play, so much so that Carrie always thought of it as play-acting. She never paid much attention to it and certainly never worried about them.

On the other hand Henry, who was big enough physically to be a real bully and had been a tough policeman as well, was something of a bon-bon. Hard chocolate coating, all sweet and smushy inside. Smushy...sweet...and soft. She wondered if he recognized that. Probably not.

Her thoughts began to smooth once more, and she let herself absorb the wonderful warmth of all that she and Henry were sharing. He *was* a very strong man, strong enough to take the blame for what had happened yesterday.

So maybe she should quit apologizing. A smile lifted the corners of her lips. It would be very nice to have someone else clean those gutters. But, as for sharing her whole life...

The tips of her fingers were following the black and silver waves of hair above his ears when she saw the clock.

"Oh, golly, we've got to stop; nephew Brad will be here any moment." She pulled her hands away reluctantly. Henry's hair rarely looked ruffled, but what fun it was to smooth it, to pretend it needed her touch to keep the waves in order.

She uncurled her body, shoved off the edge of the bed and stood, feeling addled.

"You never said it." His voice seemed to be coming from far away.

"Said what?"

"Never said you love me, not since that morning at the Ozark Folk Center last spring. You said it then."

So he remembered that time, and he was right, she hadn't said it since. She wasn't sure she could trust saying the words *I love you* now and mean what she knew Henry wanted. He was talking about a forever kind of thing between a man and a woman. Forever was what it should be for her too.

She did love all mankind as God's children. That wasn't what Henry asked for, but it was one type of real love.

"Can't you say it? Hey, I thought women were supposed to be the romantic ones."

Her silence was hurting him; she could tell that from the look on his face, but at the moment he was asking more than she could give.

She sat on the edge of his bed again and, feeling strangely hollow inside, said, "Henry, this isn't the time to...I just can't think about it now. I'm sorry."

He laughed, a little snort that spoke more of sadness than humor. "Maybe our problem is that we're always apologizing to each other. Wonder why that is? Well, okay, fine, let's forget it. For now."

Then he sat up straighter and was all business.

"I think a visit to the Garland County Historical Society is still important. We can look for information leading to people from our Elderhostel who might have been here, or had family members here, as far back as the '60s. We need to find connections. I'm sure there will be some—beyond Everett Bogardus, I mean. It's too bad a name search will be difficult when it comes to women who have married."

"A woman?"

"Yes, Carrie, it's possible." He smiled. "Equality extends to criminals too. So, shall we go there this afternoon? If we can get away from my nephew, the cop, that is. What's on the schedule for the rest of today? My folder is in the desk drawer if you don't remember."

"It's 'Metaphysical uses of crystals' for the afternoon. Begins at 3:00."

"Well, that sounds like nonsense. We can miss it."

"Maybe you can miss it, but I want to learn as much as possible about crystals, even if it's what other people believe about them. I want to be here for the session."

She looked at the clock again. "It's almost noon, time for lunch. What say we go eat with our group? I'm not very hungry yet, but surely they'll have salads or something light. It's paid for, after all. Bell wouldn't expect us to miss lunch because we had to wait for nephew Brad.

"After we eat we can go straight to your car if you feel up to it. I'll drive and you can navigate. I'm getting excited about this research—who knows what we may find?

"Now, before we go down, we'd better decide how to explain your shoulder injury."

"How about saying I fell out of bed, you tried to pull me up by my arm, and..."

"Oh, ha! Try again, Henry."

"Well, the truth, then. I fell in Hot Springs Creek. The truth is always safest." His face clouded. "Oh, Cara, I am sorry. If only I'd been willing to act more responsibly back there in the creek..."

She stuck her tongue out at him and made the worst face she could manage.

Everyone was evidently too polite to ask what Henry had been doing in the creek, because only murmurs of sympathy greeted the explanation for his bound arm. There were comments about the gaudy shirt—almost everyone remembered seeing it in the window of the lobby boutique—but people quickly went back to talking about the topic of the hour, the death of Everett Bogardus. Since no one had known him well and the group obviously believed he'd died from some pre-existing medical condition, there wasn't a display of grief. Lunch went on in a room full of happy-sounding chatter.

Jason and Eleanor were in the dining room with the others. They came over to say they understood sleeping arrangements were back to normal and that Henry's nephew was joining him today. Jason winked as he said this, so Carrie supposed Bell, or someone, had explained the situation to them. That was wise, because they were in a position to know who Henry's real relatives were.

She had noticed there were no police officers in the hall when they came down to lunch. Probably nephew Brad was supposed to be enough security, whatever that might mean.

While they ate she watched the rest of the group, trying to pick out a killer. They all looked so carefree, so innocent. She almost laughed aloud as she noticed that the Chicago lawyers had, indeed, paired off with the widowed cousins. She glanced at Henry and saw that he was watching them too. Marcus and Martha were carrying on a serious conversation while Sim and Oneida enjoyed some shared joke. Once Martha glanced up and noticed she was being watched. She didn't smile. Carrie decided she didn't like being stared at and couldn't blame her.

It didn't take long to eat their salads. As soon as they

were finished, Henry led the way to the restaurant's exit on the street, avoiding the lobby. They walked around the hotel to the parking lot and got in the car without seeing anyone who looked like a law officer.

"Quapaw Avenue, number 328," Henry said as she turned the key. "Give me a minute to find it on the map. I didn't want to ask directions at the desk and broadcast our destination."

Unfortunately the street grid wasn't organized to make easy sense to strangers, especially as interpreted by Henry. It was only after a few false turns and back-tracks that they found the building. Locating it was made doubly difficult by the fact that it was at the back of a shady parking lot and tree branches conspired to conceal the entrance.

When they got to the door, Carrie read the sign aloud:

"'Open Monday through Friday and first Saturday of the month, 8:00 until noon.'

"They're *closed*." She felt like wailing in frustration but instead put her face against the door glass. "Hey, I see lights inside. They're coming from a hallway off the main room. Someone must still be here. Maybe they'd let us in, at least until they finish what they're doing?" She knocked on the glass, then grabbed the handle and rattled the door.

"Carrie, the lights are probably for security. What are you trying to do, break in? I think..."

His words were cut off by the appearance of a shadow on the other side of the glass and the sound of a lock turning. The door opened a crack, and FBI Agent Willard Brooks looked through it, grinning at them. "My, what a surprise to see you two," he said.

Chapter XX

Henry

"Well-l-l," Henry said, "looks like we're on the same wavelength. So, why don't Carrie and I join you?"

There was a moment of silence before Agent Brooks said, "Guess you might as well, now you're here. Can always use help from a couple of private detectives."

The eye they could see through the small opening winked, then the door opened just wide enough to let them squeeze through and was quickly re-locked.

"I'm staying away from this reception area so lights won't attract attention at a time the building is supposed to be empty."

They followed him into the hall, where he stopped and looked them over, smiling as he studied Henry's shirt. Then he sobered, said, "Sorry about your accident," and turned toward Carrie, smiling again. "Ms. McCrite, I congratulate you on winning my 'Gutsy Broad of the Year' award for making it through that tunnel by yourself. So tell me, what are you two doing here when you should be back at the hotel, recuperating from your horrible experiences? Only FBI agents are supposed to carry on in spite of serious injury or death. Conclusion? You're fanatics—or idiots—like we are. On the other hand, maybe you have an important idea to follow up on here that you're eager to share with me?"

Henry laughed. Well, well, the man could be talkative, after all. Henry liked him more every time they were together. If he ever went back into law enforcement, he'd want to...he stopped himself, realizing how off-the-wall any thought like that was, and said, "We're here to look for previous connections between Hot Springs and people attending the Elderhostel. We wanted to learn if any of them, including Bogardus, were here for a length of time in the past. There must be at least one more person in our group who knows about hidden money, and that person is probably a killer.

"I assume we all agree with Carrie now, that there *is* money hidden somewhere in the basement of the Fordyce? I think what you found in Bogardus's suitcase indicates that. I am also assuming you found one or more recently broken wall tiles in the mechanical area?"

Brooks tilted his head and looked at them. "Hmmm, could be. And you're right, we are on the same wavelength. If Bogardus was here during the '60s and knew about at least some of the money that was likely spirited away before or during the raids, I figure his killer must be connected to those times too. Otherwise, why come all the way here to kill him? Could have done that back in Massachusetts if it had nothing to do with Hot Springs.

"Right now I'm searching copies of court records, births, marriages, and so on, plus looking for names of people with suspected criminal connections. In the '60s that was a lot of folks. Next, I'll get into the reminiscences of those who were here back then, which means I might be up all night. Where did you want to start? Reminiscences, maybe?" He sounded hopeful.

"Yearbooks," Henry said.

"Okay, if you say so. Actually, it's a good idea. I think they're kept in the reception area. I'll ask the historian who's been kind enough to stay and help me if she'll show us. We can move a stack of books to a table in back." He stuck his head through a doorway. "Listening in, Ms. Warner? Can you help us here for a moment?" He turned back to Carrie and Henry and winked again. "She loves this 'cloak and dagger' research stuff," he whispered.

A severe-looking white-haired woman in a business suit appeared, and Brooks introduced her as May Lee Warner. He asked about yearbooks.

"Front room," she said, and her pencil-thin form led the way back down the hall. She flipped on a tiny flashlight and moved to a group of shelves filled with yearbooks. "What time period, please?"

"How about the '50s and '60s to begin with?" Henry said.

"Our set for that period is almost complete, with only two missing. Members of three classes, sophomore, junior, and senior, were photographed each year, so if you're searching for a specific name it will probably be here, unless the person attended only during one school year of course and that happens to be a missing book. As you know, Agent Brooks suggests we stay out of the front room, so we'll take what you wish to peruse to a room in the back."

She removed several books from the shelf and handed them to Carrie. Then, sizing up Henry's one-armed condition, she lifted another stack herself and went toward the hall, followed by Carrie.

Henry stayed behind in the dim window-fed light and studied the shelf. Seeing the gap left by books Ms. Warner and Carrie had taken, he used his right hand to shove a few of the volumes on each side of the opening together, leaned over, and tucked them under his right arm. Then he headed after the women.

Ms. Warner opened a door, turned on a light, and stacked her books on the table centering a room with shelves full of boxes on all four walls. Saying she needed to continue assisting Agent Brooks, she swished out, leaving them alone. Henry looked at the piles of books, put them in order by date, then pushed one stack toward Carrie. "How about beginning with these from the late '40s and working forward. I'll start at 1970 and work back. We'll meet in the middle."

For a while silence in the room was broken only by the turning of pages and the murmur of conversation between Bell and Warner in the next room. The smell of old paper, dust, and ancient cigar smoke mingled in the air; voices hummed, paper rustled, and before long Henry's head jerked as he lost the struggle to stay alert. He glanced at Carrie. She was bent over a book, and he hoped she hadn't noticed. Lack of sleep was catching up with him.

He went back to looking at pages of faces and names, but was about to doze again when Carrie said, "Bingo! I've found someone. Marcus Trotter graduated from high school here in 1953! Sure doesn't look like him—skinny kid—but the name is unusual enough that I think it must be." She faced the book toward Henry and pointed.

"Yep, same beady eyes. Peculiar he didn't mention he'd lived here when we all talked about ourselves on Sunday night, isn't it? His graduation year is early for our purposes, so now we need to know if he was here in the '60s. Could be he left to go to college and law school, then came back. Phone books would help us if they have them here. Why don't you ask while I keep slogging through these year-books?"

"'Kay," Carrie said and disappeared down the hall. In a minute she was back. "They have them. Ms. Warner showed me where. Do you think we should finish the yearbooks first and see if any other name pops out?"

"Yes, I do," Henry said as he continued to turn pages, pinching himself on the thigh every few moments to help keep his eyes open. "Well, now, here's a Mary Trotter. A sister or cousin, maybe."

"She'd be a lot younger—1967," Carrie said, reading the date upside down. "Does she look anything like Marcus?"

"I can't tell from this picture, especially with the ridiculous hair-do. She might look familiar, kind of does, in fact, but who can really tell? Of course it's possible she's no relation at all. I'll work a friendly question about his family into a conversation this evening. I was already planning to manage a talk with him, casually of course, before or after the meeting."

They went back to page-turning.

A "Whoa, lookie here," from Carrie brought Henry out of another half doze. She turned a book toward him. "Guess who?"

He laughed, wide awake for the moment, because the name she pointed to was Henry King.

"See there? Class of 1955."

"Anyone could tell that's not me," he said, huffing at the photo. "The guy has stringy blond hair! Besides, I've found Henry Kings a lot of places, including in prison. The name is way too common. But see, blond hair there." He pointed to the photo and then to his own head. "Never blond hair here."

Carrie's eyes went to the salt and pepper waves over his ears. "Yes, I know," she said.

They went back to page-turning. Henry, now numb with fatigue, noticed his pages turned much more slowly than Carrie's.

No other familiar names turned up until Carrie saw Everett Bogardus in the 1963/64 book. They followed him through school until graduation in 1966. "Maybe Vietnam next," said Henry. "He'd be the right age."

They finished the books without finding any more familiar names. "We have thirty minutes left," Carrie said. "Let's try phone books."

Because of the short time remaining, they narrowed their search to the period from 1954 on. A "Bogardus, V. F." was listed in all the books. There were several Trotters but no Marcus until 1960, a listing at the same address as "Trotter, Stephen."

"So he's back home from somewhere, probably law school given the time gap, and moved in with his folks," Henry said.

They quickened their page-turning, following Marcus from the listing at his parents' home to a separate address in 1962. Then, in 1968, both Stephen and Marcus, as well as the Bogardus family, disappeared from the books.

At no time had Marcus been listed as a practicing lawyer.

"So they were all gone after 1967," Henry said, "and,

according to Curator Sandemann, that's the year the biggest close-down of gambling and other 'entertainments' began. I had time to ask her about it yesterday when we were waiting for Agent Brooks in her office. Of course the date could be a coincidence, but somehow I think not."

"Shall we tell Brooks about this now?" Carrie asked. "We have to go soon if I'm to make the afternoon session, but maybe he can follow up and find out exactly what business all of them were in. Gambling, maybe? I'll get him."

After showing Agent Brooks the yearbooks as well as the phone book listings, Henry asked if his research had turned up anything so far. Brooks grunted, said, "Not much, but what you've found is a help." Then he looked down at the open yearbooks and, appearing to be lost in thought, said no more.

After realizing the agent wasn't going to tell them anything, Henry turned away, said, "Thanks, hope you'll keep us in the loop," and he and Carrie left the building.

As soon as they entered the Downtowner lobby, the receptionist called them over and handed out new room keys. She said that, in their absence, Agent Colin Bell had supervised the moving of their possessions.

"I completely forgot about the room change," Carrie said as soon as the elevator door closed. "I wonder what kind of a mess we'll find, though come to think of it, if Bell was in charge, I bet everything will be super-neat. Still, I hate the idea of other people, especially men, moving my stuff."

Their doors were mid-hall, which suited Henry fine as a security measure. Doors too close to either a stairwell or an elevator seemed more vulnerable to outside intrusion, though come to think of it, trouble for them was more likely to approach from the floor they were on than from outside.

Thoughts about security reminded him of his pretend nephew, Hot Springs Police Officer Brad Jorgenson. He must have arrived by now, had probably helped Bell move them to the new rooms.

But there was no sign of a second resident anywhere. Henry had just begun to look around when he heard unlocking sounds from the connecting door between his room and Carrie's, and he opened the companion door to find her standing there holding out something that looked like a muddy rag bag.

"My purse is back," she said. "It was sitting in the bathtub. I checked inside; the contents look pretty much okay. I'll have to call the catalogue people I bought it from and tell them this fabric really is durable, just like they said. The purse will probably be good as new after washing. For now, I've stuck my billfold and a few other essentials in my book tote."

"Had the geologist's pick rusted?"

She looked at her toes. "A little."

Henry backed away from the door and she came through, glancing around. "Your room is as neatly arranged as mine, no surprise, but I don't see any sign of Officer Jorgenson. I thought Bell meant he was to be here early this afternoon. Do you suppose he came, found us gone, and is out looking for us? Oh, gosh, I hope not."

"I was wondering about him too," Henry said, "but I'm sure Brooks informed on us the minute we left the historical society building, if not before, so the FBI knows where we've been. I suppose Brad will show up soon."

As soon as Carrie had left for the afternoon Elderhostel

meeting, Henry eased down on his bed, avoiding the injured shoulder. For a minute he wondered why Brad Jorgenson was late, wondered also if he should phone Bell and ask. Before he got as far as deciding, his thoughts turned to Carrie.

He had been so sure he was doing the right thing, taking blame for his fall in the creek. In truth, it *had* been his fault, given the train of events, and he felt darn guilty. But his every word about it, every apology, back-fired. It was like he'd been talking to a wall, and the more he talked, the higher the wall got.

He supposed he should have let her accept all the blame for causing his fall and left it alone. Maybe this woman, maybe every woman, enjoyed playing martyr.

Would he ever understand Carrie? Understand any female? But then he didn't care all that much about other women, only about Carrie. He wondered if... Before he got as far as forming another thought, he'd fallen asleep.

Once he dreamed Carrie had come back from the meeting. He heard her walk to the open door between their rooms. Maybe she would come in, lie down beside him, and... But she didn't come closer, and, in sorrow, he heard the door to her room click shut as she left.

The next thing he knew, Carrie was touching his hand. "Sorry, but it's time to wake up. I need to drive you to the hospital for your check-up, then we can have supper with the group before the session on how to hunt for crystals begins at 7:00.

"I'm glad you had a nap. I could tell you needed it. Have you heard anything from Officer Jorgenson yet?"

His eyes were still closed as he struggled to come back from an uncharacteristic sleep-dusted vagueness. "No, nothing, though I think I heard...I thought..."

She interrupted. "Ummm. Henry, didn't Bell say Jorgenson would bring my purse when he came? Well, if that's
so and Jorgenson isn't here, how did my purse get here?"

He waited a moment before opening his eyes or answer-
ing. Why hadn't he thought of the purse being here without
the officer who was supposed to bring it? Of course it was
possible plans had changed and Bell himself had put it in
the tub. But still, he was beginning to feel alarmed about
the missing officer and the possibility someone else had keys
to their rooms. What was going on? He didn't want to cry
wolf or seem like a wimp, but if Jorgenson wasn't here by
suppertime, he would call Bell.

"Carrie, did you come back here during the afternoon?
Look in on me?"

She frowned. "Noooo. Maybe I should have. Did you
think someone came in?"

He sat up, shook his head. "I must have been dreaming."
He tried a smile, but her frown stayed in place. "I dreamed
you came in to lie down beside me."

"Henry, that's not funny, and you're scaring me. Maybe
someone really did come in. Someone could have come to
hurt you, or search our rooms, or...something."

"I doubt it. As you see, nothing happened. Is there any
sign someone was in your room? Searched it? That's where
the sounds came from."

She went through the connecting doors. He heard her
moving around, heard drawers open and close. Then she
came back, frown still in place.

"Nothing is missing and nothing looks different to me,
but how can I really tell? A careful searcher wouldn't leave
signs. The only thing openly out of place is my purse being
in the bathtub." She shrugged.

"Without special equipment or preparation, neither you

nor I *could* tell, assuming the searcher was clever," Henry said, "especially since Bell moved us and we haven't re-arranged things since. So, who knows? But I do know this: if Officer Jorgenson hasn't come by the time we get through at the hospital and have supper, I'm going to call Bell."

Chapter XXI

Carrie

Carrie stopped at the hotel's front desk and asked directions to the hospital even though Henry insisted he knew the way.

He just might have found it without asking directions, she thought as she drove. In daylight, and with a clear head, she located the building easily.

Doctor Abrams was on duty, could see Henry, and said the patient was mending well, though not yet ready for a boxing match. He removed the mummy-like wrappings and substituted a sling. Henry's relief at this new freedom was so noticeable that Carrie felt renewed guilt about causing his fall. The past twenty-four hours must have been a terrible challenge for him, and he hadn't complained once.

While she drove back to the hotel, Carrie shared highlights of the afternoon session on metaphysical uses of crystals with Henry, saying she was sure the presenter herself didn't believe in any individual crystal's power over mind and body—whether tabular, double-terminated, generator, Isis, or whatever.

"But the various growth patterns of crystals as she described them *are* quite interesting, and I'll watch for some of those special formations when we go on the crystal dig. The woman also told us about body points called chakras, and we learned how to put crystals there to promote health."

"Surely you didn't undress. Maybe I should have come…"

She laughed. "Nope. We looked at drawings."

"Well," said Henry, "when people believe in something, that often invests it with power."

Even more interesting to both of them was the fact Carrie had been able to have a private conversation with Eleanor and Jason during the break. She'd told them about the discoveries in the yearbooks and phone books. "They offered to help keep an eye on Marcus Trotter and will look for a chance to chat with him informally."

As the two of them got in the elevator, Henry said he was going to give his Hot Springs souvenir shirt back to Eleanor. "She can use it for a smock," he said, "but come to think of it, then I couldn't visit them unless I knew she wasn't wearing it. I don't ever want to see the thing again, not even on her."

"Let me have it," Carrie said. "I'll cut it up and make two 'Souvenir of Hot Springs' pillows we can give to Rob and to Susan and Putney. They'll get a kick out of them, and goodness knows there's enough fabric." She was already picturing the pillows. "Bright red fringe would be good with that print, but of course I'll have to tell them we won't feel hurt if they don't put the pillows on their couches for all to see."

"I didn't know you sewed," Henry said.

At first Carrie was tempted to brag about her sewing skills, but decided truth was best. "Except for mending, I don't, but pillows aren't hard to make. I wouldn't even have to use a sewing machine. I can buy enough cotton fringe to go around four sides of the pillows, sew it all together inside-out, fringe in the middle, leaving a little gap for stuffing. Then all you do is turn them right-side out, stuff with that polyester fluff, sew up the gap, and, bingo, pillows."

He was already unbuttoning the shirt to give to her as he opened the door to his room, but his light-hearted mood quickly veered a hundred and eighty degrees into swearing.

Carrie's heart was in her mouth as she hurried away from her own door to stand beside him. "Henry, what's wrong?"

The room was a wreck. His suitcase was tossed in a corner; items that had been left in it were everywhere. All the drawers were pulled out, dumped upside down, contents tossed. One drawer had been thrown aside with such force that the wood was splintered, and she wondered why someone hadn't heard the noise and come running. Shirts, slacks, underwear, socks, toiletries were scattered every which way, sheets, blankets, and pillows were off the beds, the mattresses were sideways, tilting against the floor.

Without thinking, Carrie started in, but Henry's arm stopped her. "Check your room," he said, "but go in from the hall."

Paralysis kept her still for a moment before she was able to move down the hall, insert her key, turn the knob. She shut her eyes as she opened the door, then Henry was beside her saying, "Nothing looks disturbed. Neat as before, so you can open your eyes." He handed her the cell phone. "Call Bell. Here's his card."

She moved like a zombie, feeling she had been shoved back into a nightmare after only a few hours of freedom. Why, why?

Henry went into the room, pulling her behind him, and shut the door, turning the bolt and putting on the chain. Then he went to his room and she heard the bolt click there.

She dialed the number on the card, and an unfamiliar male voice answered. She gave her name and cell phone number, said she needed to speak with either Agent Bell or Brooks as soon as possible, and was told to hang up. Someone would call her.

By the time she had finished leaving the message, Henry was sitting on the edge of her bed, staring into space. Now he spoke the same words she had been thinking. "Why? Why?"

It hit her. "*Henry King*," she said. "We're ninnies. *It's because you're Henry King.* Trotter thinks you could be the Henry King in the yearbook, and either he needed to find out for sure, or he thinks THAT Henry King holds some key to finding the money and he was searching for it. This must be like a...a group thing. Several could know about the money."

She paused for a moment, chasing her thoughts into order, then went on. "For some reason we haven't figured out yet, those who know about the hidden money chose right now, at this Elderhostel, to come back to Hot Springs. Maybe someone sent out messages, or there was a tontine, or a committee, or, or..." She stopped, realizing how overly dramatic and even silly it all sounded.

The phone rang.

"Hello, this is Carrie McCrite." She looked at Henry and nodded. "Yes, Agent Bell, we just got back to the hotel after having Henry's wrappings taken off at the hospital, and his room has been searched. Torn apart is more like it—it's a mess."

Bell's voice was sharp in her ear. "Let me speak to King's nephew."

"What do you mean? We haven't seen anything of Brad Jorgenson. He isn't here—but my purse is. Were you the one who brought it back? Have your plans chang..."

"I'll be there in forty-five minutes or less," he said, the tight urgency of his words doing nothing to calm her panic. "Lock the doors to both your rooms. Turn the bolts and put on the door chains. Stay inside; don't open to anyone until you hear Agent Brooks' voice or mine." He hung up.

"Well, for goodness' sake," she said to the dead phone.

They both paced her room, looking out the balcony window together, then walking back to the bed, sitting down, saying a few words that meant nothing, then getting up to look out the window again.

Finally Carrie said, "I might as well go ahead and take a shower. It's still twenty minutes 'til he'll be here, and I want to keep busy. I couldn't possibly read, I can't sit still, and I've stopped being able to think or talk about this sensibly."

"Better not use the tub. Could disturb possible evidence."

"I could also disturb evidence by using the toilet or washing my hands, and I am not going to stop doing that. Besides, right now I'm too upset and too tired of this whole mess to care. There will be plenty of evidence elsewhere if any is to be had."

Henry shrugged but said nothing as she picked up her Bible and a change of clothing and shut herself in the bathroom.

She sat on the edge of the tub, bowing her head for a long minute before she opened the Bible. How many problems would they have to endure here? This was supposed to be a vacation, a carefree, fun time.

But God didn't say humans wouldn't face problems. The Psalmist talked about walking through the valley of the shadow, not around it. *Too often I'm the one who gets myself stuck in that valley,* she thought. *So, I need to bring more trust in God into my life, as Eleanor reminded me.*

She shut her eyes, opened her Bible near the middle, put her finger on a page, then looked where she'd pointed:

Psalm 56: "What time I am afraid, I will trust in thee... In God have I put my trust: I will not be afraid what man can do unto me."

Okay, okay, I really do get the message. Trust.

She shut her eyes again, turned pages, pressed her finger down. *Isaiah 30: "Woe to the rebellious children, saith the Lord, that take counsel, but not of me...And thine ears shall hear a word behind thee, saying This is the way...walk ye in it..."*

Golly. She could, indeed, be rebellious.

She closed her Bible and prayed: "I *must* listen to God's message about trust. Goodness knows I've read it in the Bible often enough. I must trust God and know I am walking in His protecting love." After a pause she added, "Henry, too."

Then she closed the Bible, stripped, and got in the shower.

She was just stepping into slacks when she heard loud banging. *What...?*

Buttoning her shirt with one hand, she opened the bathroom door and said to the noise, "I'm here. Who is it?"

"Agents Brooks and Bell. Officer Gwen Talbot."

It sounded like Willard Brooks' voice, so she turned the bolt, peeked through the chained opening, then opened the door. She was pushed aside as Brooks, followed closely by Agent Bell, almost fell past her into the room. Gwen Talbot, dressed casually in grey slacks and a yellow cotton sweater, came behind them and shut the door.

"Where have you been? Where is Major King?" This from an uncharacteristically ruffled Colin Bell.

"I was in the shower. Henry's here, he..."

But, after a quick search, it was obvious Henry was not there and that the bolt and chain were off the door to his room.

Bell grabbed her shoulders. "What happened? *What happened?*"

She couldn't cry, she could not! "I went in the bathroom. Henry was sitting on that bed," she pointed, "waiting for you. That's all. He was just waiting."

The two men were already ignoring her, muttering spurts of words to each other, using a cell phone in staccato tones she didn't even attempt to understand. She sank on the bed, thinking about Henry. He was so cautious and considerate. He wouldn't have left her this way without being forced to do it.

Gwen sat beside her, took her hand.

The men came over, didn't even look at Carrie. Instead, Agent Bell spoke to Gwen. "Stay on her like glue. They got past us and somehow tricked King. Probably got Jorgenson too. Must have surprised him when he came in to put the purse in the tub. So, Officer Talbot, this is a heightened alert. It's real danger, as Brad Jorgenson could, God willing, probably tell you right now, wherever he is.

"Listen carefully, both of you. Difficult as it may be for you, Ms. McCrite, you have to carry on as if nothing has happened. We need more present information about these Elderhostel folks, and you're our best chance for getting that from the inside. So go to supper, go to that meeting. See if anyone is missing. Listen, listen, listen.

"Talbot, I don't care how you cover your presence, maybe you're a niece, but stick with her. Report to me as soon as you notice anything, and for sure report between supper and the meeting."

Gwen nodded, then bolted the door after the men had hurried out.

"Well," she said, sitting on the bed again, "shall we go down to supper?"

Carrie ignored her. She was trying hard to remember her prayers and the Bible verses she'd read only minutes ago.

"Carrie?"

"I...I..."

The room was quiet for what seemed like a long time, then Gwen said, "You love him a lot, don't you?"

Carrie stared at her and nodded as fat tears made rosy spots on her clean pink shirt and love for Henry washed over her like a baptism. Without more thought she answered Gwen in words from the Bible, "With an everlasting love."

"Good," Gwen said, "because I can sure tell he loves you. So, let's go to work and get our men back safely. Let's have supper and start watchin' all the folks."

Greta stood at her usual post near the restaurant door, and
Carrie, who was sick with worry and sure she couldn't eat,
said a weak "hello." Then, realizing she needed to explain
the presence of a stranger, she introduced Gwen as her niece,
said Henry wasn't feeling up to coming out this evening,
so could Gwendolyn perhaps take his place?

Whatever she said must have made sense, because Greta,
who seemed distracted herself, barely nodded and said, "Of
course." Her eyes went back to surveying the room.

Carrie noticed Greta's frowning focus on the group
of Elderhostelers and began to feel more alert as she, too,
made a survey of those present in the dining room. At this
moment her best help for Henry would be observing and,
as Agent Bell had said, listening.

Well, well now. She attempted a small laugh and said
to Greta, "I see Marcus and Martha aren't here. They were
pretty friendly at lunch; I bet they've gone off on a date. I
am disappointed, though. I wanted to ask Marcus about
Mary."

Greta jumped as if she'd been poked with a pin and her
gaze now focused on Carrie. "*Mary?*"

"I knew her a very long time ago, and I wondered..."
Carrie let her voice trail off.

Greta stared at her, a look that made Carrie's spine
shiver, said "Excuse me," and disappeared into the lobby.

"Was that smart?" Gwen murmured. "You may have
stirred something up."

"My intention," Carrie answered. "Did you notice? She
has some kind of bee in her bonnet. I wonder why. And
we can't just sit on our hands all evening and play lady. I
didn't realize she'd react like that, though, and now I'm
wondering why she did."

All Gwen said was "Um-hmmm."

"*Now* I'm hungry," Carrie said. "Let's eat."

They went through the buffet, then chose a small table near the back wall of the dining room so they could watch all the Elderhostelers. Carrie spoke in low tones to Gwen, who didn't know the group. "As I said to Greta, Marcus Trotter isn't here. Henry and I learned at the historical society this afternoon that he grew up in Hot Springs but has concealed that fact. Did the FBI guys tell you?"

"They were trying to bring me into the picture while we raced over here but were pretty distracted by the circumstances. Maybe you'd better give me the whole story."

So Carrie talked between bites, at times ignoring the well-remembered admonition from her father: "Don't talk with any food in your mouth." Manners were secondary right now. *Everything* was secondary to finding Henry. And Officer Jorgenson, of course.

"...And Martha Jones is a widow from Eugene, Oregon. Maybe it's just a harmless flirtation going on, but I wonder... oh, oh, there are Jason and Eleanor, headed our way. How can I explain...?

"Hi, Carrie, Gwen," Eleanor said. "Where's Henry? Shoulder bothering him, poor dear?"

Carrie's response cut off Eleanor's next words as she said, "You two remember my niece, Gwendolyn? And you must remember our experience with Habakkuk Culpeper at the Ozark Folk Center last spring? Well, this is like that, only Henry is taking my place this time."

Shock flashed across both faces. The coded explanation had been understood. Eleanor and Jason remembered the danger Carrie had been in last spring at the Ozark Folk Center when she was taken prisoner by a man bent on evil. Back then all four of them, Carrie, Henry, Jason and Eleanor, worked together to help solve a murder and save a missing child.*

But her two friends were troupers.

His voice lowered, Jason said, "What can we do to help?"

Gwen may have been surprised by the conversation and the added complication of two more people, but she was a trouper too. "Meet us in your room, fifteen minutes."

Smiling, Eleanor waggled her fingers at them as if she didn't have a care in the world, and she and Jason went back to their seats with the Elderhostel group.

It was a tense quartet that sat facing each other on the edges of the beds in Eleanor and Jason's room.

"Do you think Henry has been kidnapped?" Eleanor asked. "What is the FBI doing about it? What can we do?" She looked at Gwen.

"They're searching for him and for Brad Jorgenson. I'm going to call Bell now and bring him up to date."

She punched buttons on her cell phone. "Agent Bell, this is Officer Talbot. I thought you should know that Marcus Trotter wasn't with the Elderhostel group at supper, and a female member, Martha Jones, a widow from Eugene, Oregon, is missing too. They were together at lunch today, and the group assumes they have become an item and are off on a date.

"Yes, she's here. Any instructions? Um hmm. Any idea who you'd like her to talk to especially?" There was a long pause while Gwen listened. "Yes, I see. I'll call again after the meeting. Oh, Agent Bell, I keep an emergency overnight bag in my locker at the station. If I stay with Carrie, I'll need it. Could you...? Thanks. See you then."

* As told in *Music to Die For*

As soon as the connection was broken, Carrie said, "Who am I supposed to talk to?"

"Greta. Agent Brooks learned that Greta is Marcus Trotter's sister. She's much younger, sort of a second family for his parents, and her given name is Greta Mary. She went by Mary in school, but changed to Greta as an adult. She's married to a man named Stephen Hunt who's a reporter for the local newspaper. They've always lived in Hot Springs."

"Well, well," said Carrie. "No wonder she reacted when I mentioned the name *Mary*."

"I'd say her reaction was mild, considering, but still unusual. Why didn't she challenge you or simply explain who she is, say something like how much you've changed or she's changed or comment that she didn't remember you? But it was still foolish and dangerous to mention the name, plus now you can hardly talk to her productively."

"Why not?"

"She'll think you know she's Trotter's sister. You'll get nothing from a conversation with her now if she has half a brain. Did you suspect she was Mary Trotter, by the way?"

"Of course not, but I still might talk..."

"No. Pointless. And too dangerous."

"How can I think of danger for myself when Henry and Officer Jorgenson are missing?" Carrie said. "And I'm sure the four of us will be able to help find them. If we stick together, we won't be in any danger.

"Oh, my goodness!" Carrie hit her forehead with her palm. "I didn't tell Agent Brooks that I found the name 'Henry King' in one of the Hot Springs High School yearbooks. It isn't our Henry, of course, and it didn't seem important at the time—just a coincidence—but now I'm wondering, especially since Henry's room was searched so thoroughly, if Trotter might not think the two Henrys are the same. It almost seems as if he believes the Hot Springs Henry King has some knowledge of the hidden money that he, Trotter, doesn't have, and he's trying to find that information for himself.

"We know Everett didn't have specific information. His search was too random and mostly unsuccessful. His words to me also indicated he was angry that he would have to do a lot of searching in the Fordyce basement before he found all the money. He thought his father had put it inside baking powder tins and hid it many places.

"Melodramatic as it sounds, there must be a treasure map or instructions of some kind. What I'm wondering is if we can't somehow make Trotter think I have the information he needs and draw him out that way. Then maybe I can offer to trade information for the return of Henry and Brad."

"Whoa," Gwen said, "no way! You three simply cannot get involved here. I forbid it, and Bell would have my badge if I allowed it."

"You forget something," said Jason. "There are three of us, and..."

For a minute everyone stared at Gwen and she stared back. Carrie's mind was whirling, and, she assumed, Jason and Eleanor were thinking just as rapidly. She was sure all three of them would be watching for opportunities to help Henry, with or without Gwen's approval.

"So," Carrie said, "we'll all head to the meeting early. Gwen, as a newcomer you can chat with Greta, pretend you want to know more about Hot Springs, ask questions about bookmaking—how it worked, what it was like in the gambling clubs during the 1960s.

"Eleanor, why don't you stay with Gwen? You'll be able to provide back-up questions if needed, maybe show prurient curiosity about sin in 'Sin City.'

"I'll cozy up to Oneida Bradley, Martha Rae Jones's cousin. Jason can take on Sim Simpson, Marcus's law partner. Sound like a plan?"

After hesitating a moment, Gwen relaxed and said, "Sounds just like what Agent Bell would want us to do. But remember, no going off alone for any of us. Bathroom trips only if absolutely necessary. Watch out for anyone getting too close to you or brushing against you. Stay with the group. There are still too many unknowns, so we must be triply cautious. We'll come back here together as soon as the meeting is over and tell Agent Bell what we learned."

Everyone nodded and, huddling close, they headed for the meeting room.

It took only a few minutes for Carrie to decide Oneida Bradley was the most boring woman she'd ever listened to. But, hoping something would come of it, she waited more or less patiently through a long list of complaints about life since the death of Mr. Bradley. Finally, while Oneida took a breath, Carrie said, "Guess your cousin Martha has found a boyfriend. Did she and Mr. Trotter know each other before or just meet?"

This time the chatter was more productive. "Oh, Mattie knew him before, years ago. She was originally from this area, though she doesn't want people to know that. It wasn't a happy time for her. Hot Springs went through some awful things back when she was growing up, and her daddy was killed because of it. At least Mattie says he was killed. I've heard talk in the family that it was suicide. He was doing something *criminal* and about to get caught. Anyway, she's bitter about it all and doesn't like to be reminded. That's why I was so surprised when she called and invited me to attend this Elderhostel with her. When I asked how she felt about coming back here, she just brushed it off. 'I'm curious,' was all she said."

"When were she and Mr. Trotter friends? In school?"

"You know, I've wondered myself but doubt it. Mattie went to a private school, and I hear she didn't mix with other kids much. That's just Mattie—she's still like that."

"Does any of her family live here?"

"I think all the family is long gone from this area.

"Say, Carrie, could you partner with us when we go to the crystal dig on Thursday? Mattie needs friends, and I'm sure she isn't really interested in Marcus. She's so lonely, has been almost a recluse since the death of her husband. She always was subject to depression anyway. Add mourning for her husband to that and oh, my. I could tell from her phone calls, you know, and from what her daughter said. That's one reason I agreed to come to this Elderhostel with her, though it seemed a long way to travel for something I wasn't especially interested in, to begin with at least."

Just then Greta asked everyone to take their seats for the program on how to find good specimens at the crystal mine. Oneida went to sit with Sim, and Carrie saw that Eleanor, Jason, and Gwen were saving her a place at the end of the back row.

Carrie joined her friends, and while Greta was giving the next day's schedule and introducing the speaker, she tuned the words out and began another silent prayer.

CHAPTER XXII

HENRY

The gentle knocking preceded Eleanor's voice. "Henry, Carrie? It's me, Eleanor."

He'd been listening to Carrie sing in the shower, his heart soft and warm at the words of a hymn he remembered from childhood. Things were going to be all right after all.

Humming along with Carrie, he stepped carefully past the mess in his room to open the door. Eleanor and Jason probably wanted to eat supper with them.

A hotel housekeeper holding a parcel brushed past him and said, "Laundry delivery for Ms. McCrite." Almost immediately someone shoved a large canvas laundry cart into Henry, knocking him aside. The cart tilted and towels spilled out.

He recognized the man pushing the cart at once. He was wearing white pants, a shirt with the hotel logo, and had a paper kitchen hat pulled low, but it was Marcus Trotter who faced him. The gun Trotter held was also recognizable. It was most likely Brad Jorgenson's.

Henry's trained reaction was quick. He threw himself sideways against the wall and kicked out, but, behind him, a woman's voice that didn't sound at all like Eleanor now, said, "No, none of that. I can easily shoot her in the shower."

So he froze, watching Trotter while he cursed himself for not being more cautious about opening that door. He had to take action quickly but hadn't decided what he could do when he felt the needle prick his arm. Oh, God, they were going to put him out.

Henry waited, motionless in a tableau of horror, until the tableau grew fuzzy and the hymn from the shower changed to "Just a Closer Walk with Thee."

Had to do something...couldn't...couldn't seem to move.

He was shoved sideways and tumbled into the bottom of the laundry cart like a rag doll. Trotter and the woman lifted the cart upright and towels came in over him, some of them damp. The cart rolled, his room door clicked shut, and Carrie's singing went silent.

He was conscious enough to know he was bumping along, moving down the hallway—only a short distance. Then he heard clanging noises that sounded like a freight elevator. Whirring. A jerk and bounce. The elevator stopped.

The cart fell over, and he and the towels tumbled out. Two people tugged and lifted him into a wheelchair and tied him in. *Two people*, Trotter and the woman. Carrie must be alone and safe. Oh, God, she had to be safe.

His neck was no longer able to support his mushy head,

and it flopped sideways. He felt himself drool. Then he gave in to the drug and passed out.

The darkness was total. He'd been hearing buzzing noises in his ears for some time, had swallowed and swallowed, trying to fight the buzz. No good. Felt fuzzy-buzzy...awake enough to know his left shoulder ached, to feel his pulse banging painfully inside his head. At least he was alive.

Alive where?

He took a slow inventory of each part of his body, then used all the working parts to try to identify his surroundings.

He was sitting in some kind of metal container with his head stuck through a hole in the top. Rolling his head around proved that. All the rest of him was inside the container.

He felt fuzzy. Fuzzy-buzzy. His chuckle wobbled like a bad recording.

"You're locked in a steam cabinet," said a voice out of the darkness.

Huh? It took a minute to react. He fought nausea, disorientation, grogginess, and finally said, "Wha...what?"

"Steam cabinet. I got here the same way you did, laundry cart, wheelchair. It's Officer Brad Jorgenson in the steam cabinet next door. From what I heard the two of them say, you're Henry King? Sorry to be meeting you this way, Uncle Henry.

"You feel kinda weird, I'd bet. Don't worry, it'll pass. For a while I'll do the talking, okay? Wished I had someone to talk to me while I was coming back from buzz-land.

"We're in one of the vacant bathhouses, Quapaw, I think. I've been able to see around when they come in and light the lantern. Old bathhouse equipment is stored here, including these steam cabinets.

"An unused steam cabinet makes one heck of a good prison. I don't know why law enforcement agencies haven't thought of that. But then, it would be cruel and unusual punishment, I suppose.

"If you think it's bad now, just wait until you have to pee! I hope you didn't drink much today. You'll sweat some of it out, though. Hot inside these things."

"So you're...Brad Jorgen...son. I suppose this is where you've been...all 'long?"

"Yep. Came up behind me when I was putting Ms. McCrite's purse in the bathtub. Only place I could think to leave the thing, considering its condition. I was bending over. You can imagine where she got me. The woman is, or was, a nurse. She knows her drugs. Hope she doesn't decide to kill us with them. I have no doubt she could."

The young officer stopped talking. Probably thinking about lethal drugs.

The buzzing inside Henry's head was getting fainter. He could hear Jorgenson's breathing now, and the sound was very close. The two steam cabinets were probably pushed against each other.

The voice came again. "Trouble is, I've been here several hours and I haven't thought of a single way to get out of this stainless steel box. Yep, it sure is a dandy prison."

"Why did they put us here?" Henry wondered aloud. "What's the purpose?"

"I'll get to that. The two of them have been here twice, and they do talk in front of me, which I suppose is a bad sign. Maybe they don't plan that I'll survive to tell on them. A good sign is that they fed me cheese crackers. Made me thirsty, of course. Offered me water through a straw. I drank as little as I could manage. Feeding might indicate their purpose isn't to kill us, though. What do you think?"

"Uh-huh." No point being gloomy, Henry thought, or adding more fear to a situation that was already bad enough.

"Anyhow, from what I can understand, they think you lived here in the 1960s and know something about money that was hidden in the Fordyce during the big smash-up." Brad paused. "Shall I go on?"

Henry grunted. "Keep going."

"Okay, you got it. So, the Fordyce was empty by then; it closed in 1962. Advances in the field of medicine meant fewer people were coming to bathe as the years passed. Quapaw closed in 1968, re-opened the next year as a health service place, and that ended in '84. Been empty since. Other bathhouses along the row closed in their turn after the Fordyce went, were all gone but the Buckstaff by 1985. Today people use the baths more for relaxation, muscle relief—stuff like that—and just plain enjoyment.

"Hey, if you lived here, you know all of this anyway. So, *do* you have the key to where their money is? I'd guess it's a big amount, otherwise why bother?"

Henry said, "I've never been in Hot Springs before this week." He felt almost normal; the drug was wearing off.

Brad sighed. "That's kinda what I figured. They have the wrong guy, then, and aren't you lucky? Well, it seems the man in our evil duo—Mark, she calls him—was here back then, and the woman's father was too. During the raids. You know about those?"

"Yes."

"Okay. So, during the raids there was a ton of gambling money and other illegal cash floating around, with book-makers and so on hiding it, or taking it with them when they could get out ahead of the raids. I'm guessing the Hot Springs Police Department warned some people, and I suppose at least a few in the department got a sack of money themselves. We weren't all that clean back then. Anyway, the Arkansas State Police recovered a bunch of greenbacks, but a lot probably went missing with those who got away. Some folks here figure there's still money hidden around this area too and that most of it never will be found.

"Anyway, seems our odd couple thinks you have the key to finding *their* hidden money. They've talked about it, but what I know doesn't come just from them. A few months ago a newspaper reporter here, name of Stephen Hunt, wrote a series of exposé articles about the old times. He didn't mention real names—afraid of being sued, I suppose—but he gave a lot of what sounded like inside information. Conversation between these two pretty much confirms what Hunt wrote.

"Back in the naughty '60s four men, including Mark himself, salvaged a big wad of cash when the raiders came. Mark was a legal wizard for the Torch Club. Then there was the woman's dad, who oversaw the floor at the club, and a couple of others who were bookmakers. I don't think Mark knew the others all that well; it was just a marriage of convenience, so to speak, each doing his part taking the loot.

"Now Mark, he left town quick, scooted without any of the money. Wanted to save his reputation, he says. You can tell he's big on reputation and that he thought he was better than the other three, even back then.

"The woman's dad, undoubtedly less astute, was caught and—she says—murdered by the Hot Springs Police.

"That accounts for two in our gang of four. The other two, one of them your double, a Torch Club bookmaker named Henry King, were supposed to hide the money, then come back when it was safe and hand it out in fourths. Well, turns out this King and the second man, Victor, weren't anxious to share. Surprised? I thought not.

"By then Mark had got himself involved in a successful—and upright—business activity in another city, and he didn't care to endanger his esteemed reputation by re-associating with the two remaining guys who were, I suppose, crooked to the core. And of course the third man was dead already.

"From the talk I heard, King wasn't the one who ended up hiding the money. The fourth man, Victor, did it by himself. It seemed safer, he'd got away clear and had a place picked out. He was supposed to have shared directions with King so two of the four would know. Safety in numbers. But then Victor disappeared. Hasn't been heard of since, until—what do you know—his son shows up at the Elderhostel you're at.

"Guess who that is? Our murdered guy, Everett Bogardus. Unusual name, hard to hide. Bogardus was dumb not to use an assumed name, but maybe he had no idea there were more people in on his father's deal. Daddy is dead now so Everett wasn't getting any up-to-date news.

"Anyway...I don't know how, but Mark learned about Bogardus coming here for the Elderhostel, and that put the fox in the henhouse. Mark thought he'd let Victor's son locate the cash, then step in and take his share. Somehow the women found out about Bogardus too, and here they both are, ready to grab.

"One thing we can maybe use is that these two yahoos aren't bosom buddies, just partners of convenience for now. Might be possible to get them fighting each other instead of us, especially if they actually locate the money and a good old '*It's all mine*' argument starts.

"Or," Brad said, "maybe we can convince them neither of us knows a thing about any money and, what's more, neither of us cares about it or what they do with it. Something like in the crooked cop days? Do you think we could make that fly?"

He laughed. "I *would* like to get out of here. Man, I really gotta pee."

That's when they both heard footsteps and saw the faint glow of a flashlight bobbing somewhere in the distance.

CHAPTER XXIII

CARRIE

In spite of herself, Carrie was taking notes. Her reaction to any informational meeting was to get out pen and paper, and that's what she did as soon as the woman from the crystal mine they'd be visiting began talking.

After a few moments she realized her action might seem peculiar, even uncaring, to Eleanor, Jason, and Gwen, but it was just the opposite. Note-taking calmed her and helped focus her thoughts—not only on the crystal dig, but on the right way to help Henry. Simply sitting here stewing would cut down on logical thinking and any ability to make a plan for helping him. Therefore taking notes was the right thing to do.

Proving this, Carrie began making a list of questions concerning the need to find Henry and Brad...and, of course, a treasure seeker who was also a killer.

Or more than one? Killers?

"Questions," she wrote. *"Did someone mistake Henry for the other Henry King? Did Agent Brooks find out more that applies to people here during his research at the historical society?"* And, after some thought, *"Is the FBI withholding facts from us?"*

She was pondering this last question when she glanced up, and her pen skidded across the page, gouging a trough. Martha Rae Jones had just walked into the room.

Carrie gaped while the woman, ice-cube cool, squeezed past tables to a chair in the front row and sat down next to Greta. Where had she been? With Marcus? With Henry?

"That's Martha Rae Jones," she hissed to Gwen, who raised her eyebrows and looked puzzled.

Carrie thought a minute, then turned to a clean page in her note pad and wrote, *"She's the one who's been spending time with Marcus Trotter. The two of them were missing at supper, remember? Her cousin Oneida told me before the meeting that Martha knew Marcus years ago, here in Hot Springs. So evidently she's another one who has concealed a local connection. Don't you think she and Marcus could be the ones responsible for Everett's death and the abductions of Henry and Brad?*

"I'm going to leave now as if I had to visit the restroom. I'll sit in one of those armchairs facing the entrance to the Downtowner Bathhouse on this level. I noticed you can see the Crown Room door reflected in the glass of their entrance. If Martha leaves, I'll follow her."

She passed the note to Gwen, who scowled as she read it. Eleanor, reading over Gwen's arm, looked at Carrie and gave a small nod. Gwen shook her head and wrote, *"You can't follow her alone—too dangerous,"* then pushed the paper back.

"What, then?" Carrie wrote.

"Wait until the meeting's over."

"What if she leaves before it's over?"

Gwen hadn't replied to that when Carrie reached for the pad and pen, pushed them in her tote bag, and walked out of the room.

She went to one of the chairs facing the entry of the Downtowner Bathhouse and Spa, and was just sitting down to await events when she saw Eleanor coming out of the meeting room. Her image was clearly reflected in the glass door of the bathhouse.

Thank goodness! She'd been pretty sure Eleanor would join her, and the more she'd thought about following Martha Rae Jones by herself, the worse the idea seemed. It could be dangerous, yes, but there was an even bigger problem. If Martha did lead her to Henry and Brad—and that's what she expected to happen—how would she summon help, especially if she was too near a dangererous situation to use a cell phone safely? At least one more person was needed to keep watch while a second notified law enforcement rangers and the FBI. There would be safety in numbers, as Gwen herself had pointed out before they came down to the meeting.

Eleanor sank into the armchair next to Carrie and said, "Gwen is almost bouncing off her seat. I don't think she knows what to do. I'm sure she realizes it would be too obvious if all four of us walked out, so she probably won't dare come after us. I feel sorry for her; she's trying so hard to do a good job. She's pretty new in the department and, I suppose, has it rougher simply because she's female."

Eleanor sighed.

Carrie said nothing. She was too busy pondering a

plan of action.

Then Eleanor broke the silence again. "Never wanted to smoke but it would be handy now if we did. We could act like we were craving a cigarette and sit here sucking our lips into those wrinkled ovals and blowing puffs of smoke. That would give us an excuse for leaving the meeting and staying out. I don't suppose you happen to have any cigarettes in your tote bag?"

Carrie snorted, gave her a look, and said, "Good grief, Eleanor, I do hope you're joking. Besides, you can't smoke in this lobby."

After several minutes had passed, Eleanor pushed out of her easy chair and walked back to the Crown Room door, pulling it open to peer inside. Carrie heard chair-moving sounds as Eleanor trotted back across the elevator lobby. "The meeting is breaking up. Martha has snagged Greta and the two are deep in conversation. Jason and Gwen are on their way out with the rest of our group."

Oh, golly, Carrie thought, *all four of us following Martha will be about as subtle as a herd of buffalo.*

In a minute the would-be trackers were in a huddle by the bathhouse door. "How about this?" Carrie said. "As soon as Martha leaves, Eleanor and I will, acting casual and chatting about...cooking or something, follow her, even get in the same elevator with her in case she goes up instead of down. I suppose Henry and Brad could actually be held prisoner right here in the hotel, but I doubt it. With the housekeeping staff so attentive, it would pose problems for sure."

She looked at Gwen and Jason. "Why don't you two go to the lobby downstairs and stand at the back side of the fish tank. You'll be partially hidden there. You can follow Martha at a distance if she leaves the hotel. If you think she's seen you, Jason, you can pretend you're taking Gwen out to a bar or something. Martha knows Jason, of course, but I don't think she saw Gwen in the meeting, and she probably wouldn't recognize her in the dark anyway. I suppose it doesn't really matter if she does recognize both of you. The way Jason talks sometimes, she might well assume he's picked up a woman for some extra-curricular activity, and she'd have no way of knowing if Gwen is the type who would go along with that or not."

She glanced at Jason, wondering how he'd react to her comment. She hadn't been able to resist it. He frowned but kept his mouth shut.

Gwen's forehead was scrunched, as if she didn't know what to make of any of this, but she said, calmly enough, "Okay, it sounds like a good plan, considering our emergency situation. But as soon as we get downstairs, I'm going to try and reach Bell. Call me on my cell phone if you can manage it when you know where Jones is headed, assuming you don't pass us in the lobby. We'll provide back-up. Remember, don't approach her if she does lead us somewhere promising. Stop where you'll be out of sight, and we'll catch up to you and call for help or decide what to do next." She handed Carrie a card with a number on it, then she and Jason headed for the back stairs.

Eleanor and Carrie began an animated conversation about meatloaf recipes, with Eleanor arguing that the Times Two recipe wasn't as good as hers. Carrie was beginning to run out of things to say about meatloaf when Martha, pulling Greta along by the arm, came out of the now empty meeting room. The two of them headed for the elevators.

"Oh golly," Carrie said, "she's got Greta with her. Now what?"

"We stay with the plan," Eleanor said, walking toward

the elevators as she went back to the beginning of the Times Two argument.

They made it to the elevator just as the doors began to shut. Carrie could tell that Martha had pushed the "close" button, but she bumped against the door, risking injury by pushing her arm between the closing halves.

The door moved open again, and she and Eleanor, nodding a greeting and still talking meatloaf, got in.

"Don't know where Jason has disappeared to," Carrie said, abandoning the meatloaf discussion. "I'll bet he's meeting up with Henry so they can go cattin' around. So, Ellie, I say we have some fun too." She turned to Greta, who was staring at her, eyes wide with surprise. "Any advice about a good bar near here?"

Greta said, "I don't think..." but Martha poked her, and she cleared her throat, then said, "Green Olive. It's about half a block down the street to the right." She pointed. "Fine for single ladies. Respectable."

Carrie said, "Thanks," feeling a touch of sadness. Too bad Greta was involved in this mess; she'd seemed so sweet.

The elevator went down instead of up, and after they all got out in the main lobby, Carrie paused a moment to take a mirror from her tote bag. She fiddled with her hair while she and Eleanor waited to see where Martha and Greta were going.

Their quarry headed out the front door and turned left. *Uh-oh,* thought Carrie, *wrong direction for the Green Olive.*

She and Eleanor stayed close behind the other two women, and Carrie, laughing with what she hoped sounded like gay abandon, said, "Hey, Ellie, I don't want any lady-like bar, and I don't feel respectable. I think I saw an interesting-looking place down the street past the bathhouses when Henry and I were driving into town. Let's try that."

She hoped there was at least one bar in the area mentioned, but since she was a stranger here, surely no one would think it odd if she made a mistake. She did remember seeing restaurants and bars several places as she and Henry came along Central on Sunday.

That seemed like an age ago.

As they walked along the street, Carrie heard a familiar masculine chuckle from behind. Good. Gwen and Jason were keeping up.

Fortunately Martha was paying no attention to anyone but Greta, who seemed to be resisting her ideas. Martha's tones sounded harsh, though Carrie couldn't hear actual words.

The two women turned off Central at the corner, taking the sidewalk uphill from Arlington Lawn. Probably a good sign. Surely there was no reason for them to be going this way unless they were headed to wherever Henry was.

Oh, *no!* Carrie almost said it aloud. A car! They could drive away: there were cars parked all along the side street. She hadn't even thought of that possibility simply because they didn't go to the hotel parking lot. Some detective she was. She should have asked Gwen to request an unmarked police car, just in case.

God, be with us, guide our steps, be with us as we find Henry, she prayed. *And no car, please.*

By now Carrie and Eleanor had rounded the corner too and were trying to walk more quietly and stay out of sight. Surely the other women, intent on their conversation, wouldn't look around.

After a short climb, Martha and Greta turned right to enter the brick-paved Grand Promenade that led behind the bathhouses.

Thank you. They aren't going anywhere in a car.

Carrie moved into the shadows by a concrete wall and pulled Eleanor with her. The women might glance back along the sidewalk as they made the turn. But neither one did. As soon as they were out of sight, she and Eleanor got back on the sidewalk and continued uphill.

Now Gwen and Jason, arms entwined, passed them and turned onto the Promenade. Martha and Greta were still within view, but Carrie and Eleanor remained partially concealed by shadows between post lights and by the amorous couple bobbing back and forth in front of them.

Suddenly both women leading the peculiar parade turned around, probably wanting to see if anyone else was in the area. Jason and Gwen stopped, looked at each other, and laughed, pretending to share a joke. Carrie had to congratulate them on their acting. It sure looked real to her. Jason's ability to carry it off didn't surprise her; he was undoubtedly enjoying his role, but Gwen was as good at this as he was.

Martha seemed satisfied that the pair had no interest in anyone but themselves, so the six walkers again proceeded along the Promenade, with Jason and Gwen continuing their conversation and laughter. At least they provided a good cover for Carrie and Eleanor, who were staying as far behind as they dared.

Then Martha stopped and looked back a second time. Carrie and Eleanor pressed into the shadows as Jason turned to hug Gwen.

Gwen giggled, and Carrie heard her say, "Oh, you are some tomcat."

Before Carrie could wonder what would happen if Gwen and Jason caught up with the women and had to pass them, Martha pulled Greta off the brick sidewalk and down a grass slope toward the back of one of the silent, empty bathhouses. Evidently the couple had been dismissed as people of no consequence, simply folks out on the town.

In the glow from service lights Carrie saw Martha climb over a chain link fence guarding the sheer drop between the back wall of the bathhouse and the retaining wall against the base of the mountain. After what looked like more argument, she persuaded Greta to follow and helped her balance, first on a crossbar, then, very slowly, to crawl up until she cleared the rest of the fence. The women stepped easily over the gap between the mountainside and first floor roof covering the back side of the bathhouse. They walked across the flat roof to the wall of a second story that rose on the street side of the building. There were windows and a small door in the wall. Martha hesitated briefly at the door, undoubtedly unlocking it, then she switched on a flashlight and both women disappeared inside.

Carrie studied the back of the bathhouse. It was a large building, probably the largest of the eight on the row, and there was a dome crowning its second story. She looked for light flickering behind the second story windows where Martha and Greta had entered, but could see none. They had evidently headed to some other part of the building as soon as they were inside. That meant the door was probably unguarded. Good. Now if it was only unlocked...

"I recognize the dome," Eleanor said in her ear. "It's the Quapaw. What do we do next?"

"Are you game to follow?" Carrie asked.

"Sure. But where are Jason and Gwen? Let's confer with them before we go through that door."

In a minute the other two returned along the path, keeping up their act until they reached the shadowed area where Eleanor and Carrie stood. Then, suddenly, both were all business, intent on the mission.

"They went in there?" Gwen whispered, pointing to the door.

"Yes. I suppose an unused bathhouse would make a dandy place to hide someone. Agree?"

"It would. I guess Brooks, Bell, and Company overlooked that because the buildings are supposed to be almost inaccessible. Most of them don't have any opening in the back at all, and of course they're fenced. Well, the boys will soon learn about access. I'm calling for help."

"For heaven's sake, tell everyone to keep quiet!" Carrie said.

"Don't worry, they will know enough to do that," Gwen told her.

"I'll try to get in through that door," Carrie said, "and take a look around. They probably aren't in this part of the building. I don't see any lights. Maybe Eleanor can keep watch by the entrance while I'm inside. We'll signal for you to join us after I see where they are and what they're doing, especially if I find Henry and Brad Jorgenson. If Martha and Greta happen to catch me, well, one silly woman will seem less threatening than a man and a cop."

Jason's voice was sharp. "No, it's not safe. Wait for the FBI."

"Legions of cops and agents can't do what I can," Carrie said. "We need to find out if Henry and Brad really are there and exactly where in the building they're being held before any rescue is attempted. That's a huge place—looks like three floors including the basement. I'll be very quiet, stay out of sight, and take a look around, find out what we face. I still have my trusty little flashlight and can use it as long as I don't hear any noise or see a light. Think about it. That's the best way. I will be careful because if they hear someone coming, they could...hurt Henry and Brad."

"No! Stay here," Gwen said. "Jason's right, there's too much danger. Besides, you'd make a wonderful hostage, and we don't need any more people to rescue."

But Carrie and Eleanor were already climbing the fence.

Chapter XXIV

Henry

The footsteps were getting louder. *Had to get out! Too help-less...had to break the cabinet door, get out.*

Sweating, Henry bent his knees, braced his feet against the front of the steam cabinet and—with all the strength he could gather—shoved, over and over. The door moved slightly but showed no signs of breaking open. Finally he gave up and slumped back, defeated, though his mind still raged against this diabolical prison. Even if he could break the front door, he hadn't any idea how to open the doors locked around his neck. Why did people ever choose to get in these things? They were nothing but miniature torture chambers. Once he was out, he'd never get in one again. When he was out...when he...was anyone searching for them? Where was Carrie right now? Surely she was safe...

Bell would be with her now.

As Henry's rage subsided, frustration and regret took its place. In the face of Brad Jorgenson's comment about how effective steam cabinets were as a prison and the description of his own attempts to free himself before Henry got there, well, he was sorry he'd even tried to break out. Brad, a strong, physically fit young man, knew what he was talking about, and Henry shouldn't have doubted that. Such stuff could be humiliating to a junior officer. The ability to understand junior officers was one reason Henry had risen to the top of his unit in the Kansas City Police Department. His trust in those under him built a cohesive, effective team.

But no matter how young, the officer would also understand something about Henry...the feeling of frustration, helplessness, even fear; the need to fight against his prison. He'd know how Henry felt and why he had to keep fighting. Henry, after all, was only a man. He had to keep fighting.

They could hear voices now, two women. It sounded like one was complaining about being brought to this derelict bathhouse.

"I'll act like I'm still under the influence of the drug," he whispered. "Might help us if they thought that." He hadn't any idea how long the effects of this particular drug were supposed to last, but then, people reacted differently to drugs.

Brad didn't answer. The women were silent now and might be close enough to hear.

Henry wished, as he had several times earlier, that the edge of the metal rim circling his neck was padded. When the cabinets were in daily use attendants probably put towels around the necks of people sitting in them. Now, flopping his head over against the sharp edge hurt, no matter which direction he flopped. But then lots of things hurt, his shoulder and head included.

A flashlight beamed through the door; he could sense its light against his eyelids. The next thing he heard was a startled cry from one of the women. Greta Hunt's voice.

"*What?* Why are these men in the steam cabinets? Mattie, what is this? They're all locked up. What's going on—they look like prisoners."

"They are prisoners, Greta dear. That one is a Hot Springs cop who got in the way. You know the other guy, your old friend, Henry King. We have him so he can tell us where our money is hidden."

That voice sounded like Martha Rae Jones. Henry supposed it was the Jones woman, though she seemed able to change her voice as well as her looks at will. She had sure done a good job mimicking Eleanor and a hotel housekeeper.

He detected new noises...a clink, striking of a match, humming whoosh. He recognized the sounds. Someone was lighting a propane lantern. Steady light beat against his eyes and he heard the high *shhhhh* of pressure-fed gas burning.

Greta spoke again, her voice pinched and squeaky. "You *have* Henry King? *Have* him? A prisoner? *Money?* You think this man is Hank...oh, I don't believe what you're saying. This is crazy."

"Don't play the innocent with me, Greta. You knew what you were doing when you sent me that Elderhostel list, sent it to me and to Mark. You want your share of the money as much as we do. We all knew Victor Bogardus held the key, wherever he'd got to. If you didn't want help finding our money, why would you let us know Victor's son was coming back to Hot Springs after all these years?"

"Well, of course I recognized the name and thought you'd find it as interesting as I did." Greta's voice was stronger, incredulous, scornful. Instinctively Henry thought, *Watch out, Greta. The Jones woman is a loose cannon. Don't make her angry.*

"It sure wasn't because of that old story about some hidden money. I don't care a thing about that, and I know Mark doesn't either. Why would he? He's rich already. He has very important friends in Chicago, some of them high up in government. And we certainly weren't thinking about you doing this stupid, wicked thing, not...not putting men in steam cabinets. Mark wouldn't condone this."

Martha's voice turned to acid. "Oh, wouldn't he now? Think again, little Greta."

"For goodness' sake, Mattie, get it through your head that Mark's a big, important man. He's head of a huge law firm and has lots of famous clients. Even people from other countries have him represent them in the United States. He doesn't need money somebody is supposed to have hidden here forty years ago. Besides, Stephen says he doubts there's any money left now. He should know—he talked to Hank, he wrote the story. Stephen says if there ever was money it's already been found; whoever found it, kept it and didn't say anything."

"Oh, I don't think so."

"I could not care less what you think, Mattie, and where is Mark? You lied to me. He isn't even here. You said he needed me..."

"Oh, he does, little Greta, he does. He needs you to tell me who this man is."

"One of my Elderhostel group, Henry King, and you'd better let him and this other man out. They could sue you. You could get arrested for false imprisonment...or something. I'll call the police...the FBI."

"Shut up about the police, Greta. You're beginning to make me angry. You always were a self-righteous little snot, spoiled rotten by Mark and your folks. Well, I'm not impressed, and all I want from you now is confirmation of who this man is."

"I told you, a man from the Elderh..."

"It is Henry King?"

"Sure. And you think it's the Henry King from way back when?" Greta began laughing. "Well, there might be more than one Henry King in this part of the world."

Henry heard the sound of a slap. Brad said, "Hey!" as Greta's laugh changed to a cry of pain.

"*Who is he?*" That was Martha Jones's voice again—sharp, angry. "Mark said he's the one Stephen got all the inside information from, the man who told him what happened back in the '60s.*"

Greta was laughing again, but now her laugh sounded more like hysterics. "Oh, boy, oh, boy, Mattie, did you get fooled. Hank King, the one Stephen talked to, only told him about the money because he was dying and didn't care any more who knew his story. All he cared about was that Stephen didn't publish it until after he was dead. Stephen kept his word, and Hank King from Hot Springs was buried last spring. Did it ever occur to you that this might not be the same man?"

"Oh, yes, it occurred to me, it just didn't occur to your stupid brother. He said looks can change, hair can be dyed. That's why I brought you here, because your brother insisted this man was the key to finding our money, and I suspected...well, never mind. I've proved he isn't who Mark thinks he is."

"You're lying about Mark. He had nothing to do with

this. He wouldn't...why, he isn't even here. Now, open the cabinets and let these men go."

"I don't think so, Greta. I don't think so."

"You *aren't* thinking. Shelley said..."

"Shelley?" It was a shriek. "What's she got to do with this? I never told her about the money. I wanted her to think her dad and I..."

"Oh, it's nothing to do with some imaginary money. Shelley's worried about you, that's all. We still exchange Christmas cards, so I wrote her to get your address after Everett Bogardus sent in his registration. I thought you'd have a good time at this Elderhostel and that it would be fun for all of us to see what Victor's son was like now. I thought you and Mark might remember him as a boy.

"Shelley said you were still mourning the death of her dad and spent too much time alone. She told me inviting you here was a good idea, it would perk you up, help you meet new people. She thought you'd feel at home in Hot Springs and it would be good for you to see what the town is like today, help you get away from the past and have some fun."

Now Martha Jones sounded sulky. "Shelley always wanted to boss me, even when she was a little girl."

"Shelley only wants..."

"Stop it, Greta. My daughter is out of this. I brought you here to tell me who this man is, that's all. You'd better leave now. I'm sure you can manage that fence by yourself. And I wouldn't get smart and think you want to tell anyone about these men. Don't forget Stephen Hunt is as much involved as Mark and I are. He's the one who found out about all the money, remember? Oh, he's involved, all right, and the FBI would be very interested to learn that. You can imagine how guilty he'd look to them. "

"You can't...are you threatening me? Oh, Mattie, just look at those poor men." Greta's voice changed, quavered. "One of them, see him, Henry King from my Elderhostel, he looks sick or...dead."

"Oh, no, Greta, he's a long way from dead yet." There was a pause, a scuffling of feet as Martha Jones bent so close to Henry that he could feel her breath on his forehead and smell the onions she'd had for supper. "But you may be right, he could be *acting* dead. He should have come out of that drug by now."

"Drug? What have you done?" Feet scraped again. "I am getting out of here, and I am going to call the police. You can't do this. You can't hurt these men, so you just run now, Mattie, run. Get away from here. Your father ran from the police. You run too. Maybe you'll have better luck getting away than he did."

Martha Jones' shriek was so close to Henry's ear that only long training kept him from flinching. "Oh, no, Greta, no, you don't. Not unless you want Mark in jail for murder, not unless you want your precious Stephen's career ruined."

Greta was shouting back now. Maybe adrenaline had taken over. "This is crazy, a stupid nightmare. If you let these men go right now, I won't call the police. And stop talking about Mark. He wouldn't put up with this. That's crazy."

"Well, who do you think killed old man Bogardus's son? Use your head for once. You know Everett Bogardus was murdered even if your precious Elderhostel folks don't. It wasn't me who did that deed. I was with the tour group the whole time. Mark wasn't. He was gone for more than thirty minutes—ask anyone. I'll bet even the FBI knows that by now. It was your brother who killed Victor's son. *Mark slashed his throat.* Talk about stupid. He probably killed the only man who knew where our money is."

Greta's shout became a cry of fury...or fear. Henry couldn't tell which. Then the noise stopped as suddenly as if someone had cut her throat too.

But no one had. After a few moments the room was filled with soft, whimpered sobs and the words, "No, no, Mattie, no." Unmistakably Greta's voice. What was Martha doing?

The fear that had been bubbling just under the surface of Henry's thoughts came out full force now. Martha Rae Jones did not plan for him or Brad Jorgenson to leave this place alive. Alive, either of them could do too much damage to her and to Marcus Trotter. Dead, there would be only very silent bodies to dispose of. He was beginning to suspect that Marcus Trotter from Chicago might be very good at disposing of dead bodies.

That's when cool metal touched Henry's right ear. At the moment of contact he smelled an odor that was burned in his brain after long years of familiarity with it—the oily-sweet scent of gun-cleaning solvent. Almost before his brain could register the smell, he heard the unmistakable snap of a revolver hammer.

CHAPTER XXV

CARRIE

As she and Eleanor scurried across the flat roof, Carrie could see that the door Greta and Martha had used was obviously a utility door, put in place to allow workers access to skylights and equipment. Stile-like wooden steps led up to a sill at the same level as the bottom of the windows next to it. Probably the door had once been a window.

Carrie climbed the steps, reached for the handle, turned it, pushed. The door wasn't locked. She opened it a crack and peeked through. The building was dark and silent. She eased the door shut, climbed back down, faced Eleanor.

Eleanor looked exactly like a woman trying to appear brave and fearless. In other words, she was as scared as Carrie.

"I sure dread going in there, but..."

"Maybe we should..."

They stared at each other.

Finally Carrie broke the silence. "If it weren't for Henry, you wouldn't find me anywhere near this place, but I can't think how else we'll learn what's going on inside and do it quickly enough to be of help. Henry could be in great danger *right now.* Oh, Eleanor, if only I hadn't been so interested in what Everett Bogardus was doing in that basement..."

Resolve flew into Eleanor's face and she held up a hand. "Hush now. We have a mission to complete. You said if we stuck together we'd be okay, and I agree with that. Therefore I am coming in the building with you."

"Only to just inside the door. Maybe there will be a place you can hide while I look around. You'll be my back-up, listen for problems, and summon the agents after I case the place...search, you know? Shall we go?"

She climbed the stairs again and pushed the door wide open.

The windows next to the door were painted over, but front windows in the room they entered faced the street with its multiple lights. Since their eyes were already used to the dark, Carrie didn't turn on her flashlight. The room was empty except for bits of miscellaneous junk lying around. She wondered if there was something here she might use as a weapon. If only she'd brought the geologist's pick with her.

She listened again, heard no voices, and finally turned on the flashlight to do a more exact survey. Numerous footprints and what looked like drag marks led through heavy dust to an open door on their right. A pile of old looking construction trash was heaped against the wall next to them. Carrie saw a short piece of metal pipe sticking out of the pile and pulled it loose to take with her.

Realizing their footprints would be as obvious as the others were, she took Eleanor's hand and they walked in the existing tracks as far as the door. Eleanor stepped around it on tiptoe, flattened against the wall, and pulled the door back to shield her body from view.

Carrie inspected the hiding place. It looked safe. Unless someone beamed a flashlight directly on Eleanor from the entry door, she'd be completely hidden.

The tracks led through a small hallway to a flight of stairs. A few steps down the stairs turned left, so she couldn't see the bottom.

She turned the flashlight off and stopped to listen. Women's voices. A slapping sound. Man's voice, "Hey." Not Henry. Brad Jorgenson?

Faint light from below, voices barely audible, so the stairs didn't open into the room where the speakers were.

She started down the stairs, bracing a hand against the wall, feeling carefully for each step.

The stairs ended in another hall. Bright light came through a door on her right. Propane lantern? Evidently the room had no outside windows. If it did the light could probably be seen from the Promenade, perhaps identified as a fire. That would sure get attention.

The hallway she stood in was between the front of the building and the lighted room. There were several closed doors on her left and, testing, she turned a knob. It moved silently, and she opened the door to see the glow of Central Avenue lights through the window of a closet-like room.

What next? She moved into the small room, pushed the door partly closed, and wondered if she should go back and tell Eleanor where she was. She could send her to let Gwen know it would be easy for her to signal anyone on Central.

But first she had to see if Henry was in that lighted room.

The women were talking about Henry King and she recognized both Greta's and Martha's voices. They were discussing just what she had assumed, that Marcus Trotter thought her Henry was someone who knew where money was hidden back in the '60s.

Henry must be in there because Greta was telling Martha this Henry was not a local man, but only a member of her Elderhostel group.

Carrie had heard enough. Time to get help.

She started out of her hiding place but was stopped by slow, measured footsteps coming down the stairs. Eleanor? She ducked back to wait and see.

She was about to risk another look when a dark shape went past in the hallway and moved silently to stand in the shadows at the side of the lighted door. The person was listening as intently as she had been. A man. Was it Marcus Trotter? She couldn't tell.

Oh, if only it could be Agent Bell. How was she going to get out now and alert everyone? Once more she had let her impulses drive her into an impossible situation, and the drumbeat of her heart was keeping time to words banging in her head, *What now? What now? What now?* She hoped Eleanor had seen the man and gone for help.

She could tell, even in the semi-dark, that the man was agitated by what the two women were saying. He shifted his weight from one foot to another and moved his hands rapidly up and down the sides of his body. Finally his hand jerked into a pocket and came out with a hand gun. Light from the lantern was strong enough to reveal its unmistakable shape as he attached a silencer to the barrel.

Now Martha Jones was telling Greta that her brother

Mark was the one who killed Everett Bogardus!

The watching man jerked to attention, lifted the gun. He could see what was happening in the room, but Carrie couldn't.

Oh, God, what am I going to do? Help me, help me! Help all of us. Oh, please, please.

The man brought his other hand up to steady the gun and walked into the room. Greta cried out and a male voice grunted. Was that Henry?

Carrie hurried out of her hiding place to stand where the man had been, but she was afraid to risk a glance around the door frame. He must be just inside, and everyone would be looking toward him.

Was there a second entrance? She backed away from the opening and went around the stairs to the opposite end of the hall. Yes, another door. The light wasn't as bright here so that must mean the action was centered around the door where the man had been standing. Should she go get Eleanor now, alert the FBI?

The man and Martha were yelling at each other. He sure sounded like Trotter, and he wasn't pleased that she had brought Greta here, or that she had a gun herself. "You fool," he said. "A shot can be heard. Use your drugs."

"I remind you your gun makes noise too, even with that silencer. But I had no intention of using mine; I was simply entertaining your baby sister. I fully intend to get rid of these people the quiet way."

A thunk and a cry from Martha had Carrie hugging the door frame to peer carefully around its edge.

Henry! He was locked inside a steam cabinet angled to face the other door, and a young man, presumably Brad Jorgenson, was inside a second one. Martha Jones was slumped on the floor next to the cabinets. She seemed to be unconscious; evidently Trotter had hit her. Greta huddled against her brother's chest, sobbing.

NOW! Go for help. Carrie went up the stairs as fast as she dared, grabbed for the door Eleanor was hiding behind.

Eleanor? She was gone! Gone for help?

Where...? Quick, turn on flashlight, where, where? Search... there, footsteps, new drag marks, no, oh, no. ELEANOR! Follow the drag marks...another empty room.

Oh, Holy God! NO! Carrie almost shouted her friend's name, but choked the sound off in time.

One end of Eleanor's bright red scarf was around her neck...slip knot, Carrie recognized that. The other end was tied to an exposed ceiling beam. Eleanor's wide, terrified eyes pleaded with her. She was gagged with a handkerchief, her hands were tied, her ankles too. The tips of her toes were braced against the back of a broken, three-legged chair that was almost, but not quite, out of her reach.

Dear God, oh, help us, help! Have to get her down.

Something to climb on...I'm not tall enough...something to cut that scarf.

She jerked her flashlight around the room, saw nothing to stand on except the chair balanced so precariously under Eleanor's toes. Was Eleanor breathing?

Hold on just another minute, dear, dear Eleanor.

Hurry, hurry. To the door. Up the steps, jump down. Could Gwen and Jason see her? Wave arms. Hurry to edge of roof. There, there! They were running toward her.

"Gwen, Jason—Eleanor needs help. Inside. Quick! On the left."

As they rushed forward she continued, "I've been hiding on the floor below. Quiet—Marcus Trotter has gun—Henry and Brad there—locked in steam cabinets. Greta Hunt,

Martha Rae Jones there too—Jones is down now—not for long, I think. Be careful. Help Eleanor."

As soon as Gwen was close enough, she reached for Carrie's hand and, this time, Carrie didn't resist. Instead she pulled the young woman across the roof of the building and up the wooden stairs. Jason had run ahead of them and was already through the door.

Were they in time? How awful that Jason would have to see Eleanor like this and know her best friend Carrie had brought this danger and pain to her. Terrible, terrible thing for a friend to do.

She waited long enough to see Jason grab his wife's legs, lift the weight of her body. Eleanor was still strong enough to keep her knees locked as he lifted.

She was alive, alive!

Gwen had her knife out and was balancing on the broken chair, reaching up to cut the red scarf.

Oh, please, let her be unhurt!

As they eased Eleanor down, Carrie began tip-toeing toward the stairway. This room might be directly over the room where Henry was.

Nothing looked different when she returned to her place by the doorway. How was it they hadn't heard the commotion above? These old buildings must have thick walls and floors, and maybe Greta's sobs, still loud in the silence, had masked any noise the three of them made. After all, she hadn't heard that evil man drag Eleanor away and tie her to the beam, and Eleanor wouldn't have gone without a fight.

Trotter was still holding Greta and had turned away from where Martha Jones lay. There was no sign of her gun. He obviously didn't consider the woman a threat to him, conscious or not, and was more interested in comforting his sister. Greta's eyes were shut, her head lying against his chest.

Neither of them could see Martha Jones when she began to move. She lifted her head, only inches at first, then slithered backwards across the floor like a snake in reverse. Where was she headed? To get something? Whatever it was must be on the other side of those steam cabinets.

Could Henry or Brad see Martha? No, she was crawling against the wall of the cabinet Henry was in, and the metal itself would shield her from their view.

Carrie wondered if she should scream something about Martha. Trotter could stop her movement; he still held his gun in the hand that wasn't holding his sister. But, she decided, if he was alerted he'd want to shoot Carrie McCrite, not Martha Jones. And all she had for her own defense was a piece of pipe.

Martha had slithered out of sight, and Carrie began to shift from one foot to another just as she'd seen Trotter do earlier. *What was the woman up to?*

Brother and sister were talking; he was urging her to go back to her Elderhostel group and forget all that she had seen tonight. He would take care of Martha Jones, he would take care of everything. She shouldn't worry.

"Will you set these men free?"

"Of course, little Greta, right away, as soon as you're safely gone."

But Carrie didn't believe a word of that. He couldn't afford witnesses.

And neither could Martha, who had now come back into view just behind Henry's head.

There was a hypodermic needle in her hand, and she was reaching toward Henry's neck.

...get rid of them the quiet way...

Wild heat raged through Carrie and, without a second thought or consciously willing it, she cried out as loudly as she could and vaulted across the floor, holding the pipe in both hands. She swung toward Marcus Trotter's head as she passed him, connecting with something, then leaped behind the steam cabinet, flinging herself against Martha, lifting the pipe to aim a blow at the arm with the deadly-looking needle.

"Don't you touch him!" Carrie yelled as she brought the pipe down on Martha's arm with a horrendous, bone-breaking crack.

CHAPTER XXVI

CARRIE AND HENRY

For an instant there was no sound at all.

Then Brad's voice said, "Wow, oh, wow, did you *see* her?"

That was just before Martha Rae Jones began shrieking and Greta Hunt's wails joined the racket.

Henry didn't blame Martha for crying. Her arm had to be broken, and Carrie was now grabbing her by the hair to drag her away from the steam cabinets, the hypodermic needle, and the bag of lethal drugs.

Would Carrie be able to tie her up, tie Marcus Trotter too, all by herself? Trotter lay on the floor and, for the present at least, he wasn't moving. Carrie's pipe had connected with his head, so he probably posed no immediate threat, and Henry saw Carrie pick up Trotter's gun as she tugged

Martha past him.

Henry began to undo his belt. If he and Brad could get their belts out of the neck holes of these confounded cabinets, Carrie would then be able to use them for securing Martha. With Martha tied and Trotter unconscious, she'd have time to undo the cabinet locks and let him out so he could help her with the rest of it.

The rest of what? She was doing okay by herself.

Next to him, Brad cleared his throat. "Um, who *IS* that woman?" he asked. "You know her?"

"Yes...guess I do," Henry said. "And I've decided I'm going to marry her."

"Well, um, okay then, if it's what you want. But buddy, you don't ever wanna make her mad at you..."

Brad went on—talking to himself now. "All she had was a pipe. Gotta get me one of those."

Henry began laughing, and that changed to a smile of relief as Agent Bell slid into the room, looked around quickly, then put his gun away. He went to lock handcuffs on Marcus Trotter and the weeping Greta Hunt. Gently, Henry noticed, he pulled Martha Jones away from Carrie, looked at the woman's arm, and handed her over to one of the FBI agents who, along with two park rangers and Gwen Taylor, had come into the room behind Bell.

He hoped someone let him out soon; he needed to go to Carrie. She'd slid down the wall where Bell left her and was sitting on the floor, arms loose, legs extended like those of a limp rag doll. Her eyes looked glazed, staring out at the room. She was probably in shock and needed him to hold her in his arms.

Over. It was over, and she felt like a rag doll with the stuffing leaked out. All of a sudden her stuffing had drained away somewhere in this room, and she couldn't even lift her hands.

Languidly she watched Gwen go over to Officer Jorgenson...Brad. Hmmm. Gwen and Brad. She wondered if they were friends—or was this just one police officer helping another?

Why didn't someone let Henry out? If only she could walk, she'd...

Gwen was talking to the good-looking young officer as if they knew each other well. She'd managed to open the top doors on his cabinet. Now their conversation seemed more intense, as if she were trying to convince him of something.

Oh. Oh-oh. Gwen opened the lower door, helped Brad stand. He must have been in that cabinet for what... ten hours? Gwen put Brad's arm around her shoulders so he could lean against her back. Together the two of them moved out of the room.

Carrie smiled. Their positions almost shielded the big wet spot on the front of the young man's pants. Under the circumstances, she was probably the only one who saw it.

She wondered about Henry. There were public restrooms up on the Promenade. If she could just get her stuffing back, she'd be able to take him there. She shut her eyes and wished someone would let Henry out of his box and that Agent Bell would come back to talk with her. She needed to tell him Greta Hunt was an innocent bystander in all of this and he should let her go.

He had to let her go; they couldn't continue the Elderhostel without her. The trip to the crystal mine was coming up, and Carrie didn't intend to miss that. It was, after all, the main reason she was here in Hot Springs.

Chapter XXVII

Carrie and Henry

Law enforcement ranger Jake Kandler was the one who finally freed Henry. The big man opened the steam cabinet doors easily, helped Henry stand, helped him take his first steps. After a brief interlude outside, Kandler accompanied Henry back into what he identified as the former men's dressing room in the Quapaw Bathhouse.

Ignoring the activity in the room, Henry sat on the floor beside Carrie and, without a word, pulled her onto his lap, holding her against his chest. That's when the tears started. She was still limp as a rag doll, and eventually he had to help her look in her pockets for the tissues she always carried.

After a blessed period of quiet she was just beginning to wiggle when Agent Brooks appeared beside them.

"Hear you're quite a menace with a pipe," he said to

Carrie, "if what Trotter and Jones say is true, that is. Feel ready to talk about it?"

She lifted her head far enough to shake it, then leaned back against Henry.

"Okay, we'll talk later."

"You must release Greta," she said then, finding her voice. "It's true she was the one who told Marcus Trotter and Martha Rae Jones about Everett coming to the Elderhostel, but that was innocent, nothing to do with money. Her brother rarely came to visit her, and I bet she hoped that the chance to meet Everett, whom she knew to be the son of one of his old-time friends, would bring him here for a visit. As for Martha Rae, Greta talked with her daughter, and they believed getting her to come would erase past ghosts and help Martha find new friends. Greta may be naive, but criminal stuff couldn't be further from her thought. She's not like that.

"I saw Bell put handcuffs on her...you've got to let her go."

"What Carrie says is true," Henry added. "I was here while Jones and Hunt had the conversation that proves it. Carrie evidently overheard the same thing."

"I'll see what I can do," Brooks said. "You two wait here."

Henry managed a laugh. He doubted either of them could get five steps away from this spot without being stopped by some agent or ranger anyway, though Carrie's strength seemed to be returning and he was sure she'd soon be able to walk.

"What now?" she asked.

"I don't know what now. Guess we just wait."

In a few minutes Agent Bell came back into the room with Greta, sans handcuffs, and a strange man who hovered over her. Husband, probably.

"Got to get up, talk to Greta," Carrie said as she slid off his lap, braced a hand against the wall, and stood. She insisted on walking to Greta on her own. Henry followed, expecting to hear her offer gentle words of comfort to their Elderhostel coordinator. He was touched by this concern in the face of all Carrie herself had undergone.

He'd noticed, though, that Greta looked more resigned than sad. He suspected she'd known at least something about her brother's criminal connections, no matter how innocent she seemed. Nevertheless, as Carrie touched Greta's hand, he tried to think about words of comfort he, too, could say.

But Carrie began briskly, talking to Greta as if this evening had never happened. "We haven't had a chance to thank you for all your work organizing this wonderful Elderhostel," she said, "and I wanted you to know how much we're looking forward to the crystal mine trip. You're doing a great job, Greta. Keep up the good work."

What the... Carrie was talking as if they'd had nothing but a pleasant vacation for the past two days. She was simply saying thank you.

Henry's own words of sympathy died in his throat as he saw Greta perk up and lift her chin. "I'm so glad you're having a good time," she told them. "The rest of the week is even better. Don't forget, on Friday we have the bus trip to the herb farm and a boat tour on Lake Ouachita. I've planned a picnic by the lake, too.

"I'll see you two tomorrow," she finished as she let her husband lead her away. It was as if the entire evening's events had been erased from her mind.

Henry was sure Greta would still grieve—however privately—but, thinking about it, he decided there was nothing like being needed—and knowing that what you do is important to others—for helping anyone through a bad patch.

I guess that's how mothers make it through many of the problems they face, he thought.

Finally agents Bell and Brooks took pity on them and said they'd delay hearing their reports until the following morning. Would they be available at 8:30?

"We'd miss the 8:30 session. It's about cooking with herbs," Carrie said, "but I don't really mind."

Henry didn't mind at all.

He already knew too well that the agents had a long night ahead of them and plenty of other people to talk with. Poor Gwen and Brad weren't likely to get much sleep, and Eleanor and Jason, who were in the room now, seemed to be all fired up and eager to talk. The danger and excitement they had faced was new to them, and they both said they were willing to stay. "Couldn't sleep anyway," said Jason, who was treating his "brave detective" wife with a deference that bordered on awe.

As Carrie and Henry waited for Agent Brooks to bring a car around to the front of the bath house, they listened to their friends tell Bell the story of their evening.

Eleanor had seen Marcus Trotter come into the building while Carrie was on the floor below, and she'd tried to get to Carrie with a warning. Marcus caught up with her as she started down the stairs, grabbed her in a choke hold, and dragged her away. He gagged her with his handkerchief, tied her ankles and wrists with her own shoelaces, and used the red scarf she was wearing to tie her to the ceiling beam. Then he left her to hang herself.

Hearing this, Henry was almost sorry Carrie's pipe hadn't done more damage to Trotter. The man had known

Eleanor would drop the minute her feet slipped inside her loose shoes and her toes lost their ability to support her weight, or when the chair tilted. He'd cruelly left her to await her own death.

But the chair held, and so did Eleanor's toes. She'd fought for her life against all odds, and Jason had come in time to save her.

That sort of thing can improve any marriage, Henry thought as he watched Eleanor and Carrie wrap each other in a goodbye hug.

Agent Brooks drove Henry and Carrie the short distance to their hotel, repeating that he and Bell would be back to question them at 8:30 the following morning.

"'Kay," Carrie said, sounding sleepy now, "but a class called 'Scientific and Industrial Uses of Crystal' begins at 10:30, and I plan to be in that class."

"I imagine we can get through our discussion in two hours," said Brooks. "I'll keep your deadline in mind."

Henry had forgotten about the chaos in his room.

Carrie evidently had too. They stared, speechless, at the mess and the crime scene tape closing it off. They turned back to stare at the one queen-sized bed in Carrie's room. Then they stared at each other.

Finally Henry spoke, trying to be as cool and matter-of-fact about this situation as Greta and Carrie had just been about the coming Elderhostel events. "You can have the bathroom first. While you're getting ready for bed, I'm going under the tape to grab my razor and a few toiletries, then I'll call for room service breakfasts."

She wasn't long getting ready, nor was he.

They chose sides and climbed into bed. After a moment

of quiet, two hands reached out and touched. Then, feeling the comfort of each other's warmth, they fell asleep.

Agents Brooks and Bell, tired-eyed but crisply dressed, arrived just after the room service breakfasts were delivered. Carrie and Henry were still in night clothes, but both had put on robes, and they sat together on their bed eating breakfast while the agents pulled up chairs to talk.

"First," Bell said to Henry, "Officer Jorgenson told me what he could about your abduction, but would you describe it again for me?"

Henry described between bites while Bell took notes, occasionally nodding encouragement. Meanwhile Brooks was watching Carrie eat. After asking him if he'd had breakfast and receiving a "Yes, but," answer, Carrie piled eggs and a slice of bacon on a biscuit and offered it to him with a bathroom tumbler full of coffee.

The men asked question after question, alternating between Carrie and Henry, until they'd heard the entire story, and Henry learned how Greta and Martha were followed to the Quapaw. It had been very hard not to laugh during Carrie's account. It sounded to him like she was trying to relate every detail accurately, though she'd stumbled a bit during the part where she described Jason and Gwen's play-acting.

Finally Bell asked Carrie, "Why did you take the risk of subduing Trotter and Jones with that pipe? The fact you managed to hit them both was...unexpected...a gamble."

"Maybe, but I thought Martha was going to kill Henry with whatever was in the hypodermic needle. I had the pipe, I had the opportunity, *and I had to do something.*"

"You could have failed. What you did was dangerous."

"That didn't even occur to me. In fact I didn't have time
to think. I just did what I needed to do. You face danger too,
Agent Bell. We all do every day, one way or another."

Subdued, Agent Bell stared at her for a moment,
glanced at Henry, then said only, "Yes, ma'am, I guess we
do, I guess we do."

After a silence Henry asked, "What more have you
learned about Marcus Trotter and Martha Rae Jones? I've
begun to suspect he's mob-connected. What about that?"

"You're right, he is. The connection was through his
former wife. She's Carmen Landau, the daughter of Rollo
Landau, who died in a Federal prison last year. Things have
been going downhill for Trotter since the father died, partly
because Carmen walked out on their marriage shortly after
his death.

"We hear from Chicago that her brothers never liked
him as much as the father did—jealousy, maybe. I gather
Trotter has been on rather precarious ground with the family
since separating from his wife, no matter how much they
may have depended on his legal talents in the past. He's
kept more than one of them out of prison, but this last
time the evidence against the father was too damning for
him to overcome.

"I suspect the problems looming there are one reason
Trotter was interested in finding money in Hot Springs
when the opportunity presented itself."

"What about Sim Simpson? They're from the same
firm."

"Different departments. Simpson is in corporate, Trotter handled many of the big-deal criminal cases. They did
build the firm together, starting with just the two of them
many years ago, but we haven't found that Simpson is in-

volved in anything illegal.

"I'm guessing Trotter urged his partner to come here with him because he thought that would make the trip seem less unusual to those who worked with him as well as to the Landau family. Being with a friend would also help him 'hide in the crowd' while here, so to speak. Greta Hunt says he asked her not to mention their relationship. He told her he wanted to be seen as just one of the regular guys, not as her brother."

"Ah, yes. And Ms. Jones?"

"She used to be a geriatric nurse but was fired about a year ago because she was making too many mistakes with patients. When one woman died, some misuse of drugs was suspected, though no one followed up on it. Folks at the nursing home where she worked said yesterday that the family wasn't inclined to prosecute, and on their own they couldn't prove anything. The woman who died was nearly a hundred years old, and wealthy, which probably had quite a bit to do with her family's disinclination to pursue the matter.

"According to Jones's daughter, who lives near her mother in Oregon, the woman has been more than a little unsettled since the death of her husband two years back. Evidently she's always been flighty; the daughter says her dad was the stabilizing influence in their family. Losing the nursing job last year put her over the edge, I'd guess, though I'm no psychiatrist. Daughter says she's been acting very depressed lately and was especially worried about money, though, again according to the daughter, she had no reason to be.

"By the way, it is a good thing Ms. McCrite took Jones out with that pipe when she did. The drugs she had were dangerous, and the stuff in that hypodermic could certainly have killed you and Brad in the dosage she planned. So, King, it looks like Ms. McCrite saved your life."

"Oh, my," Carrie said as Henry took her hand.

Brooks looked at his watch and then at Bell. "Well, that about wraps this up, doesn't it, Agent Bell? It's 9:45. You two should have plenty of time to get ready for the session on crystals."

"Will we see you again?" Carrie asked.

"Oh, yes," Bell told her. "There will be some follow-up to deal with. But, for the most part, you can enjoy the rest of the week—if you stay out of trouble and try not to notice anything peculiar, that is."

He winked at her. "And please don't call us if you do see something out of the ordinary."

"What about the money in the Fordyce?" Carrie asked.

"Hmmm. Guess we'll leave that up to the National Park Service," Bell said. "If more of it exists, and to be honest I'm inclined to think it does, well, then, it's on their property. If they want to tear up the Fordyce basement, their choice."

"Oh, dear," Carrie said. "Then we'll probably never know..."

"Probably not," Bell told her firmly as he and Agent Brooks rose to leave. "It's out of our hands...and yours, Ms. McCrite, *and yours*."

"How about my room?" Henry asked.

"Okay to go back in. Thanks for reminding me," Bell said as he went to take down the crime scene tape. "My suggestion is that you retrieve your possessions and let the hotel people take care of the rest of it. They'll put things back together for you."

Henry and Carrie shook hands with both agents, and Henry shut the door firmly behind them.

"Well," he said. "Well." *Was now the time?*

"Well?" She was sitting on the edge of the bed, and he stood looking down at her for a moment before—moving very slowly—he got down on his knees. Did men still do it this way?

At first she looked startled. Then, for probably the first time in her life, Carrie McCrite blushed.

He took both of her hands in his. At last she smiled, and it was a smile like the one he'd seen on her face while he was telling the Elderhostel group about his friendship with her...explaining why he was at this Elderhostel. A quiet, knowing smile.

Guess it was meant to be. Carrie believed in things being meant, being part of a big, overall plan.

So, say it, Henry King. You've thought about it enough, say it.

"Carrie...dearest Cara, I've known you a couple of years now, and we've become very close friends. More than close. I've known I was in love with you since...since that time we were trapped in the cave last November.

"This week we both proved, not for the first time, that we care enough to be willing to die for each other. Therefore, I think—hope—we're ready to celebrate *living* for each other and to share our happiness in being together as partners in life."

She stood and, holding his good right arm, helped him unfold and get to his feet. *She was still smiling...were those tears in her eyes...?*

"So, Carrie, will you be my wife? I, uh, don't have a ring to give you yet, and I know I should, but..." The words rushed out. "Will you marry me anyway?"

The smile was still there and got bigger and bigger until she began to laugh through tears now streaming down her cheeks.

"Yes, Henry, yes, I most certainly will."

They *almost* missed the crystal session at 10:30.

As it was, Carrie didn't hear much of what the presenter said. Her mind was busy; she was planning *A Wedding to Die For.*

RECIPES

Magic Two Meatloaf
(Quantities are easier to remember,
Carrie believes, if they all have
the same number!)

2 lbs lean ground beef
Scant 2 cups dry stuffing mix (Note from a friend: *very
scant.*)
Scant 2 cups tomato juice, or enough to just soften stuffing mix
2 eggs, beaten until uniform yellow in color
Scant 2 tsp salt, or salt to taste
Pepper to taste
2 heaping T. ketchup (Cheat, put at least three.)
2 heaping T. prepared mustard (See above.)
2 quarter-cups minced onion. (For everyone but Carrie,
that's a half cup. Use more if you like onions.)

Soften stuffing mix in the juice. Beat eggs and add to stuffing mix. Add remaining ingredients and mix well. Shape
into loaf in roasting pan. Bake, covered, 350 degrees for
1½ hours.

Suggestion: Put medium potato chunks around loaf for
last hour of baking. Carrie serves this with her home-made
peach, apple, or pear sauce (peel, slice, cook fruit, add sugar
and spices to taste at end of cooking and stir until sugar
dissolves, whir in blender), green beans cooked with a bit
of chopped onion, and crescent rolls.

(continued on the next page)

No-Thaw Hamburger Meatloaf

Use approximately 1 lb lean hamburger, frozen in a lump just as it came from the grocery store. (If the hamburger isn't frozen, reduce baking time 30 minutes, but this recipe—trust Carrie—tastes better made with frozen hamburger. Who knows why?) For larger amounts of hamburger, increase baking time.

1 can beef broth. Carrie buys the no-fat kind from a health food store.

1 small can tomato juice or similar tomato product. Carrie uses the seasoned tomato sauce she makes from her garden tomatoes, but use your imagination here. Have fun experimenting. How about salsa, picante sauce, or seasoned canned tomatoes for example? If sauce is very thick, add water. Quantities of all additions are flexible, according to taste. Just make sure there is plenty of liquid around the meat at all times.

1 medium to large onion, cut in strips, and 1 green pepper, cut into strips with membrane and seeds removed. You can also add crushed garlic, or other seasonings that please you, to the sauce. Salt and pepper to taste.

Unwrap the meat and put it in a large casserole dish (3 quart or larger) or a roaster with a lid. Salt and pepper the meat lump, arrange onion and pepper slices on top. Pour the mixed broth and tomato product around the sides. Bake, covered, 350 degrees, for an hour and a half. For more than two or three people, increase the amount of hamburger and test for doneness after the hour and a half. (The meat will have a pinkish tinge throughout because of the tomato.) If not done, cook an additional fifteen or twenty minutes per pound, being sure there is plenty of liquid around the meat. When done, thicken gravy by adding a tablespoon or so of corn starch softened in small amount of water and stirred thoroughly into the liquid. Return meat and sauce to the oven until the gravy thickens. Serve with potatoes or rice, vegetable and fruit.

One possible variation is *No-Thaw Meatballs*. After meat has softened during baking process, use a teaspoon to break into rounded meatball-sized chunks. (For this version, cut pepper and onion into smaller chunks and let it float in sauce.) Use a larger proportion of tomato product for the liquid, spaghetti sauce, for example. Serve with pasta, garlic toast, and a tossed salad or raw vegetable platter.

ABOUT THE AUTHOR

Award-winning Arkansas writer and journalist Radine Trees Nehring and her husband, photographer John Nehring, live in the rural Arkansas Ozarks near Gravette.

Nehring's writing awards include the Governor's Award for Best Writing about the State of Arkansas, Tulsa Nightwriter of the Year Award, and the Dan Saults Award, which is given by the Ozarks Writers League for nature- or Ozarks-value writing. The American Christian Writers named Nehring Christian Writer of the Year in 1998, and the Oklahoma Writers Federation, Inc., named her book *Dear Earth* Best Non-Fiction Book and her novel *A Valley to Die For* Best Mystery Novel. *A Valley to Die For* was a 2003 Macavity Award nominee for Best First Novel.

Research for her many magazine and newspaper features and her weekly radio program, *Arkansas Corner Community News*, has taken the Nehrings throughout the state. For more than twenty years Nehring has written non-fiction about unique people, places, and events in Arkansas. Now, in her Something To Die For Mystery series, she adds appealing characters fighting for something they believe in and, it turns out, for their very lives.

OTHER BOOKS BY ST KITTS PRESS

PO Box 8173 ► Wichita KS 67208
316-685-3201 ► FAX 316-685-6650
stkitts@skpub.com ► www.StKittsPress.com

Music to Die For by Radine Trees Nehring

LIBRARY JOURNAL "As inviting as an episode of *Murder, She Wrote*, this follow-up to Nehring's Macavity Award-nominated *A Valley to Die For* delivers a good, old-fashioned whodunit that should please any fan of Christian cozies."

THE OKLAHOMAN "The Ozark Folk Center...is the setting for the second in a series of 'to die for' mysteries by a former Oklahoman who obviously loves the Ozarks..." (REVIEWED BY KAY DYER)

THE TULSA WORLD "...hooks [readers] with a story they can't put down." (REVIEWED BY JUDY RANDLE)

MIDWEST BOOK REVIEW "...[leaves] the reader sighing in satisfaction." (REVIEWED BY SHELLEY GLODOWSKI)

MYSTERY SCENE MAGAZINE "A nicely woven cozy by a writer who knows both the music and the hill people of Arkansas." (REVIEWED BY MARY V. WELK)

COZIES, CAPERS & CRIMES "In this character-driven story, heroes have their values straight and fight for what they believe in." (REVIEWED BY VERNA SUIT)

I LOVE A MYSTERY "Highly recommended." (REVIEWED BY EDEN EMBLER)

OZARKS MONTHLY "Happily, rumplyness takes nothing away from the cleverness of gray-haired heroine Carrie McCrite..." (REVIEWED BY LEE KIRK)

GRAVETTE NEWS HERALD "Action, plot twists and wonderful characters..." (REVIEWED BY GAYLE WILLIAMS)

THE BENTON COUNTY DAILY RECORD "...Nehring's specialties—intrigue and suspense, unique characters and situations—all set in the gorgeous Ozarks."

JOE DAVID RICE, ARKANSAS TOURISM DIRECTOR "...a compelling read."

BARBARA BRETT, AUTHOR OF *BETWEEN TWO ETERNITIES* AND, WITH HY BRETT, *PROMISES TO KEEP* "...murder and mayhem in perfect pitch!"

JULIE WRAY HERMAN, AUTHOR OF THE THREE DIRTY WOMEN GARDENING MYSTERY SERIES "Endearing characters make you want to come back to visit soon!"

MARY GILLIHAN, HARMONY MUSICIAN; PARK INTERPRETER AND ELDERHOSTEL COORDINATOR, OZARK FOLK CENTER STATE PARK "It was such fun to read about our Ozark Folk Center and picture where *the murder* took place."

A Valley to Die For by Radine Trees Nehring

LIBRARY JOURNAL "With flair, Nehring, an award-winning Arkansas writer, launches a cozy series that will appeal to mystery readers..."

THE TULSA WORLD "The skill...the character development, the place, the pace and the action tell the true story." (Reviewed by Michele Patterson)

SOUTHERN SCRIBE (MEMPHIS, TENN.) "...a warm and enchanting tale. Carrie is charming as a woman who wants to be recognized as spunky, independent, and a hero. Casting the book in the Ozarks is...well, icing on the cake." (REVIEWED BY ROBERT L. HALL)

FORT SMITH TIMES RECORD (FORT SMITH, ARK.) "...a delightful mystery with appealing characters fighting for a cause. Throughout the story I grew all the more attached to Carrie, marveling at her strong faith and silently chastising her for her stubbornness. A... bonus is Carrie's cooking." (REVIEWED BY TINA DALE)

GRAVETTE NEWS HERALD (GRAVETTE, ARK.) "...kept my heart pounding...a page turner with no easy stopping places." (REVIEWED BY GAYLE WILLIAMS)

THE BOOKWATCH "...a smoothly written novel that grips the reader's attention from first page to last, and documents Radine Trees Nehring as a mystery writer whose imagination and talent will win her a large and dedicated readership."

I LOVE A MYSTERY "The suspense is grabbing, but the book is as relaxing as living alone in the forest... Very highly recommended." (REVIEWED BY EDEN EMBLER)

JANE HOOPER, PROPRIETOR OF SHERLOCK'S HOME BOOKSTORE (LIBERTY, MO.) "Weeks later, I'm still thinking about the book and characters. I can't wait for the next in the series."

CAROLYN HART, AUTHOR OF THE DEATH ON DEMAND AND HENRIE O MYSTERIES "A pleasure awaits mystery lovers."

DR. FRED PFISTER, EDITOR OF THE OZARKS MOUNTAINEER "It's great to read fiction about the Ozarks that rings true."

MIKE FLYNN, PRODUCER AND HOST OF THE FOLK SAMPLER, HEARD WEEKLY ON PUBLIC RADIO "...a fascinating mystery that gets better and better as the pages roll."

Irregardless of Murder by Ellen Edwards Kennedy

CHICAGO TRIBUNE "...good writing and solid plotting don't need a famous imprint...a satisfying cozy..."

THE MIDWEST BOOK REVIEW "...a signature mystery..."

THE BOOKDRAGON REVIEW "A delightful cozy mystery peopled with eccentric characters with the prospect of more in the future." (REVIEWED BY MELANIE C. DUNCAN)

BOOKBROWSER.COM "...a wonderful puzzle, complete with all its pieces; clever, entertaining and hard to put down."

I LOVE A MYSTERY "A warm and cozy evening's read."

MYSHELF.COM "...an absolutely delightful mystery."

BOOKREVIEWCAFE.COM "...one of the greatest mystery books of the year!"

THE DROOD REVIEW OF MYSTERY "...a treat and a triumph..."

ANNE GEORGE, AUTHOR OF THE SOUTHERN SISTERS SERIES "A delightful read. The characters are wonderful."

SARAH SHABER, AWARD-WINNING AUTHOR OF *SIMON SAID* AND *SNIPE HUNT* "It's got everything a great cozy story needs — a charming and sympathetic heroine, a colorful supporting cast...a little romance, and, of course, a murder that challenges the reader..."

JOANNE FLUKE, AUTHOR OF *THE CHOCOLATE CHIP COOKIE MURDER* "A wonderful debut mystery with a delightfully appealing amateur sleuth. Ms. Kennedy's characters are so well drawn, you can almost hear them breathe."

ROSEY DOW, BEST-SELLING AUTHOR OF CHRISTY AWARD-WINNING *REAPING THE WHIRLWIND* "Tight plot, fascinating characters and a tantalizing mystery. I couldn't figure it out or put it down."

N.J. Lindquist, author of *Shaded Light* "...a satisfying traditional cozy mystery with an interesting cast of characters, more than a touch of romance, and moments of brilliance."

B. Lynn Goodwin, editor/interviewer of *Writer Advice Newsletter* "Wonderfully refreshing. With quiet humor, Miss Prentice follows her instincts, protects her students, and cautiously opens her heart to an old love."

DorothyL "...a book that I read, and then wanted to re-read, to see all that I had missed... This one is worth buying and keeping." (reviewed by Tom Griffith)

The Writer's Hood "...a novel that ticks neatly along with all the jeweled clockwork of a Christie. If you're a fan of the cozy, Kennedy is an author you're sure to enjoy." (reviewed by Charles A. King)

A Clear North Light by Laurel Schunk

Library Journal "Schunk solidly launches a new 'Lithuanian' trilogy, following one family's triumphs and tragedies through the generations."

Booklist "Schunk, author of the well-regarded coming-of-age story *Black and Secret Midnight* (1998), drops back to 1938 with *A Clear North Light*, the first installment of her Lithuanian Trilogy."

NWSBRFS (Wichita Press Women, Inc.) "...notable as much for its excellent character development as for its story line...Good reading..."

Gretchen Sprague, author of *Maquette for Murder* "... dramatically illuminates the effect of deadly global politics on the private lives of all-too-human individuals caught up in events not of their making."

James D. Yoder, author of *Lucy of the Trail of Tears* "...pulls one into an historical drama with excitement and moral persuasiveness as Petras fights and searches for faith, meaning, and love..."

Shaded Light by N.J. Lindquist
(available only in PDF format from St Kitts Press)

Publishers Weekly "...a cozy that will delight fans who appreciate solid, modern detection."

Library Journal "Detailed characterization, surprising relationships, and nefarious plot twists."

Rapport Magazine "A very good novel by an accomplished writer."

The Pilot (Southern Pines, NC) "This most enjoyable novel is written in the style of Agatha Christie...Follow the clues to a bang-up ending."

The Mystery Reader "...an admirable first outing for a pair of detectives readers will look forward to hearing from again." (Reviewed by Jennifer Monahan Winberry)

The Charlotte Austin Review "With any luck, we'll see more of Manziuk and Ryan in years to come." (Reviewed by PJ Nunn)

I Love a Mystery "This excellently plotted novel is the first in a projected series of Manziuk and Ryan mysteries."

Internet Bookwatch "Paul and [Jacquie] make a fabulous team as their divergent personalities harmoniously clash to the benefit of the reader."

Midwest Book Review "A cozy reminiscent of the best Agatha Christie had to offer." (Reviewed by Leann Arndt)

THE BOOKDRAGON REVIEW "...a well-plotted crime novel that should appeal to all those who especially like this sub-genre." (REVIEWED BY GENE STRATTON)

ABOUT.COM "...a fast paced book that was really hard to put down." (REVIEWED BY LORRAINE GELLY)

DOROTHYL "...we are treated to varied and carefully delineated characters that hold our attention, to good, uncliched, lucid writing, and to a well-sustained pace as we try to match wits with the detectives." (REVIEWED BY GINGER WATTS)

LINDA HALL, AUTHOR OF *MARGARET'S PEACE* "...a page-turning, keep-you-up-all-night mystery where the murderer isn't revealed until the very end."

JOAN HALL HOVEY, AUTHOR OF *NOWHERE TO HIDE* "...an excellent mystery in the classic sense — a who-dunnit in the tradition of Agatha Christie, but for the 21st century."

Under the Wolf's Head by Kate Cameron

GRIT: AMERICAN LIFE & TRADITIONS "You'll laugh at the sisters' relationship and grow to love the two women just as Callista's plants grow through her loving care."

PUBLISHERS WEEKLY "The gardening tips seeded throughout the narrative are a clever ploy, echoing the inclusion of cooking tips in the ever-popular culinary mysteries..."

LIBRARY JOURNAL "Plenty of gardening filler and allusions to inept local law enforcement lighten the atmosphere, as do the often humorous sisterly 'fights' and the speedy prose."

NORWICH BULLETIN (NORWICH, CT) "Schunk in the past has tackled child abuse and racism; her first gardening mystery provides a message about ageism and the value placed on elderly lives..."

THE CHARLOTTE AUSTIN REVIEW "Highly recommended." (REVIEWED BY NANCY MEHL)

ABOUT.COM "...a wonderful new release..." (REVIEWED BY RENIE DUGWYLER)

THE BOOKDRAGON REVIEW "...evokes in the reader an understanding of the atmosphere of a small town, where everyone is important and interesting." (REVIEWED BY RICHARD ROYCE)

NWSBRFS (WICHITA PRESS WOMEN, INC.) "...a quick and pleasant read..."

JAMES D. YODER, AUTHOR OF *BLACK SPIDER OVER TIEGENHOF* "Kate Cameron brings this murder mystery to a finale, murders solved, villains implicated and captured, with the added bonus, protagonist Callie Bagley discovers new love in her life."

Death in Exile by Laurel Schunk

LIBRARY JOURNAL "What could have been a straightforward Regency romance is elevated by apt social commentary in this offering from Schunk..."

THE PILOT (SOUTHERN PINES, NC) "Schunk is a good writer who has a good grasp of story and character."

THE CHARLOTTE AUSTIN REVIEW "This beautifully written Regency novel...will throw you into another time, and you won't want to leave." (REVIEWED BY NANCY MEHL)

MURDER: PAST TENSE (THE HIST. MYS. APPREC. SOC.) "Laurel Schunk is a masterful storyteller."

Black and Secret Midnight by Laurel Schunk

LIBRARY JOURNAL "Beth Anne's appealing child's-eye view of the world and the subtle Christian message should make this appealing to fans of Christian and mainstream mysteries."

PUBLISHERS WEEKLY "Beth Anne is at times touchingly naive..."

SMALL PRESS BOOK REVIEW "...a memorable picture of racism that is variously stark and nuanced."

THE PILOT (SOUTHERN PINES, NC) "...a good look at racial relations in the south...with a mysterious twist."

MURDER: PAST TENSE (THE HIST. MYS. APPREC. SOC.) "The story is so gripping that I worried [Beth Anne] would be killed before the end."

NWSBRFS (WICHITA PRESS WOMEN, INC.) "...Schunk's adult novels are serious, skillfully crafted works."

THE CHARLOTTE AUSTIN REVIEW "...a light in the darkness and a novel to sink your teeth and your heart into." (REVIEWED BY NANCY MEHL)

AMAZON.COM "...a great regional mystery that will excite fans with its twists and turns." (REVIEWED BY HARRIET KLAUSNER)

DOROTHYL "...skillfully mixes a story of segregation in the South and deep, dark family secrets with the plot of Shakespeare's 'MacBeth' in a very unique way." (REVIEWED BY TOM GRIFFITH)

SANDY DENGLER, AUTHOR OF *THE QUICK AND THE DEAD* "MacBeth and mayhem in the 50s. What a mix! I love Ms. Schunk's characters, and I remember the milieu all too well. It was the era you love to hate, beautifully brought to life."

LINDA HALL, AUTHOR OF MARGARET'S PEACE "Indicative of life in the South in the 1950s when racism and bigotry were around every frightening corner, *Black and Secret Midnight* is a great mystery with plenty of foreshadowing, clues, and red herrings to keep you reading far into the night."

The Voice He Loved by Laurel Schunk

THE CHARLOTTE AUSTIN REVIEW "...a masterful tale that reaches into the inner workings of a bruised and battered psyche, while keeping the plot moving at a breathless pace." (REVIEWED BY NANCY MEHL)

The Heart of Matthew Jade by Ralph Allen
(available only from St Kitts Press)

PUBLISHERS WEEKLY "...a compassionate view into religious, familial and romantic love..."

KEVIN PATRICK, CNET RADIO, SAN FRANCISCO "Fabulous!"

THE MIDWEST BOOK REVIEW "...an obliging and magnificently written mystery which is as entertaining as it is ultimately inspiring."

THE EAGLE (WICHITA, KANS.) "...Allen's book will inspire many who believe in the power of faith — and enjoy a good story."

THE CHARLOTTE AUSTIN REVIEW "...an eye-opener. *The Heart of Matthew Jade* is a compelling novel that will stay with you long after you put it down." (REVIEWED BY NANCY MEHL)

THE BOOKDRAGON REVIEW "...this novel's strength is in the behind the scenes glimpses of faith behind bars." (REVIEWED BY MELANIE C. DUNCAN)

THE LANTERN (BUTLER CO. COMM. COLLEGE) "...destined to become a classic. Its mixture of love and hate, religion and fallacy grabs readers from the very beginning and never lets them go."

LAUREL SCHUNK, AUTHOR OF *BLACK AND SECRET MIDNIGHT* "This compelling story chronicles the faith journey of a simple accountant from his sanitized office building into the maw of Hell as chaplain in a county jail."

Hyænas by Sandy Dengler
(available only from St Kitts Press)

LIBRARY JOURNAL "Highly recommended."

INTERNET BOOKWATCH (THE MIDWEST BOOK REVIEW) "...a terrific murder mystery and a work of unique, flawless written exploration of prehistoric antiquity."

THE CHARLOTTE AUSTIN REVIEW "Dengler has crafted a masterpiece. *Hyaenas* proves that there are still new slants to the mystery genre." (REVIEWED BY NANCY MEHL)

AMAZON.COM "For anyone who wants something a bit different with their mysteries, *Hyænas* is the answer, hopefully with future novels starring Gar and company." (REVIEWED BY HARRIET KLAUSNER)

DOROTHYL "...I had a hard time putting the book down when I needed to do some work." (REVIEWED BY TOM GRIFFITH)

PAT RUSHFORD, AUTHOR OF THE HELEN BRADLEY MYSTERIES "Dengler is masterful at creating characters that come alive in any era."[